The Keepers

Part 1 "The Beginning"

M. A. Samms

ISBN: 0991393201
ISBN 13: 9780991393206
Library of Congress Control Number: 2014912975
M.A. Samms, Richmond, New Hampshire

I would like to dedicate this book to the following people:

My husband, who faithfully loves and encourages me.
To my children who always give me the reason.
To my dear friend Michelle who never loses faith in me and lets me laugh at myself.
To my siblings who support me behind the scenes with encouragement, laughter, and advice.
To my dear departed friend Howie who inspired me with the words, "Just keep going!"
Collectively, you have all inspired me in your own ways to see me to the finish line. I thank you so much and love each and every one of you.

one

"One of the most interesting things in life is the likelihood that unforeseen things can come your way and change you forever, either for the good or for bad. That depends on you."

~M.A. Samms~

Rain again. I have been in Boston for only a day, and the rain has been persistent. The relentless patter on the roof above me has attributed to my waking much earlier than I prefer. My surroundings are unfamiliar. I feel out of place here. It's different from anything I have known. I have to ask myself if I did the right thing, pulling up stakes and moving to an unfamiliar city, unfamiliar apartment, unfamiliar everything. Boxes fill the rooms I now call home, beckoning and taunting me to empty them, a job I was not looking forward to. Before I could fully grasp what time it was (and not really having the slightest desire to know), I somehow managed to open one eye halfway. My eyelid felt heavy and I wanted to close it again and go back to sleep, forgetting about the day ahead of me. Bailey, my pesky but faithful canine companion, wasn't about to let that happen. He had other intentions. Through the hazy vision of my slightly opened eye, I gazed straight into a big brown eye that was hoping to get my attention. I could feel his panting, hot breath on my exposed arm hanging off the side of the mattress. Was it really time to haul my carcass out of bed? It felt as if I had been asleep for only a few hours. Bailey continued to stare, his anxiety starting to show in his expression. His internal clock was telling him it was time to wake me up. I opened the other eye, and that's all it took for Bailey. He started to show signs of an impending desperate need to go to the bathroom, and my dallying was not going to be tolerated. Without a doubt the prancing back and forth from the bedroom to the front door would now begin.

"Okay, okay, I'm getting up, just hold on."

My voice was scratchy and gruff, which caused Bailey to give me a strange look. My day was starting, like it or not. Throwing back the covers, I placed my feet on the cold floor and made my way sluggishly to the bathroom. Bailey sat by the door waiting patiently for me, his tail wagging. My morning did not belong to me until I gave Bailey the attention he needed. I dutifully pulled on the sweatpants and sweatshirt I had left on the floor from yesterday and readied myself for the cold, rainy jaunt outside. The apartment felt cold and damp, so I could only imagine how it was going to feel outside. Bailey's leash was somewhere in this mess, and I realized I should have left it in an obvious spot. I had been tired and overwhelmed with everything last night and hadn't thought about getting out of bed early to take Bailey out. I had told myself to keep important items together, knowing the difficulty I would have finding something in the mess of boxes littered throughout the apartment. After taking Bailey out last night, I remembered taking his leash off and that's where my memory ended. Bailey was now anxiously nudging me to hurry. I stood in front of the door and gave myself a minute to recollect last evening. I had pulled my sneakers off around the corner from the door because they were wet from the rain. And that's where I found the leash, buried under my sneakers and wet socks. Thank goodness. I shoved my feet into my shoes and followed Bailey to the door. I snickered to myself thinking of what he would say to me if he could speak. On second thought, maybe it's better that I didn't know. I latched his leash as he waited patiently. City life was going to be an adjustment. In Cleveland, I only had to open the back door, let him go and unfailingly, he would show up back at the door within a few minutes. That's definitely not going to happen here. I pulled my hood over my head and we finally made our way carefully down the long but wide flights of stairs and across the street to a small open area where Bailey would mark his spot. After taking way too long sniffing around his new environment, I tugged on his leash to let him know I was still making the decisions on how long I was willing to stand in the rain. I glanced back toward the house and noticed another dedicated dog owner walking a small dog who was obviously not liking the rain any more than Bailey or I did. The dog's owner was dressed much more logically than I was in a full-length coat, hat, and gloves. I couldn't quite make out the face to see if it was male or female. In an attempt to be friendly, I gave a wave as Bailey and I made our way around the back of the building and up the flight of stairs, stumbling a bit on the last step from hurrying. I was more than ready to go back inside. The rain was cold and it seemed to seep into every crevice of my joints, rendering me chilled to the bone. Bailey never seemed impressed one way or another with the cold. His only thought was his next plan of action, which was my getting his breakfast, and he exhibited no patience when it was breakfast time. Or dinnertime for that matter. As soon as the food hit his dish, he practically inhaled it and then chased the bowl across the floor in an attempt to get the very last morsel. After realizing there was no more to be had, he settled down and decided to explore his new surroundings. He calmly walked around the apartment, sniffing each spot with his keen sense of smell, finding each and every unfamiliar scent from the previous tenants. We were both going to need some time to get comfortable here. I sat and watched him wander from one room to the next. I yawned and considered going back to bed as I still felt tired and unwilling to pour myself into unpacking. But instead, I realized that an early start would mean an early finish and I was relishing the thought of getting the worst part of moving over with. I moved a few boxes around, frowning at the lack of good labeling. While packing I had thought I would remember what each box contained and now I stood among them, realizing that they all looked identical. But I had labeled the all-important box. After sifting through several large boxes, I found the priceless one labeled "kitchen." It was no secret to anyone who knew me that without coffee in the morning, I was no prize to be around; I had no problem admitting to that fact. I quickly opened the box, knowing that inside was the coffee pot and a bag of coffee. I opened it as if it were a fragile gift. I wasted no time getting my first pot brewing. I knew I was going to have to push myself to accomplish anything today. Once the smell of coffee permeated the apartment, I started to feel revived. With the only coffee cup I owned in my hand, I looked down at Bailey and realized how much our worlds were alike. While the coffee brewed, I waited patiently at the counter. Yesterday's paper, which was given to me by the friendly waitress, was right where I had left it last night. I knew it would take few cups of coffee to fully wake up, so I decided I might as well use this time to read the local news. The coffee finally ready, I took my seat at the table near the window that looked out over the sidewalk below. It dawned on me how old this house must be after noticing the windows, which appeared to have the original wooden frames, the paint peeling a bit. This house must be closing in around one hundred years old. The window was quite tall with a huge ledge, which I decided I liked. I'm sure if the walls could talk, they would tell some great stories. It raised my curiosity and I thought maybe one of these days I would have the chance to talk to Mr. Tyler, the owner and my land-lord, about the house. I felt sure he would know a great deal about his home and the area. Stories about life and times that you can't read in history books were my favorite. I hoped he would have some personal stories of the older days when times were changing and people were struggling to survive. I would definitely find time to pick Mr. Tyler's brain, and in the long run, learn some facts about where I now lived. As I savored my first cup of coffee, I glanced out the window at the steady rainfall and noticed only a few folks quickly mak-ing their way from here to there. The tops of umbrellas were all I could see from my second story view. Soon that would be me, racing frantically to a new job and stepping into a position I was qualified for but for some reason doubted if I could really do. I realized at that moment how stressful it would be navigating a new city and a new job, and meeting new people. Even with my doubts, I felt sure I had made the right decision. I didn't regret leaving a dead-end job where I was always hoping for advancement to no avail. I took a risk and moved to Boston with my faithful Beagle companion to make a better living and maybe advance my career. Around every corner would be a new adventure, something more exciting than Cleveland had to offer. Little did I know as I sat there, feeling both anxious and excited about the unknown, what would be in store for me.

With my small savings and even smaller window of time, I had to make decisions that limited my options of getting the prime apartment with a lot of space. With only two weeks to relocate after my last day of work at Bristle Financial Group in Cleveland, I had a limited selection of available and affordable apartments. One had been located above a pizza shop and, aside from the thought of the constant wonderful smell, it looked small and outdated in the photos. It didn't seem to warrant the rent price or the limited apartment size, plus there was nowhere for Bailey to roam. When I saw the ad for the furnished apartment on Miner Street, its' cost drew me in, and it was near the ballpark and not far from where I would be working. I went on instinct, which is not always the best idea, but it was all I had as I had no connections in Boston. Not unless you count the "should be retired" guy at the ticket booth off Interstate 90 who stepped up to assure me I submitted the right amount of change, or the green-eyed, apron-donning waitress at Bill's Smoking Burgers who smiled a little too nicely my way when I ordered a burger, mustard, no onions, and a side of fries. And least of all, my landlord, Mr. Tyler, who I noticed as we climbed the wide, steep and somewhat unlevel stairs at the back of the building, had a bad leg that must be related to an injury of some sort. He was very well dressed, with a short, recently trimmed haircut, and a clean shaven face. He was soft spoken and had an ear-to-ear smile that lit up the room. His "please" and "thank you" manners indicated he was a man with impressive social graces. I noticed a ring on his finger, which indicated he was married or was at one time. He did not speak of his wife when we first spoke. He allowed me to roam from room to room and answered all of my questions. He was eager to fill the apartment and happy to see that a "strong young man," was moving in. I took an instant liking to Mr. Tyler and had respect for the gentleman. I felt comfortable with him, and Bailey seemed to approve as well. He lived in the building, in the front section of the first floor of the two-story house, which he said was plenty of space for himself and his dog, George. He was open to having Bailey live in the building; he understood the company a dog could provide to someone on their own. There was a slight cost for Bailey, but Mr. Tyler said he would consider dropping the extra charge after a few months. We would take it one month at a time. I also appreciated that the apartment was secluded enough to buffer the sounds from the street below and from the noise of the sometimes crazy crowd attending the ball games. I knew I would be able to hear the occasional roar of the ballpark crowd but I wasn't too worried.

After two cups of coffee, the day drifted along slowly as I emptied box after box into a pile in the corner of the living room. Bailey stopped following me from room to room once he got bored. He lay down and decided it was more worthwhile just to watch. The rain continued through the afternoon, but I kept my nose to the grindstone, eager to get this process over. My stomach was telling me with each grumble that I had bypassed breakfast and lunch and was heading toward dinner. It occurred to me that I had no food in the house. With the last box of the day almost empty, I decided a trip to the store was in order. As Bailey was my captive audience and the only one I had to talk to, I found myself asking him an all-important question.

"I don't suppose you would know where I can find a piece of paper and pencil, do ya? I think I should make a list if I'm going to the store."

Bailey cocked his head as if he understood every word, looking from the door back to my face and wagging his tail as usual.

"That's what I thought. You don't really know what I'm talking about, do you?"

Again, the cock of the head, but this time he assumed it meant a ride in the car. Up on all four legs, he was ready. I was sure he was feeling a little out of place with the new surroundings. It would take a while for him to adjust. I bent down next to him, hugged him, and petted him for a minute to reassure him that I was not leaving him. Just then my cell phone rang. I remembered seeing it several hours ago but with all the unpacking, I couldn't remember where it was.

"Please keep ringing, please keep ringing so I can find you." After four rings, I found it...on top of the blankets piled on the bed that I never made this morning.

"Hello?" No answer on the other end. "Hello?"

"Hi, Sam, it's Jake."

A familiar voice! Jake and I had known each other since seventh grade. He moved to Cleveland because his parents had divorced and his mom wanted to be closer to her own parents. Jake had no choice but to come along. His dad moved to Phoenix to remarry and that didn't sit too well with Jake. So they rarely saw each other during Jake's school years. Jake and I became instant friends from his first day at school. We did everything together. We were both on the football team, we got into trouble together, ate meals together. Since we lived close, we spent most of our time when not in school at each other's houses planning our futures. We had made plans for the next eight years of our lives and we would do it all together as best friends. We were going to have everything: the money, the sports cars—all the good stuff. We would get married after college, have great kids, and nice houses. But the college years came and went. Neither of us got married or had kids. And neither of us lived away from home. But we both did land jobs with Bristle Financial Group. Finance was Jake's strength. He could clean up any financial worksheet in the bat of an eye. I, on the other hand, worked hard at what I did, made a lot of mistakes, and didn't excel the way I would have wanted, like Jake. He had natural ability; I had none. I don't know what possessed me to take accounting in college. Maybe to do the same things that Jake did. After all, we were in it together for life. Isn't that what best friends do? As for me, I ended up taking night classes to further my education and that's what helped me land this position in Boston. It didn't surprise me that Jake was calling so soon after my leaving. He would need to know every detail of my life away from Cleveland.

"Hey, Jake, how are ya?"

He sounded far away. Cleveland seemed like the other side of the world today for some reason.

"Well, I can hardly hear you. You don't have good reception. Where you are?"

"You're the first person to call since I got here. Maybe it's just the weather. It's been raining since I arrived and you know how much I hate the rain!"

"Yeah, you were never one for rain or for snow. Just suck it up, man. Did you find an apartment yet?"

I answered, knowing he was going to want to know if there were any women living nearby...that's just Jake. "Yeah, I did, a second floor apartment in an older home not far from work. An older gentleman owns the house and rents part of it out to support himself I'm guessing. I got here yesterday and he took me right in, worked out great. Plenty of room for me and it works for Bailey."

"Man, I'm glad for you, didn't want you sleeping in your car."

"Yeah, yeah, I hear ya, very funny. No, I was just unpacking and making my way to get some food. How's everything with you?"

"Oh, you know, things are good. Just wanted to see how you were making out. I'm a little jealous you took the step and got out of this place. I was thinking once you get settled and start working, I could come out and see Boston."

"Sure, I can let you know. I got a place not too far from the ballpark. Maybe we can catch a Red Sox game. Boston is a big place, I'm sure we can find something to do. I'm just unpacking the few boxes I brought with me. The apartment is furnished, which is what I needed. Bailey is trying to find his comfort zone. He's doing okay though. Too soon to know for sure."

"Yeah, you know, it just takes time. At least you have Bailey to keep you company. That Sox game sounds good. Just let me know. I have some vacation time coming up in May, maybe then."

As I was about to answer, I thought I heard a knock on my door. It seemed a little strange that someone would be at my door since I hadn't even been here twenty-four hours. No one knows me. And who would know where I live? It sent an odd feeling through me. I'm not usually paranoid, but it seemed a bit strange.

"Listen, Jake, gotta go, there's someone at my door. I'll try to give you a call later."

"And you have only been there one day! What's her name?"

Wise guy, always was, always will be. Maybe that's why we get along so well, he is quick with the jokes, and I always seem to be a good target.

"No, seriously, Jake, knock it off. I will give you a call later. Someone is at my door."

"Okay, talk to you later."

I ended the call, apprehensive to answer the knock, but nevertheless, moved toward the door. Bailey scrambled to his feet and came with me, but he didn't bark, which is unusual for him. He whined and put his ears back, not like him at all. As I reached for the doorknob, there was the knock again. I pulled my hand back and a strange, creepy feeling went through me. Stop being a wimp, I said to myself, taking a deep breath. Answer the door, you chicken, what are you afraid of? Who would be interested in doing you any harm? I grabbed the doorknob and turned the handle. The door creaked as I opened it, the chain dangling across that would stop absolutely no one. I opened it a small crack, just enough to get a glimpse of who was on the other side. I exhaled a sigh of relief to see it was Mr. Tyler.

"Hey, Mr. Tyler, how are you?"

"I am sorry to bother you, Sam, but I just wanted to make sure everything was okay and to your liking. I know how sometimes new places can make even the slightest thing difficult, especially when you are new to the area."

His voice was very apologetic and sincere. He had a gentle nature and I somehow felt he was going to be a good landlord.

"Mr. Tyler, please come in, no need for you to stand out in the rainy weather." I unlatched the chain and opened the door wider.

"Oh, no, there's no need for me to interrupt your unpacking. You must be very busy. I only wanted to see that the apartment was all right and there were no problems getting everything up those stairs. Moving everything to a second level can be such a bugger you know. You also let me know if there is anything I can help you with. Finding your way around the city can be confusing at first. I would be glad to help you out if I can."

"Please, come inside, Mr. Tyler," I said. "Actually, I was just telling Bailey I need to get out to the store. Maybe you can tell me where the nearest store is. I just need a few things to get me by for the next few days."

He stepped inside, slipping his wet shoes off at the door so as not to track in the rain.

"I will only stay for a minute, son, I don't want to keep you. But if you are looking for a local store to pick up a few things, you could stop at Baker's, it's just a few blocks down on St. Mary's Street. They have just about anything you might need to get started. But if you are looking for a larger grocery center, you might want to try The Liberty. But it's a few miles down from here at the intersection of Parkman Street and St. Paul on the left-hand side."

"Thank you, I'll try Baker's. It sounds like they will have what I am looking for. Can I get you something to drink, Mr. Tyler? Maybe a cup of coffee?"

He looked tired. No doubt the hike up the flight of stairs could not be easy for someone with a bad leg.

I asked if he would like to sit down for a minute.

"Oh, no, I have kept you long enough, Sam. I will be on my way. You let me know if there is anything you need or if any problems come up. Don't you hesitate to give me a call."

He smiled that broad smile; he was a cheerful gentleman. And I couldn't help but smile back at him. Bailey was at his side, ears back, wagging his tail as if he had known Mr. Tyler for years. He usually didn't respond to people quite so fondly, and I was amazed at his reaction. It's usually a battle to get him away from strangers at the door and his bark can continue for at least five minutes before he finally gives up and lies back down. But not this time. As odd as it was, I liked the change. Mr. Tyler turned for the door, stopping to slip his shoes back on before stepping out onto the small stoop that led down the staircase. I thanked him for stopping by to see me and for his help with directions.

As he turned to step out, I thought I heard him mumble quietly to himself. "Did you say something, Mr. Tyler?"

He replied calmly, "Oh, it's just the mumbles of an old man. Good day, Sam. See you soon."

I asked him if he wanted help getting down the stairs.

"No, no, I am fine. I have made this climb many times, my dear boy. Thank you very much though."

And with that, the oddly charming gentleman made his way with no hesitation down the flight of stairs. I waited until I couldn't see his figure any longer and then stepped back inside and shut the creaky door. Bailey was sitting with his ears back, paw up for a shake, eager to show his affection. This was not the normal behavior of my dog when he was around someone he barely knew. Maybe I was just being crazy, maybe Mr. Tyler has a way with animals and Bailey sensed his gentle manner. Either way, I was glad I did not have to control his barking and send him off to be quiet.

I took Bailey out for a quick walk before I left for the store. I had become so engrossed in my own work unpacking I had forgotten to take him out in the early afternoon, and he now welcomed the extra time to walk and stretch his legs. The rain was still coming down, letting up just enough every few minutes to give the false hope that it may be coming to an end. But it continued. Bailey was taking his time. I tugged on his leash to let him know his time was up, and he obediently followed my lead. As I turned to cross the street, I noticed the same person I had seen earlier wrapped in the same coat, hat, and gloves and walking the same small dog. There was no acknowledgement, no hello. Bailey and I crossed the street and headed back upstairs. Bailey took charge up the stairs, nearly stumbling near the top step as I had done in the morning. I decided I should put something down to keep from tripping at the top. That could be a dangerous fall. Inside, Bailey was hoping for an early dinner and performed all his tricks to get my attention. I had to tell the old boy, "Dinnertime is later. Right now, I am leaving you here for a while." I made my way through the stack of empty boxes thrown about the living room to get through to the bathroom. I thought it best to shower and change before I made any public appearances. Bailey kept guard at the door. The hot shower felt good on such a cold day and I was already chilled to the bone. I got dressed quickly, assured Bailey I would only be a few minutes, and patted him on the head goodbye. Last night I had set my keys on the shelf by the door, that much I did remember. Losing the keys to the apartment would be substantially worse than losing Bailey's leash. Bailey returned to his bed and lay down, not getting any indicators from me that he would be eating anytime soon. With keys in hand, I made sure I locked the creaky door behind me and made my way down the flight of stairs to my car, which was parked in front of the building. Each tenant was allowed two parking spaces, for a spouse or for company, neither of which I had at the moment.

Baker's was as Mr. Tyler described, a small store with a lot of everyday items. It actually was in walking distance, but I figured for my first shopping trip it might be too much to carry home. The trunk of the car would serve me better. The store was busier than I expected. In an effort to put my best foot forward, I tried to make eye contact with several people I passed in the aisles, hoping to find a friendly face. But most seemed too concentrated on finding what they needed and getting to the cashier to pay.

The kitchen in the apartment was small so getting just a few things until I had space figured out seemed like the right plan of action. I got what I needed and made my way to the checkout. It was then that I noticed the familiar coat, hat, and gloves phantom standing several people ahead of me. I was sure it was the dog walker. It was becoming an obsession with me to see the face and say hello. I didn't want to bring notice to myself, so I quietly stood in line, moving from one foot to the other, hoping the person would turn around to grab something from the cart or speak to the person behind them—anything that would allow me to make eye contact. But as I stood waiting patiently for the opportunity that would put this mystery to rest, an older gentleman with a nearly empty cart bumped my leg. As I turned to ask if he was okay, the coat, hat, and gloves phantom disappeared out the door.

As I waited in line, I wondered if asking the cashier whether she knew the phantom would be inappropriate. I didn't want to seem like a stalker. The more I tossed this around in my mind, the more I felt it would not be the best idea. I said hello to the cashier, who could not have been any older than I was when I worked in a grocery store, the finest job ever. She had a pleasant face but seemed to be elsewhere in her thoughts.

"How are you today," I said to her, hoping to engage in conversation with someone.

"I'm good, how are you? Did you find everything you needed?" she asked.

I told her I had and then added, "Is Amber your real name, or did you switch your tag with someone else to keep the customers guessing?"

She gave me a strange look and I quickly tried to explain the question.

"When I was a freshman in college, we used to switch nametags so no one knew our names and it was sort of funny to confuse the customers. It was just a practical joke, sort of, in a weird kind of way." Once the words left my mouth, I immediately felt foolish.

I could see that my humor had struck a sour chord and I was about to go down.

"But I can see that it's not that funny anymore. Never mind, sorry I asked."

And then before I could stop my mouth, I said, "So, is your name really Amber?" I chuckled as I said it.

Despite my efforts to share a funny story, the girl, perhaps Amber, did not think I was remotely funny and obviously preferred that I didn't speak to her at all. She rolled her eyes at me, as if she had heard that story before. Or maybe she thought I was making a move. Either way I could sense I was treading on delicate ground. In the next moment, as though things were not uncomfortable enough, the store manager suddenly appeared. He was a very large man and his nametag read Max. I did not feel compelled at all to ask him if that was his real name.

"Is everything okay here?" He was trying to be pleasant but looked me directly in the eyes with a stern, cold stare.

Strike one for the new guy. I remained silent for the rest of my checkout. My groceries cost a measly $26.90 and I paid the cashier. Amber (if that was her real name) dropped the change into my hand without making eye contact. In town for less than forty-eight hours and I've already humiliated myself. Suddenly I missed Bailey. He appreciated my sense of humor and always laughed at my jokes.

I decided I would probably never shop at Baker's again.

The rain had finally stopped, the sky was clearing to expose a bright glow of the moon hiding behind the branches of the trees. Although eerie at first, I welcomed it.

two

"One should never underestimate the power of positive thinking...I am positive of that."

~M. A. Samms~

No rain—that was a sign of a good day.

Monday morning was at my doorstep much sooner than I wanted it to be. I finally had to confront the demons of my own doubt about my new job, with a new boss and new co-workers. It always looks greener when you are at a point in an old job when things aren't going your way, and you don't feel the rush of satisfaction you did the first few months. You finally decide to take that step and start your plan of action to look elsewhere. Yes, the grass is always greener at that point. But it doesn't last long. And that is what I was afraid of...how long would I feel that this was the right move for me? Leaving everything I was familiar with, my family, my friends, co-workers, my hometown. I had lived there all my life, in a suburb called Garfield Heights, and grew up with two sisters and a brother. Aside from the fact that it's cold, rainy, windy, and snowy, the city life isn't great, and the Browns haven't won in years, I still miss it. I even miss my sisters, which I didn't think I would ever admit. Ruth is my mean sister, I probably shouldn't paint her that way, but she is sharp with her tongue and doesn't think about the consequences of what she says. I love her but she is mean. I admire the man she married, Roger, and their two children. They live about five miles from my parents' home, and they visit them every Sunday. They are happily married and I am fortunate to have a great brother-in-law like Roger. He's a diehard Browns fan and we have made many treacherous, snow-filled journeys to football games. He's a great guy and treats my sister, who is sometimes undeserving, very well. Growing up with Ruth was not always easy. Mean sisters have a way of making brothers feel embarrassed about girls, facial hair, odors, big feet, and anything else they can think of. So on the day she got married and moved out of the house, I felt liberated to say the least. Her two daughters, Anna and Amelia, are twins, and they look exactly alike. I mix them up sometimes but they forgive Uncle Sam no matter how many times I get it wrong.

Then there is Grady, my older brother. Charming, well built, and quarterback of his high school football team, he taught me everything I know about football. Grady was always an A student, and the best brother a guy could ask for. He met Shelby his first year in college at Cleveland State. He made it through the first semester, dropped out after that, and landed a job at Shelby's dad's sports memorabilia store over by the football stadium. I'm not sure if that is what he envisioned for himself, but it's where he is. I only see him once in a while, as he spends a great deal of time with Shelby's family. I can't help but feel that some of the dreams he had in high school have passed him by and I feel sorry for him in a way. But that's what happens in life sometimes.

And then there is Hannah, the quiet one of the family. She's three years younger than me and lives in New Hampshire just outside of Keene in a town called Peterborough. She owns and operates a successful bed and breakfast named "The Old Door Inn." My parents make the trip every fall to stay at the inn and help out in any way they can. Mom loves to help with all the room linens, and Dad is a great cook so he lends a hand in the kitchen. There's always a lot to do at the inn. Mom and Dad always come home feeling that they have contributed to their daughter's business venture, even if it's only for one week. Hannah refused any financial help from Mom and Dad. She felt it was just not right for them to work all their lives and then spend their money on her dreams instead of theirs. She seems to be one of the most successful innkeepers in the area. She asked the bank for a loan, bought the old house and converted every inch of it. Each room has an old door, either original to the house or taken from one of the deconstructed houses in the area. She restores them and uses them in her inn along with any lumber she can find from old structures. She's the creative one in the family and is the most grounded by far. Hannah is not married yet, but I think whoever marries her will be one of the luckiest guys alive. She has a kind, gentle nature that I am sure has attributed to her success as an innkeeper. I never had to run and hide from Hannah when I was growing up. She never wanted to embarrass me about my awkwardness as Ruth did. Maybe she felt the same awkwardness growing up and for that reason never could find it in her heart to be cruel. I often thought my friend Jake had a crush on Hannah. He never flirted with her but I never saw him treat her with anything but respect. Jake and I visited Hannah one weekend and he became a whole different person, a real gentleman. Maybe that's just the effect Hannah has on people. Or maybe there is something there I don't know about.

Even though growing up with my family was sometimes challenging, I love and miss them, especially now that I am alone in Boston on my first day of work.

The trip to the office was only three blocks away from the apartment and it took me a mere five minutes. What were the chances that I would get this lucky to live so close to work? I didn't even have enough time to talk myself out of going. I gave myself one last pep talk and took a deep breath.

The office building was just as impressive as I remembered from my interview. There were no offices facing the front of the building in order to eliminate employees arguing over getting an "office with a view." The front of the building on each floor was an open waiting area that included a lounge and a conference room.

Ms. Hansen was the first person I came in contact with at Berkley and Sons. I interviewed with her prior to meeting anyone else and she determined my fate. She was a pleasant woman and was dressed very conservatively but sophisticated. I would guess she was somewhere around her mid forties and married as she had a ring on her finger. She made me feel at ease during the interview. She had a good sense of humor and I felt relaxed while talking with her. Auditing is not a pleasant job so having a good sense of humor is an advantage.

I entered the building and found Ms. Hansen waiting at the front desk. She offered me a cup of coffee before we took the elevator up to the fourth floor. I declined because I was nervous enough and didn't need anything to add to my agitation. I wished Jake was here because he was so casual. This would have been a breeze for him. We took the elevator to the fourth floor and stepped out into a room full of people already busy at work. It was time to dig my heels in and get rid of all the self-doubt that has been creeping into my thoughts for the last few weeks. I could do this job as well as anyone here and I was set to prove it. Ms. Hansen showed me to my office, a small, orderly room containing all the necessary equipment for the job. I left my briefcase on my desk and moved on to my first task of the day, which was to meet my new boss, Clive Howards. Mr. Howards was the junior executive of operations for corporate audits. To my surprise he seemed to be no older than me, give or take a few years. I wondered how someone his age gained that position. How had he climbed the ladder so quickly in such a large company, unless he had his foot in the door another way? He was on the phone when Ms. Hansen knocked and you could tell in his voice that our meeting was not a top priority. Nevertheless, he motioned us in to take a seat. A choking feeling started to make its way to my vocal cords, and I was sure I was going to either throw up or make a sound that resembled the tight squeeze of a balloon. Please God, let this yellow-belly chicken attitude of mine leave my thoughts.

"Sorry for keeping you waiting. I had to take that call; it was a matter of urgency. You must be Sam. Nice to meet you," Clive said as we shook hands politely. His grip was lame and I noticed he made no eye contact. Maybe I made him nervous.

"Nice to meet you, Mr. Howards," I said.

He grinned and chuckled under his breath.

"Please, Sam, call me Clive. One reason is it's just easier for me to communicate with everyone on a first-name basis and I will assume it's the same for you. Second, I am pretty sure we are the same age, give or take a year. It doesn't seem likely that you are comfortable calling me Mr. Howards any more than I am hearing you say it. Our job here is taken seriously; we are not friends or friendly to many of our clients, so I figure the least we can do is work in a casual environment. Besides, I feel like you are talking to my father when you say Mr. Howards.

There it was, the reason I had been waiting to hear, the door that led Clive to his high position in such a prestigious company. Dad was the boss. I knew it. I had noticed quite a few older people working in the office, many of whom looked like they had some years of experience in their positions. But blood is thicker than water and so here sits Clive next to Dad in a probably undeserved position. I wondered how that was received by the employees with twenty or thirty years' time in here.

"Okay, Clive it is. Thank you for taking time today, I know you are a busy person."

"Welcome aboard. I trust Ms. Hansen has shown you around and made you feel welcome. There are a few meetings I would like you to sit in on for the next couple of days just to get you acclimated to how things are run here. There's also some paperwork for you to fill out and get back to our human resources department. Take this week to get to know the office and the people you will be working with most of the time. Ms. Hansen is the staff supervisor as you already know, and she can help you with any questions you may have. Your direct supervisor is Paul Gibbs, but he's not in today so I will have Martha work with you. If you have any critical questions save them for Paul, he will be back in tomorrow."

He was scuttling through some papers as he talked, looking up only once briefly, maybe to see if I was listening. He seemed preoccupied and rushed through the preliminary politeness. Maybe he was meeting with Dad. He apologized for needing to leave so quickly, but confirmed that we would meet later as he would be back in the office around 2:00 p.m.

After the brief meeting, Ms. Hansen smiled apologetically and led me to the other side of the office to introduce me to other staff members. "Martha, this is Sam Wylkes, he is joining us from Cleveland, and this is his first day here so please make him feel welcome."

"Hi, Sam, I am going to work with you today because Paul is out. He and his wife just had a baby and he won't be back in until tomorrow. So, my apologies for our last minute change, and I will try to show you as much as I can today. I have a few reviews I need to get through before tomorrow, so I will do what I can for you," Martha explained.

It's nice to meet you, Martha," I replied.

Ms. Hansen told Martha we would be back shortly and led me down the hall.

"Sam, let me show you the break room in case you want to get yourself a cup of coffee. I just have a few calls I need to make and then I am free to show you around. And by the way, you can call me Gail."

She left me standing alone in the break room and I noticed a man sitting at the table. I couldn't decide if I should introduce myself or leave him alone as he seemed to be deep into reading the book he had with him. I decided to make a cup of coffee and get back to my desk. As I started toward the door, I heard him say something that was obviously directed at me.

"You don't have to run out on my account. I can read this book anytime. Come on over and sit for a while. I'm Keith, I started here a few months ago and don't know anyone too well yet. I just stay to myself and do my work. It's best that way. All this "have to know everyone" stuff drives me crazy and doesn't have anything to do with my job here. I audit people's financials, that's all I do and I don't need everyone to be in my business, you know what I mean?"

Keith was a biggest, burliest guy I think I had ever met. He towered over me and had the gruffest voice of anyone I knew. I think I was going to like this guy.

"Hi, Keith, Sam Wylkes. I just started here today."

"Yeah, I see you are getting the grand tour. Trust me, it's not that grand, just another office building loaded up with folks doing their job, taking care of other people's problems. I have been in audits since I was twenty-five. I'm now fifty-two and nothing has changed—money problems are money problems. It's not a popular profession and you don't make many friends. But the IRS likes you a lot. How many years have you been doing this?"

I was embarrassed to say I had only five years under my belt, and I thought that had been grueling. How could I identify with this gentleman who obviously hasn't made many friends in a very long time. Honesty, as usual, was the best policy here.

"I have only been in audits for five years, not much in comparison to your years of experience, Keith. I admire how long you have been doing this."

That didn't seem to gain much ground with him.

"Don't be impressed, you're young yet, still making friends as you go along, nothing wrong with that. I have been married twice and divorced twice. Neither wife could take the boring, impersonal lifestyle of an old stick in the mud like me. I just stay to myself now and I can live with that. I have my faithful dog, Stanley, he's a man's best friend, you know."

"Oh, yeah, I know what you mean. I have a dog, too. Bailey. He's a beagle. I've had him for a couple of years now, faithful boy. We just moved here over the weekend, found an apartment, and are trying to settle in"

"How did he handle your moving here, you know, sometimes dogs don't take as well to a different environment as we do."

I laughed. I don't handle moving and relocating very well either so I can only imagine how an animal must feel when nothing is familiar.

"He's doing as well as I am, I suppose. I feel bad that he doesn't have a chance to go outside as much as he's used to. I live only three blocks away though, so I might try to get home during lunch and let him out, keep him company for a little bit. Don't want him to get lonely."

"That's probably not a bad idea. That will make him a bit more comfortable, I suppose. You live just a few blocks away, huh?"

"Got really lucky finding this place, it's got lots of room, nice landlord. Haven't met anyone else who lives there yet but after all, I just moved in...so."

"Well, good luck to you in settling in. Don't try to do too much too fast. It all takes time. There's a small store not far from there, a couple of blocks down, called Baker's. Might want to try it if you need a few things to get by."

I couldn't help but chuckle, remembering the embarrassing attempt to break the ice with the cashier.

"Yes, I've been there already, it's a great little store. It's been nice talking with you, Keith. I should get over to my office and settle in as much as I can on my first day."

I couldn't help but smirk at the suggestion of Baker's and how repulsive I must have appeared to an innocent young girl. I am sure I will not be going there ever again.

"Yes, nice meeting you, Sam. Take it easy. I'm sure I'll see you around."

He went back to his cup of coffee, head down so as not to encourage conversation with anyone else. He seemed like a nice person. I wondered if he had any children from either marriage. He didn't indicate as much, but it seemed like he kept his personal life, other than a dog, to himself and that's the way he liked it.

I made my way back to my new office to focus on getting myself organized. I passed Martha's and Gail's offices and both were empty. I guess it was not a priority to stick with the new people if you were busy. I guess it's a "learn as you go" system. My office was situated on the opposite side of Gail's and Martha's, which would give me some privacy. I sat in my chair to get a feel for things. Taking a deep breath, I tried to relax. I realized I couldn't set up my computer since I did not have passwords or access information until I met again with Gail. I wondered what I could do while I waited. I could call Jake, he must have some funny story for me or some words of enlightenment to share. But I didn't want to get caught on a personal phone call on my first day. I wished I could just speed up the hours until I could go home. Bailey would be waiting for some companionship. Being alone for long periods was not something he dealt with well. He was all I had here and everything was unfamiliar to him. Maybe I would give Jake a call; a cheerful voice would be welcome right now. I felt like I was back in school, making a fatal decision that would send me to the principal's office for reprimand. Shaking my head, I decided to take my chances. Just as I put my hand on my phone, it started ringing. I jumped.

Was this a sign, a premonition of sorts? It rang a third time before I looked down to see if I recognized the incoming caller. Nothing looked familiar to me, and I thought about letting it go to voicemail. It must be a call for whoever had this office before me. Fourth ring, I still couldn't decide if I should answer or let it go. Fifth ring, I picked up the phone and hit the connect button.

"Hello?"

"Hi, is this Sam Wylkes?" It was a woman's voice on the phone, no one I recognized.

"Yes, yes it is. Who am I speaking with?"

"Sam, this is Nurse Paterson at Massachusetts General Hospital. You were listed for us to call in the event of any emergency for Mr. Abraham Tyler. Do you know this person?"

"Yes, I do, he is my landlord."

Why would Mr. Tyler list me as an emergency contact for him? We barely knew each other outside of our rental agreement. He must know dozens of others, even family members who could help him in the case of an emergency. Why would he choose me? We hit it off pretty well and he was a nice gentleman, but I hardly knew him well enough to be helping with medical issues. There were other tenants in his home he must have had longer relationships with. Why, the guy on the other half of the first floor has lived there for three years, according to Mr. Tyler. He made mention of that to let me know there were folks who regarded his home as a sensible place to settle in, a comfortable family atmosphere. So why me? I suddenly realized I had a nurse on the line who didn't much care about my reservations in this matter. She was only calling the person listed and that person was me. I would have to figure out the reasons why later.

"Well, Sam, Mr. Tyler has been admitted for observation to the hospital. He suffered what may have been a heart attack this morning at his home. He called 911 and was transported here for observation. Because of his age, Sam, we were wondering if you could come down to the hospital to help us make some decisions for your friend. He doesn't seem to be lucid in his thoughts right now, and we are concerned about his condition. Can we expect your help with this?"

Not lucid in his thoughts...what's that mean? Mr. Tyler seemed very "with it" when I spoke with him just yesterday. He showed no signs of senility or forgetfulness. Was this something that had just happened today due to his heart attack? I wasn't sure I was the right person for this responsibility. I could hardly make decisions for myself much less another person. He must have family somewhere nearby that could do better than I could. I felt panic setting in. What if he dies because of me? Why would anyone list me as responsible? The best I could do was take care of Bailey. What types of decisions was I expected to make for him?

"Yes, I will be there as soon as I can. I'm at work but I'm sure I can leave if this is an emergency. Can you give me the address please, I just moved here and I'm not familiar with the area. But my office is only three blocks from my apartment, Mr. Tyler's address.

"Yes, the address is Fifty Five Fruit Street Where is your home located, Sam? I can give you directions from there if you'd like."

"The address there is 14 Miner Street"

She gave me directions as if she could see it mapped out in her mind, not missing a detail. I wrote frantically as she spoke, turn here, go three lights down, turn right, enter the circle. I already felt lost. The hospital was about a fifteen minute drive from my office.

"Let me find my supervisor and let her know I have an emergency and that I need to leave. This is my first day of work so please forgive me if I seem a little hesitant. Is Mr. Tyler going to be alright?"

"He seems to be very stable right now. We are watching his vital signs very closely, but in case of any changes, we will need you to be here, Sam. I cannot say any more over the phone. Please come through the emergency access doors at the left-hand side of the building for the ambulance entry and we can direct you from there."

"Thank you, Nurse Paterson, I will be there as soon as I can."

My mind was going crazy with thoughts of Mr. Tyler passing before I could get there. What about his dog, George, and his home and the folks who rented from him? What about Bailey and me? We just moved in and would need to find somewhere else to live. I had no idea how to handle any of this, let alone make any decisions regarding life or death situations. I headed over to Gail's office but she was not there. Next I checked Martha's office but she wasn't in either. I felt panic in my chest, but kept moving to find anyone who could excuse me to leave. Opposite Martha's office was a small, dark and cluttered cubby with a desk and chair. I noticed memos stuck on the walls and piles of paper on the desk. What poor soul did such an awful deed to deserve this space, I thought to myself. As that thought traveled across my mind, someone appeared behind me. It was Keith, the only other friendly face I knew so far.

"What's up, Sam? You have a look on your face like you just saw a ghost."

"Keith, oh man, you are the only one I can find. Listen, I don't mean to put this on you, but I have to leave. I have an emergency at the hospital. My landlord suffered a heart attack and listed me as the 'go-to person.' I just want someone here to know I had to leave. I know it's my first day and I haven't been here more than two hours, but I have to leave. Could you please let Ms. Hansen and Mr. Howards know? I appreciate your help here, Keith."

"Sam, I can't make that kind of decision to let you leave, I don't have any authority here. It could cost me if I just let you leave and they didn't know about it."

"Do you know where Ms. Hansen, I mean, Gail is or Martha?"

"No, I haven't seen them this morning at all. It's not my business to keep track of where they are or what they do. I'm sorry, I can't get involved in your leaving."

I stared into his face for what seemed like minutes, the face of a man who chose to do nothing, be nothing, and feel nothing. I could see I was invading his comfort level, pressing him into an uneasy position.

"That's fine, Keith, I will try to find them to let them know I have to leave. I can't wait any longer."

I turned, realizing that I may have to leave the office without any one of my supervisors aware of where I went. It was a risk I would have to take as I felt I couldn't waste any more time worrying about it. It would be worse if I did not get to the hospital for Mr. Tyler in time. I decided to leave a note on Ms. Hansen's desk and it would have to suffice. I would take the consequences. I scribbled the words down quickly, left my cell phone number if she needed to call, and taped it to her computer screen where I knew she would eventually look. I felt about as unprofessional as I possibly could, but at that moment, it didn't really matter much. I gathered my things; cell phone, car keys, briefcase and directions to the hospital. I left without anyone knowing except Keith.

three

"Think like a man of action and act like a man of thought."

~Henri Bergson~

Sitting in my car, waiting for traffic lights to turn green, for other cars to move out of the way, for "Walk now" signs to change to, "Wait," is a mind game played every day when getting from place to place. But today was different. If I was not panicking, feeling the responsibility of someone's life hanging over my shoulders, I could confidently manage a fifteen-minute ride without sweating. But I was sweating. Notes on computers, no one around to give me affirmation that I was doing the right thing, making life choices for someone I hardly knew...this was not my world. My world was walking Bailey three times a day and feeding him two times a day. I had never had anyone's fate in my hands, and I was not dealing with this concept very maturely.

I pulled into the emergency entrance parking lot seventeen minutes from the time I left the office. No phone calls on the way saying I was too late. I was still feeling that panic sensation in my chest and I was breathing heavier than normal. An alarm buzzed as I passed through the sliding doors of the emergency room just like on those television hospital shows with all the gorgeous doctors and nurses rushing to meet you at the door to take your pulse and monitor your statistics. Not today though, today was the real deal and there I was walking through doors that were going to change who I was, only I didn't know it yet.

The woman at the desk stopped me. "Sir, can I help you with something? This is emergency at Mass General."

Did I look that dazed and confused? I had to pull myself together. People were going to think I needed to be admitted if I didn't get a grip. There was a little old man lying in a room somewhere who thought I was going to handle taking care of some decisions for him and here I was appearing to be the one who needed help. I prayed something brilliant would come out of my mouth.

"I am Sam Wylkes. I was called as an emergency contact person for Mr. Abraham Tyler who was brought into emergency a short time ago. A Nurse Paterson I believe was her name, called me."

"Alright, Mr. Wylkes, yes, let me look this up for you. Can you show me your I.D., please? It's just precautionary."

She looked at my license and then looked at me. She looked at her computer and then looked at my license. I swayed from side to side, trying to be patient. Finally she gave me the green light; everything was in order.

"Everything looks good, Mr. Wylkes, Mr. Tyler is in Section Fourteen, Room Sixteen. I will let Nurse Paterson know you are here. Go left at the end of the hall and the elevators will be on the right. You're going to the third floor."

I thanked her and headed to the elevators. It still felt like I was walking in someone else's shoes. I would only stay a few minutes with Mr. Tyler. I was sure he did not mean to have me make decisions for him. They must have confused me with someone else in the house. Perhaps they just saw my rental contract on the table and figured I was someone they could call. I was sure there had been some mistake and that it would all be cleared up as soon as I talked to Mr. Tyler.

Section Fourteen was easy to find, but Room Sixteen was quite a walk down a very long hallway. It smelled like rubbing alcohol, bedpans, and old people. I didn't like where I was and was eager to get this over with. It felt like death everywhere.

I found Room Sixteen. The sign on the door had Mr. Tyler's name in the slot. But with so many rooms filled with sick people, they could easily make a mistake. Hospitals always made me feel uncomfortable and today was no exception.

I took a deep breath and pushed the door open slowly, as quietly and unobtrusively as I could. I did not want to disturb Mr. Tyler if he was resting. Once inside, I could see his small figure lying in a bed with rails on the sides to prevent falling. To my surprise his hair was tousled and he looked different from how I saw him yesterday, so clean cut and tidy in his appearance. His face was a pasty pale color and his lips were dry and cracked. His mouth was open slightly as his breathing must be more labored for him than normal. His head was turned toward the window and he looked as if he was speaking in a whisper to someone, but there was no one else in the room. His eyebrows were raised as if in conversation and he was using facial expressions as he spoke. Then a small smile came across his face and he nodded his head, gesturing an affirmation of some type in a make-believe conversation. He then closed his eyes so I remained quiet and frozen in my position, not sure if he was asleep or had passed away. Either way, he looked peaceful and content. I didn't want to disturb the moment if it was his last. I dropped my head to my chest and felt a stirring of sadness. I was too late. I took too much time and was too worried about myself and my job. How could I ever justify this? How could I have failed when someone needed me? At that moment, I felt a tear run down my cheek.

"Are you Sam Wylkes? I'm Nurse Paterson."

I jumped when she spoke. How had she snuck up so quietly behind me? My heart was pounding out of my chest.

"Nurse Paterson, oh, hi. I have to tell you, I think Mr. Tyler has passed. I just got here and opened the door and there he was talking like he had someone in the room with him and then he closed his eyes and that was it. I never got to talk to him or ask him any questions. I'm sorry. I am too late to help him."

"Nonsense, Sam, he's drifted off to sleep," Nurse Paterson said. "We gave him medication a little while ago and it makes him sleepy. He's not gone, just sleeping."

"Are you sure? Check his pulse, go on, check it."

I felt the rush of panic returning, the uncertainty of why I was even here. And here I was telling the nurse to check on him. Who did I think I was? I couldn't even tell the difference between death and sleep.

"Sam, just calm down. Mr. Tyler is fine."

She confidently walked over to his bed and checked his pulse for me. I had been so focused on his face that I didn't notice the monitor, working away tracking each beat his heart took. I felt like such a fool.

"If he had an attack, it was extremely mild, but we were concerned because he was mumbling the whole time they put him in the ambulance and also when we settled him into his room. It was as though he was hallucinating, having a conversation with someone. Your name and phone number were in his wallet so you were the one we contacted."

I stepped closer to his bed and could see for myself he was breathing. I felt relieved that he was still alive and I had not witnessed someone's last moment. He seemed to be in a deep sleep as our talking did not stir him. I looked up and saw Nurse Paterson looking at me with a grin on her face.

"Does it make you nervous to be here, Sam? Do you know Mr. Tyler very well?"

"Mr. Tyler is my new landlord. I have only spoken with him on a few occasions regarding the rental at his property. He is a pleasant gentleman and lives with his dog, George. There are people in the apartments of his house who probably know him much better than I do. So you can see why I'm surprised that I would be the one to be called. I will gladly help him in any way I can, it's just a surprise to me. I moved here from Cleveland two days ago. Today was my first day of work. Things have just been a bit hectic."

"He did specifically ask for you while in the ambulance and he did have your name and phone number listed in his wallet to be his contact person. I understand your situation, but we try to honor the request of someone who specifically is asking for one person in particular. There was no other name he gave us. You understand, right?"

"I do. I don't mean to make it a difficult thing. What is it I can help you with regarding Mr. Tyler?"

"It's his state of mind, the hallucinations or pretense he acts out. We just want to observe him regarding that, along with the possible mild heart attack. His vital signs all seem to be back in line to where they should be for someone his age. But it's the other things we are concerned with," Nurse Paterson explained. "We didn't find any drugs in the test we ran on him. Would it be possible for you to take a look around his apartment for anything that may help us determine what is bringing on these visions he has? If it is dementia or some similar condition, we can deal with it through medication and he can live a normal life. He seems to be healthy otherwise."

"I'm not comfortable going through any of his belong-ings, I really don't know this guy well enough. I just can't do that. I can talk to him and try to get some information that way, but I am not going to go through his home and invade his privacy. I would prefer not to be asked to do that."

"He does need to stay here for a few days for observa-tion, Sam, and I understand he has a dog that someone will have to take care of. I think it would be logical for you to do that and it would give him peace of mind to know that you are there. He will sleep for a while now, but we would like you to be here when he wakes up. You'll see what I mean. Can you stay for a while, Sam?"

I considered my new job and how I was going to make this work. What would I say, that I needed time off? I might as well pack it up now. I needed to figure something out and do it quickly. And I really needed to earn a living here because I didn't have much to fall back on. The little amount of money in my bank account wasn't going to last very long. I am not the one in my family who handles these things with ease. Maybe I should call Ruth and get some advice. No, not a good idea, she would never let me live it down. Couldn't handle a little bit of pressure when it came my way. No way will I tell her anything about this. I should call Hannah, she's pretty levelheaded, she must have some experience dealing with a dilemma. She is a compassionate person and has always been there for me. Yes, she's the one I'll cry to. She'll have some good, solid advice.

"Yes, Nurse Paterson, I can stay for a while. It's early yet and I have time before George and Bailey will need to go out and be fed. I will make some arrangements to take care of things."

There, that sounded pretty mature. I will make some arrangements. What she doesn't know is that my sister will solve this for me and I will look like I knew what I was doing. She doesn't need to know any better. I was feeling quite pathetic at the moment after crying when I thought the guy died, and now faking maturity to help him out because he's still alive.

Suddenly I really miss Cleveland.

Nurse Paterson suggested I get a cup of coffee in the cafeteria and wait for Mr. Tyler to wake up. I could talk with him then. The cafeteria didn't have that sterile, rubbing alcohol smell. It was messy and busy. It smelled like strong coffee and sandwiches. And dill pickles. People with stethoscopes around their necks and charts in their hands hurried around in between handling life-threatening situations and pending operations. There were families waiting to hear news, good or bad. Since it was almost 10:00 a.m., I ordered a fruit salad and a cup of coffee. I thought moving to Boston was a big step for me, a mature step, a "taking the world on by myself" step. And the first thing that happens that puts me in a grown-up situation, I run for help.

The ringing of my cell phone brought me out of my thoughts. I looked at the number on the screen and saw it was the office. I couldn't let it go to voicemail. I had to man up and answer it. Take the consequences.

"Hello, this is Sam."

"Sam, this is Ms. Hansen....Gail. Is everything okay? I got your note on my computer. Tell me what's going on."

"Gail, hi. Sorry I had to leave you a note, I know it's not very professional of me. I received a call from the hospital that my landlord suffered a heart attack and they needed me to come right away. There was no one around when I had to leave. Sorry about the note."

"Oh, is he going to be okay? Are you okay?"

"Yes, he's fine for now, they are observing him, they think it was a mild heart attack. I'm just a bit at odds with the whole thing. I mean, I know him but not really well. I am just confused about why I would be called because he has lived here all his life. He probably knows a lot of people much better than he knows me. But, anyway, he's all right, just confused, I guess. They are observing him for a while. Please tell me I'm not in trouble and didn't jeopardize my job."

"No, don't give it another thought. You had an emergency and had to leave, that's understandable. Take all the time you need. We can get things taken care of here another day. Is there anything I can help you with?"

"Thank you Gail, I think everything is okay for now. Thank you for understanding. Like I said, I am a little surprised I was called, but here I am and I will do what I can for the guy. I will give you a call tomorrow and keep you posted with what's going on. Will you pass this on to Mr. Howards, I mean Clive?"

"I will take care of everything. I hope your landlord will be okay. Just give me a call and we will go from there."

"Will do, thanks again."

I hung up, feeling relieved that I was working for understanding people. Could have been fired, I guess.

I finished the last drop of coffee and ate the last bite of my fruit cup. The room had emptied out without my even realizing it. It was time to go upstairs and see if Mr. Tyler was awake. I have come to the conclusion that I don't deal well with hospitals or near death experiences. This day cannot get over quick enough in my opinion. But I would do for Mr. Tyler whatever I could to help him. He has been very kind to me and it's the least I can do for him.

There were no nurses in the room when I returned and Mr. Tyler was sitting up in his bed, looking out the window. He appeared to have a smile on his face, so I figured he was feeling better. I didn't want to startle him so I knocked lightly on the door and called his name.

"Mr. Tyler, it's Sam Wylkes. Can I come in or if you are resting I could come back another time?"

"Sam, son, come in, of course. Come in and sit down if you would. I am feeling much better. Sorry to give you such a scare. I hope this did not inconvenience you in any way. I would feel just awful if coming to my aid interfered with your new job. If you would like, I can speak with your supervisor or boss and explain the situation to them. I would feel just awful if anything were to happen with your new position."

"No, no, Mr. Tyler, there's no need for you to concern yourself about my job. You absolutely did the right thing.

I got here as soon as I could. Is there anything I can do to help you out, Mr. Tyler, anything at all?"

I couldn't help but smile at the old man. He seemed so helpless.

"Actually, Sam, there is. George is home alone and I am very worried about him. Would it be possible for you to take care of him for me until I can come home? I am so worried about him, he's not used to being alone."

I knew the question was coming. Not that I didn't want to help Mr. Tyler, I just get nervous about going into someone's home who I don't know that well. But how could I tell him no, he needed help and he had for whatever reason put his trust in me.

"I will help you in any way I can, Mr. Tyler, you just tell me what I can do for you. I don't want you to worry about anything while you are getting yourself healthy again. Is there anyone in your family I should call, anyone who you would like me to contact for you?"

"Well, I cannot think of anyone, Sam. My dear wife, Elle, is no longer with me. I have a few friends but no one that I see or speak with on a regular basis."

He looked away and turned his eyes toward the window, his thoughts traveling somewhere else as he spoke. For the first time in my life, I looked intently at someone's face, and his eyes seemed sad and lonely. He was such a quiet soul and when he spoke it was with calmness and peace. The laugh lines around his eyes signaled years of smiles and joy from happy times with Elle.

I watched a smile spread across his face and he began to speak.

"When I met Elle, I thought she was the most beautiful woman in the world. She was shy, quiet, so pleasant and sweet and I believe I fell in love with her immediately. Of course, there are a lot of people who don't believe that's possible, but I believe God brought her into my life for me to love and care for. He knew exactly who I could give myself to for my whole life."

He folded his hands gently over his chest, reflecting on the memory of their first meeting. I noticed the skin on his hands showed the signs of old age, folds of skin that had cracked over years of work and toil, displaying the fragile condition of his aged body. Again, a smile spread across his face, an obvious sign that a pleasant memory was crossing his mind.

"I remember our first meeting. She was so unsure if she should talk to me without her father nearby. She took great comfort in her father's protection; she was very close to him and had a great love and respect for him. We courted for a few months and finally she realized I was safe to be with outside of her father's shelter. She had a sweet sense of humor, giggling as we spoke about the warm weather and the way the summer bugs truly assumed their names... bugs! But no matter what, she never lost her poise as a young woman. I remember asking her dad for her hand in marriage, I was so nervous. He shook my hand and said there couldn't be a better man for his little girl. I had a full time position at a bank in town and she worked at the hospital as a nurse. He knew I would work my hardest to support her and take care of her till the end. And he knew I already loved her dearly."

"You must have loved her very much. She sounds like a great woman," I told him.

"Oh, she was. She was loving and strong. We never had any children but we had many wonderful years together. Being a nurse, she cared for children at the hospital and somehow it filled the emptiness of having no children of her own. She spent many hours volunteering, working with handicapped children as well. She was just a loving soul, and I miss her very much. More than you could possibly know."

"If you don't mind my asking, how long has she been gone?"

His eyes changed, and a look of pain and sadness took over his entire demeanor. But, he pressed on with the story.

"It's been almost ten years. It was a Wednesday, the worst Wednesday of my life. Elle had been up almost all night, coughing and achy. So she stayed home from work. She had several bouts of pneumonia in her lifetime and she felt another may have been coming on. I decided to go to work. I kissed her goodbye that morning, told her to rest and that I loved her. I asked her to call me if she needed anything or if she started to feel worse. Little did I know that would be the last time I saw or heard from Elle again. When I got home from work, I pulled the car into the driveway and noticed the front door was wide open. I scrambled, panicked, and made my way inside the house. The living room was in a shambles; an obvious struggle had taken place. I yelled over and over for Elle, going from room to room, asking her to answer me. But there was nothing, no response. I froze right where I stood, I didn't know what to do. I was in shock, I didn't know where to begin, I needed to find Elle, I needed to know what happened to her, I needed to call the police. I fell to my knees on the living room floor, tears pouring down my face, asking God to please lead me. I felt my whole world falling apart. After what seemed like hours, I finally pulled myself together and called the police. They came and asked me questions that to this day,

I vaguely remember. I was devastated as you can imagine, Sam. They never found Elle, there was not enough evidence at the house to give them much to go on. The police and I talked to friends and family and people she worked with but nothing surfaced as far as concrete evidence. Elle was gone and no one had any answers. No one saw or heard anything. I didn't know which way to turn and suddenly my life no longer had the same meaning."

I could see tears in his eyes as he spoke, the sadness still very evident, and the pain of losing the woman he loved for so long, the person he shared every day with and dedicated himself to. I was beginning to understand this man. The many years they were together meant everything to him, made him the person that he was now. I sensed that he relied very much on his faith in God and his prayers.

"Do you have any brothers or sisters, Mr. Tyler?"

"I had a sister, Madeline. She died in the winter shortly after her ninth birthday. I was eleven years old. I had just gotten home from school. Dad met me at the door to let me know she was seriously hurt, that there had been an accident on her way home, and that she may not make it. I could see her but I had to be quiet. I remember I started to cry. Dad put his hand on my shoulder, told me to be strong. He wanted me to see her before she passed. The doctors said it would be soon. Her injuries were too severe and life threatening, there was nothing they could do for her."

I watched the expression in his eyes, the unbearable sadness that took over his entire person. I could not imagine what it must feel like to lose a sibling, one of my family members. The times we had growing up, the memories, even the challenging ones, they have made me who I am and have shaped me. The tearing apart of a family is life changing and the rebuilding must be exhausting. Mr. Tyler's strength was coming through in his words and expressions. I felt my problems were so insignificant, so small. It made me feel selfish and self-centered. I had no reason to complain after listening to his heart-wrenching story.

He continued and I was glued to every word.

"I felt like I was in shock and knew I only had a few minutes to talk to my sister for the last time. I went into her room. My mother was sitting in a chair next to the bed, holding her hand, trying to restrain from breaking down for Madeline. Tears were running down her face and leaving stains on her cheeks, but she smiled down at my little sister and reassured her it was going to be okay. I walked over to the side of the bed. Madeline looked up at me with those big blue eyes she had and smiled that sweet smile that was her signature. I thought at that moment I would never know her beyond that day, no future memories, that what we had done up to that moment was all we would have to hold on to, that she would always be in our minds nine years old. I would never know her as an adult. She would never marry or have children. It all stopped right there that day. I remember her telling me to take care of Mom and Dad and that I could have her bike if I wanted it. I gave a smile and chuckled at that comment. We didn't own bikes; we only talked and dreamed of the day we might have them. We laughed about it, challenging each other with which one of us would have the best color, the fastest bike. My mother gave me an empty glance and nodded for me to go along with what Madeline said. She was getting little oxygen and hallucinating as she drifted in and out of reality. We looked each other in the eyes with tears between us. I promised her I would be there for Mom and Dad and I would finish school and be nice to her friends. Those were the worries she had at that very moment, not about herself, not about dying, not about her pain, but about the people she was leaving behind. I leaned over and kissed her on the forehead and said she should rest. She reached for my hand and squeezed it with what little strength she had and told me not to cry; she would see me again someday in heaven, she promised. I looked down at her tiny hand and saw she had colored her fingernails with crayon. She loved coloring her fingernails. That is still very vivid in my mind, the pink crayon color of her small fingernails. It surprised me how gracefully she exited this world, quiet, peacefully, and with faith that we would meet again. She lived a short life but a life where each day was filled with laughter and smiles. Lots of smiles. It became who she was. She passed just a few minutes after I left the room. I remember my mother for countless days and nights sobbing when she didn't think I could hear her. I promised Madeline I would take care of my mother and father and I knew what she meant when she asked that of me. She meant to fix the hole in their heart, to comfort them if I could. It broke my mother's heart to lose her little girl. I would sit with her and hug her more often than I ever had before. After that day, I never left the house without telling her how much I loved her. Thinking back it must have scared her for me to leave the house every day. I always tried to reassure her I would see her later. It was a tough time and lasted for several years before we readjusted to our lives without Madeline. Dad was a man of strength. He was loving and caring for Mother. He taught me how to give till it hurt, and he always put her before himself.

In my teenage years, I grew to truly admire my dad for his courage, how he hid his own feelings of loss and hurt so my mother could heal. They taught me about patience, togetherness, sacrifice, and faith in God. They gave me my first Bible at the age of fourteen. They knew that I would need it as I got older and searched for answers; they knew I would need something to give me solid ground to turn to. I wanted to understand losing Madeline and heaven and what peace I could find in it all. The years went by and somehow we lived happily, the three of us. And we knew in our hearts that Madeline was always there."

I was mesmerized with his life story. I felt I had been insensitive in asking him about this family. It amazed me that he had such vivid recall of those years so long ago. I was learning little by little about this man of strength and grace, the years of sorting out emotions and tragedies. I listened intently as he continued to speak. I felt my own emotions welling in my throat, that lump that doesn't go away, leaving you on the verge of tears. He was a story-teller, and he held my interest like a good book. I couldn't take my eyes off his face. I wanted to hear more about his life and his Elle, how he grew up, and what the years were like for him and Elle. I felt I could listen to him for days. I was so captivated. There was truly something about this man that took me in, like he was some long lost relative I was just getting to know. I must have appeared mesmer-ized as he shared the story of his childhood. I held on to each word. I was like a sponge every time he spoke, I was eager to soak up every word he said. I had completely forgotten about my new job. It wasn't even on my mind. My focus had completely switched gears from my career to helping this man. I didn't even notice when the nurses came in with Mr. Tyler's lunch. His eyes met mine and he smiled and nodded that all was well. Time had helped heal and conquer the pain of those events. His attention moved to the meal before him. I decided this would be a good time to see about George and let Mr. Tyler get a hot meal in him and maybe some rest. It had been an eventful day and he was probably tired, physically and mentally. I cleared my throat, hoping that any emotion I was feeling would not show. I asked him for some instructions on what to do for George, where his leash was, and how much to feed him.

"Sam, I cannot thank you enough for taking care of George for me at a time like this. I feel I am inconveniencing you, dear boy, but I just was not comfortable with anyone else to tend to him. That's why I had them call you. I know you have Bailey and you care about dogs so I called upon you. I hope you don't mind."

"I will do whatever I can do to help you, and George will be fine. Don't you worry about him at all. You just work on getting yourself better and coming home. I know George will miss you so anything you can tell me to make him comfortable would be helpful."

"Well, I talk to him a lot. I know that will help him be comfortable with you. And just pet him and tell him what a good boy he is, that always calms him down. I sing sometimes, not that you have to, but these are things he is used to. I do hope this is not asking too much of you, Sam."

I chuckled a bit, not because of Mr. Tyler's suggestion, but at the image I had in my mind of me singing. And to a dog, no less. But if it helped George become comfortable with me, I would do it. I just felt sorry for anyone who might hear me. A singer I am not.

four

Mr. Tyler handed me the keys to his home without giving it a second thought. He was trusting me with everything he owned, including George. It took me by surprise because I would not be so trusting of someone I barely knew. But this man had remarkable faith that all would be well with me in his home and with me attending to George.

I pulled into the driveway and parked my car this time behind Mr. Tyler's car instead of in my reserved spot as a tenant. It felt awkward, but I was staying for only a few minutes and it was convenient. I could hear George barking and I was sure he knew the difference in sound between my car and Mr. Tyler's. Dogs are smart and intuitive animals. They could sense something different before we even knew it was coming. I stepped out of my car and heard Bailey chime in, letting everyone know that someone was there. He was probably not used to so many sounds—the traffic, different voices of people going by. Poor old boy, I wondered what he really thought of all this. I had assumed he would just adapt, but animals go through stress when their routines are upset. I figured that the only thing comfortable to him right now was being by my side at all times. Loyal dog, loyal friend. The barking became more intense as I walked up the porch steps to Mr. Tyler's house. George was in the window. He saw me and his demeanor changed. He started to calm down, the barking subsided, and his tail was wagging a mile a minute. I thought that was very strange as this dog didn't know me at all and hadn't even met me through Mr. Tyler. But it eased my mind to know I was entering the house of a friendly dog. I fumbled for the keys and it was at that moment I hesitated. The thought went through my mind...what kind of home would I find inside. Is Mr. Tyler a neat freak? Would everything be in its place, neat as a pin? Or would there be disarray? Dirty dishes and un-mopped floors? I pushed the thoughts aside and decided that whatever I found inside didn't matter. I was here to help this kind gentleman who called upon me today and the rest was irrelevant.

I turned the key in the lock and heard the shuffling feet of a dog just on the other side of the door. George was waiting. I pushed the door open and there he was, sitting down, tail wagging, acting like his master had just returned home after a long day. He seemed happy to see me and not at all upset that I was not Mr. Tyler. George's coat was black, brown, and white and his eyes were big and brown. His bushy tail was wagging up a storm. His ears, a little long for his small head, were covered in soft fur. I couldn't wait to pet him. He seemed so docile and friendly. I was actually looking forward to taking care of him for a short time. Right on the wall by the door was George's leash, just as Mr. Tyler had told me. George nudged it with his button black nose, making sure I knew it was time for him to go out. I reached down to pet him and let him know I meant him no harm. His ears went back and he came right to me. I knelt down for him to get closer and he practically jumped into my lap, licking my face with a warm welcome. I could tell we were going to get along just fine. It took him just a minute more to thoroughly sniff my shoes and then perch himself back on his hind legs, wagging uncontrollably. All was good.

"George, old boy, I'm going to take care of you for a while, so you can expect me here every day until Mr. Tyler comes home."

He cocked his head to the side as I talked to him, appearing to understand my words. He was a gentle animal but this did not surprise me considering his master. He sat wagging his tail, waiting for the leash to be attached and his walk to begin. And then it hit me. The apartment smelled clean, fresh, and well kept. I looked around and saw a tidy home. I grinned. This should not surprise me because everything about this situation has been unusual. George was looking up at me wondering what the holdup could be. I was taking more time than he was used to. I bent down and hooked the leash on to his collar. He led the way out the door and down the steps to the sidewalk. He kept looking back, checking to make sure I was still following. It was a quick walk and in a matter of minutes we were making our way back into the house. George seemed satisfied with the short jaunt. Bailey could learn a thing or two from George. Bailey was too young to give up his wandering and snooping. I took George's leash off, making sure I put it back where I found it. Mr. Tyler appeared to be very neat with his surroundings and I wasn't about to let him down. A thought occurred to me as I stooped down to pet George before I left. Mr. Tyler had left abruptly this morning for the hospital and may have mistakenly left something on. I decided to check around the house before I left. Although it didn't set well with my gut instincts and snooping wasn't my thing, I made my way to the living room where I noticed a huge bookshelf with framed photos on top. Upon closer inspection, I decided the couple in the photos was Elle and Mr. Tyler. She looked just as sweet as I had imagined from Mr. Tyler's description. She was a small woman with big blue eyes, high cheekbones, and beautiful structure to her face. I didn't usually notice those things about people, but this photo of Elle drew me in. Her eyes were a cool blue color, very lovely. Her hair was a soft brown and swept across her brow in a very demure fashion. I could see why Mr. Tyler fell in love with her. She had such a sweetness about her that came through even in a photo. I noticed another framed photo of a young girl and a boy who looked to be a few years older. This one appeared to be very old. I guessed it was Mr. Tyler and his sister Madeline who had died so many years ago. She had similar features to Mr. Tyler. The facial structure, the eyebrows, and shape of their eyes were the same. Her complexion was darker, but her eyes were the same shade as his. She was a beauty, to say the least. Mr. Tyler must have felt lonely without his sister, having to finish growing up on his own. Even though he loved his parents and they did everything they could for him, the void of losing a sibling must be difficult. Another photo, black and white, was perhaps Mr. Tyler's parents. It appeared to be a husband and wife sitting next to each other. The woman's head was tilted toward the man and she smiled sweetly, but her eyes looked sad. Next to that frame was yet another black and white photo of parents and two children. The younger child looked to be about two or three years old and the older child, a boy, no older than five or six. This was Mr. Tyler's family photo; the treasure of all photos. I wondered if Mr. Tyler's parents had given it to him when he left home to marry Elle, so that he would never forget his only sister. This was a loving family and the joy in their eyes and smiles was evident. It would have only been a few years later that they would lose Madeline. Suddenly I felt that I was invading Mr. Tyler's privacy, snooping into his personal life when he wasn't there. I felt I was taking advantage of his trust in me by looking at his family photos. I needed to leave. I continued my walk through the house, checking out the kitchen for anything left on. It was spotless. It looked like a housekeeper had already come through. Everything was in its place and it looked almost unlived in. Magazine perfect—that's what it looked like. I walked down a hallway and into a bedroom. The bed was made, pillows fluffed, everything looked too perfect. The blankets on the bed were tucked in as though done by a professional. What the heck was going on here? Maybe he did have a maid and she had already came for the day. That was the only explanation I could come up with. Things seemed a bit too perfect for the home of an elderly gentleman who lives alone with his dog. Even the dog was in good shape. I continued my walk-through but nothing seemed to be of concern. In fact, there was probably more to be concerned about with the way I left my apartment this morning than there was here. My skepticism mounted as I passed the bathroom. Nothing appeared to be touched in there either. Towels hanging perfectly, everything spic and span. No one lived in this house, that's how it felt to me. Again, the question kept running through my mind. How does someone the age of Mr. Tyler live so immaculately? I wandered back to the front room of the house. George was lying on the floor looking at me with a questioning expression. I decided it was probably strange for him to have someone he doesn't know walking around his house. Any other dog would be anxious and would follow me around. George just lay there quietly, unbothered by any of this. I looked at him and he looked back at me, tail wagging. I noticed there was no dust on any of the tables and the floors were immaculate. Something very strange was going on. I decided it was time for me to have a talk with Mr. Tyler. Maybe the other tenants would know something. Maybe I should pay them a visit and see if they had some answers. Was this elderly gentleman just a neat freak and I couldn't accept that? Perhaps I was mistaken and giving my imagination something to work with. I could be tired. After all, it had been a very stressful few days with moving and the new job. Maybe my mind was on overload. Suddenly, I missed Cleveland again, missed my friend Jake, and my old, boring job.

I decided to lock up and go upstairs to take care of Bailey while I was there. I was sure it would be a nice surprise for him to get a walk in the middle of the day. I needed to feel normal and being with Bailey would help. I made sure the key was in my pocket before I left. George was sleeping soundly. He never even looked up as I pet him on the head and then left. None of this bothered him. Strange. Bailey would be shaking and nervous if he was in this situation. I walked around the back of the house and up the stairs to my apartment, my foot catching on the top step as usual.

What was it about that top step? Maybe I could find some boards in the garage and replace that step with a new one. I would talk to Mr. Tyler about it when I got back to the hospital later. I unlocked the door and Bailey was already barking to ward off any intruders.

"It's just me, boy, home early to take you out for an afternoon walk. How about that, huh? You want to get out for a short walk?"

He looked at me in disbelief. His tail was wagging and he was running himself in circles by the time I got his leash ready.

"Sit down and sit still, give me a chance to get this leash on you."

His excitement was getting the best of him. He couldn't sit still no matter how many commands I gave him. This was a treat he almost never experienced: a walk in the middle of the day. I got the leash on and we were on our way out the door when my cell phone rang. Bailey was all geared up. I didn't think I could keep him from running down the steps if I tried. I let it go to voicemail. I would check it when I got back upstairs. Bailey was bolting down the stairs, his excitement overtaking anything I could say to calm him down. Instead of trying to contain him, I decided to move with him, hurrying myself down the stairs in order to keep up. He's not usually this desperate when I come home from work to take him out. This was not like him at all. One more thing to make this day a very strange one. Bailey was acting unusual, George was simply way too calm, and Mr. Tyler's house was way too perfect. Bailey was practically pulling me along on his leash. I needed to step it up to keep up with him. He found a good spot, and I got to catch a breather. He wasted no time, did his duty, and now was interested in sightseeing. There weren't too many people out and about this time of day. Bailey was in hunt mode, trying to scope out any strange smells of unfamiliar dogs. I took this chance to look at my phone to see who called. It was Jake. Now I wished I had picked up the call, it would have been great to talk to someone who was normal in my life. As soon as we got back inside, I would call him back. Maybe hearing from a friend would settle my mind from everything that happened today. I tugged on the leash to give Bailey the signal we were done but he resisted and chose to go about his business. I tugged a little harder this time and he understood and came to my side. Just as we started to cross, a car came around the corner with the windows down and music playing excessively loud. I could barely make out what type of song it was as it flew by us. Bailey was startled and took a few steps back. He started to bark, reacting to the danger. I caught a quick glimpse of the person behind the wheel, a young man wearing sunglasses, sitting tall in the seat. He was looking straight ahead and never noticed us. The next thing I heard was a crash close enough for me to wonder if it was the reckless car that just sped past. The sound jolted us. Bailey's ears went back. A few people were starting to head in the direction of the noise. It couldn't be more than a block up the road. I didn't want to take Bailey into a situation where there was a lot of commotion. I quickly crossed the street to Mr. Tyler's house and got Bailey back inside the apartment. I would feel much better not taking him with me to check out what happened. I made my way back downstairs and across the street to where the accident was now drawing a crowd of onlookers. I wanted to see if I could help; I was in no way a curious bystander. I realize many people make their way to the scene of an accident just to be curious, to somehow be a witness to a fatality. I could never understand that type of curiosity, it seems rather morbid to me. As I came upon the crowd forming, I saw the car that had sped so quickly past Bailey and me, the music no longer playing. I made my way along with the crowd and heard sirens blaring in the distance. Someone had contacted the police, and it sounded as if they would be here in a matter of minutes. As I walked past the frozen onlookers, a strange feeling overtook me. I didn't know what I was about to see. Steam rose from the hood of the car, and its front end was mangled, making it look much shorter than it had when it sped past me moments ago. Traffic had started to pile up in all directions, and onlookers were taking up space along the sidewalk. I was hesitant to look into the vehicle so I kept my sights on the front fender and broken light. A bystander was quick to give his account and as he spoke, I tried to envision what had happened.

"Can you believe this? I have never seen anything so strange in my whole life."

A young woman standing beside the gentleman seemed to be in complete disbelief. No doubt the police would hear several renditions of what took place. I turned to face the car and saw the smoldering steam still seeping out from under the hood. It seemed like a lot more smoke than there should have been. I dared not look any further than the mangled vehicles themselves, knowing inability to deal with disaster.

"Please, folks, step aside, let me through."

The police officers arrived quickly and I was thankful they were finally on the scene. Anyone who was there at the time would surely be asked questions as to what they saw and what they remembered. The officers walked around both cars. The first officer stayed with the vehicles and the second one approached the crowd of spectators.

To my surprise, I was the first to be questioned.

"Sir, can you tell me what you saw, if anything?"

I had never in my life had to give my account of something like this. I had never witnessed an accident. I felt nervous and my throat was tightening up. But I knew I had to offer whatever information I could.

"I was out walking my dog not even a block away and the car came around the curve in quite a hurry. The radio was blaring and it seemed to me even then he had no intention of slowing down. I don't recall seeing him hit his brakes. I remember backing away from the curve in order to keep my dog and myself from getting hit. We just moved in a few days ago, and I don't really know anyone around here so I can't really help you with recognizing anyone. My landlord and a few folks I have met today at my new job are the only people I know so far."

Suddenly I felt that I was babbling, talking to save myself from blame, giving an alibi to mark my whereabouts. The officer and I both turned toward the car to find the driver's seat empty.

The police officer turned to question someone else, to see whether or not our stories were the same. I felt relieved. I glanced at the other car and there was someone sitting in the front seat. It looked like a young woman but she didn't look hurt. One of the officers was making his way over to her car, glancing at the headlight and the crushed hood of the abandoned vehicle as he walked past it. The young girl would be able to give the details from her point of view but it still wouldn't clear up the fact that the driver of the other car had now disappeared. I saw the car go around the corner, I saw the guy sitting in the driver's seat, and I heard the crash. Not much of an account, but it was an honest one. This all seemed too strange, too spooky. I woke up today with one concern: my new job. And at this point, it is at the bottom of my list of concerns. The officer was talking to the young lady. She was shaking her head, using her hands to describe the collision, how the car came around the corner at high speed, and smashed into her. Her flailing arms were probably telling the story of how he crossed into her lane. She put her hand to her throat as if to express surprise. She was a very demonstrative individual. The officer pointed toward the other car, probably asking her where the driver was and if she saw anyone leave the car. I wondered if her answer would be the same as mine. I saw no one leave the car. One minute he was there and the next minute he was gone. I decided this would be a good time to call Jake. I needed to talk to somebody who was saner than I was right now. I grabbed my phone out of my pocket and scrolled down to his number. It rang two times, three times...then, "Hello?"

"Jake, it's me, Sam. Listen, I have to talk to you. Do you have a few minutes or are you busy?"

"Hey, Sam, I've been trying to call you. I got a call from the hospital today. They have my mom there and they think she had some type of heart attack. I don't know. I'm on my way over to the hospital. I don't know what to think, it just came out of the blue. I don't have the whole story yet but I will call you when I do. Is everything all right with you? You didn't answer your phone."

"Yeah, everything's fine."

I didn't have the heart to put more stress on the guy with my problems. He had enough to handle right now.

"Has your mom been sick or anything like that? I know these things can happen all of a sudden, you know. Are you okay, Jake?"

"I'm okay. No, I don't think Mom's been sick, but you know, she wouldn't tell me if she was. That's just who she is. But I'll be better when I find out what's going on with her. I'll touch base with you later, okay?"

"Yeah, man, don't worry, everything will be okay. Hang in there. Maybe it's just something that's causing some stress. You know how it is."

"Yeah, listen, I will call you later. Thanks for calling back."

"Sure, talk to you later. And Jake, take it easy, call me if this turns out to be serious."

"Alright, talk to you later."

We hung up and I felt no better than I did before the call. In fact, I felt worse. Poor Jake, handling his mom's heart attack by himself. His dad lived in Phoenix last I knew and had remarried. So Jake's mom was all he had. I should have suggested he call my mom and dad. They knew him as well as his own parents did and they certainly would be there for him. He and I practically lived at each other's houses growing up. I remember summertime, you could bet we were either having dinner with my family or at his mom's house. She was an awesome cook. She could make the best meals out of nothing. I always told Jake he had the best mom in the world because he would never go hungry. Not that my mom couldn't cook, but nothing like Jake's mom. It's odd, I never called her by her real name, which is Esther. I always called her mom. And since she was not married to Jake's dad any longer, I didn't really have a formal name to give her. Should I call her Mrs. Harmon, which is her ex-husband's last name, or do I call her ma'am? She was a pleasant woman but somehow, to me anyway, always had a sad way about her underneath that smile. And she tried to hide it when Jake and I were together. I felt bad that she had to raise Jake alone and that she had such a crappy situation. Maybe that's why Jake and I were so close, we both needed to have someone we understood, that person we didn't feel inferior to. I never thought much about the emotional stuff. We just naturally hit it off. I would do anything I could for Jake; he was like a brother to me. And now this was happening when I wasn't there to help him. I should call my mom and see if she could be there for Jake just in case it turns out to be bad news. I would hate myself if something serious happened and Jake was alone. I didn't even know what hospital his mom was in, I hadn't thought to ask. There are four major hospitals in Cleveland and it could be any of them. And I didn't want to call if he was driving to the hospital. I decided it would be best if I waited it out. If I believed in prayer, I would be praying right now, not just for Jake and his mom, but for all the things that had happened today, for the situations that didn't make sense.

The police officer made his way back over to his car. I faintly heard him talking to his fellow officer in the car with him. He didn't seem to spend much time with the girl in the other car, probably not much to tell. The officers did a lot of mumbling. I had just stood there. I had nowhere to go and no one to talk to. The people standing around were talking among themselves. For just a brief moment, I got a good feel for all these folks from the community, coming out of their houses when something happened. It gave me the feeling that if anything happened to me, perhaps they would be there to help me. The young girl was standing outside the car and she seemed shaken and confused. She was on her cell phone. I felt the least I could do was go over and ask her if I could drive her anywhere. I would see if I could help in some way.

"Sam Wylkes, is that you?"

I turned quickly, but didn't see anyone I recognized.

"Sam, hey, it's me, Casey. You remember, I was in the same night class you took for accounting? Are you serious, what are you doing in Boston?"

For the life of me, I could not place this person. That class was over a year ago and I didn't remember anyone by the name of Casey. I didn't make many friends during that time; I just wanted to get through the course and move on. I looked into the face of this guy but nothing was coming back to me at all.

"I'm sorry, but do I know you? You don't look familiar to me at all. I don't mean to be rude but really, it's not coming back to me at all. Can you refresh my memory a little?"

"Casey Burns, don't you remember? We studied together that one weekend right before finals. A whole group of us ordered pizza and had some beer. It was at Paul's house, down on Creek Street. You remember, there were about eight of us that decided to study together, for all the good that did us, right? We studied and then went out for midnight bowling with Jim and his girlfriend? You remember now?"

"I'm sorry but I'm not remembering any of this. Are you sure it was me and not someone else? I don't know anyone by the name of Paul and I haven't bowled in years. I think you have me confused with another person. I was in the class, but I really don't remember you."

"And here I thought I had the face no one would ever forget. I suppose I could have you confused with another person, but I am pretty sure it was you. There was Paul, Gregg, Brett, Ryan, Glen—none of those guys ring a bell with you? How about Rita, you have to remember Rita...short, blond, brown eyes, real smart, we all fought over who would sit next to her in the hopes she would let us see her answers. I think she liked you more than any of the rest of us."

"Nope, I am not remembering any of this. I think you have the wrong person. I mean, my name is Sam Wylkes, but I was not a part of that study group. And for the life of me, I do not remember a Casey Burns, no offense. I'm real sorry, wish I could remember this stuff, but, I'm not your guy."

"Okay, if you say so. Pretty weird though, it's clear as day to me. Well, sorry to have taken up your time here, wish we could have caught up with each other under better circumstances. Looks like someone's going to be in trouble for this mishap."

He peered over my shoulder at the two banged up vehicles. I turned to look with him. When I turned back around after a few seconds to shake hands with him regardless of my memory loss, he was gone. As quickly as he came over to me, he had left. Where did he go? I took a few steps to look around, but he was nowhere. I turned and faced the two vehicles, shaking my head in disbelief, knowing in my gut that something was going on here that didn't add up. I decided to leave the accident scene. Traffic had begun to back up and police were diverting vehicles to go around the accident scene. Several trucks were insistent on making their own decisions on where to go, creating more havoc than necessary. Things were just too strange and I doubted very much this girl needed any help from a stranger. I needed to get back to Mr. Tyler anyway. He needed my help—that I was sure of.

five

I walked back to my apartment, confused about what had just occurred. This whole day was filled with unusual events. I was trying to make some sense of the bits and pieces, from Mr. Tyler's heart attack to people disappearing from the scene of an accident. I made my way upstairs to see if Bailey needed anything before I drove back to the hospital to check on Mr. Tyler. I wasn't even sure what I was going back for. I wondered if he needed me to stay at his house, or if I would keep George at my place during the night. Upstairs I found Bailey sleeping. Even as I opened the door, he lay still, breathing deeply, probably in a dream state. Good old boy. I went into the bathroom to splash some water on my face. I really needed to get a grip. I wondered how Jake was doing and what he had found out about his mom. I didn't want to wait. I wanted to know now so I could rest assured that Jake was okay. I dried my face and headed back for the door. Bailey was still asleep. I knelt down to pet him goodbye. He lifted his head, ears back, tail wagging, and gave me a sleepy look. My good old boy, how lonely I would be without him.

Traffic back to the hospital was bumper-to-bumper. I didn't have the patience to be waiting in a long line of cars. The headache that had started this morning was now making my whole head throb. I was looking forward to going to bed tonight. I hoped that if they released Mr. Tyler, he would rest through the night and that George would only need to go out once until morning. I felt selfish thinking it, but I really needed some sound rest. I was looking forward to this day being over and I hoped that tomorrow would start without incident or chaos. Perhaps I would go to work and all of this would be a faded memory. A few more blocks and I would be at the hospital. I wanted nothing more than to get through the next couple of hours. My phone rang and I immediately thought of Jake. I was worried about his situation, and on a day like today, I felt anything could happen. I fumbled for the phone on the passenger seat but it stopped ringing before I reached it. I decided to check it when I got to the hospital. I pulled up to the stop light and waited, paying no mind to my surroundings. I yawned. The stress of the day was taking its toll. My eyes felt tired and they stung when I blinked. I took off my sunglasses and rubbed them to clear my vision. I began feeling impatient, as the light was not changing. The "walk" sign was green and people crossed in front of me. I looked up to see the long, dark coat and hat. It was the phantom from the grocery store crossing right in front of me, but the face was turned far enough away for me to miss even a glimpse of who this person was. I rolled down my window and yelled to the phantom, but the person kept on walking, never glancing over at the fool yelling out the window. I suddenly felt embarrassed. People in nearby cars were staring, wondering who I was yelling at and why. I looked away, wishing that I could become invisible. This scene was as bad as the grocery store episode with "Amber" or whatever her name was. I wondered if I would ever meet this phantom person and end the mystery. I felt certain that they must live nearby, and possibly worked somewhere between Mr. Tyler's house and the hospital. As much as I wanted to know, now was not the time to focus on this mystery person. Finally, the light turned green and traffic began moving. I noticed people staring at me as they passed, hoping to catch a glimpse of the loon who was yelling at random pedestrians. I wished this bizarre and unnerving day would end. I was a block away from the hospital. I hoped Mr. Tyler would be awake and ready to go home. I could get him situated and get back to life as I knew it. Tomorrow I would go to work and make a living helping other companies with their finances or at least explaining their lack of finances to them. No more hospital runs, no more George, no more strange accidents and people disappearing, no more phantom figures roaming the street to peak my curiosity. Just normal stuff like walking Bailey twice a day, buying groceries, talking to Jake, and watching a good baseball game on television. The hospital came up quickly on the right. Thankful to be out of the traffic, I turned into the parking lot and drove around a few times looking for a parking space. My head was still pounding. I checked the glove compartment for some aspirin and found nothing. I could ask one of the nurses if they would give me something to ease the throbbing in my temples. I stuffed my keys in my pocket and grabbed my phone, remembering now that I had missed a call. It was Jake, darn it, I didn't want to miss his call. He left a message but all it said was, "Leave me a message and I will get back to you." I didn't know what to think. I wondered if his mother was okay.

I called back and it went straight to voicemail. I thought of what I should say, not knowing if something serious had happened. My words were stuck in my throat. All I could get out was, "Jake, hey, sorry I missed your call. I was driving at the time, but give me a call back when you get this message or when you get a chance. Hope everything is okay. Talk to you later. Bye."

It was so generic, so meaningless and rehearsed. I could have been talking to an associate at work or a stranger for that matter. But because of the uncertainty of the situation, I wasn't sure how much to say. It had been a strange day and I didn't want to take my chances saying the wrong thing to a close friend. He would call me back when he got a chance. Hopefully I would be home resting in my chair with Bailey at my feet when he called and his mother would be okay, nothing serious, just a case of bronchitis or something. I hoped.

The double doors opened automatically as I entered the hospital. I stopped at the desk to remind them that I was there to see Mr. Tyler. They remembered me and let me go right through. I asked the receptionist if it was possible to get a couple of aspirin for a headache. She declined and reminded me of the legalities of handing out medication to people who randomly walked through the doors. I accepted her answer, gave her a smile, and decided to just deal with it. I walked to the elevator and waited for it to reach my floor. It seemed to be taking forever. Either that or I was experiencing anxiety. My level of patience was running low. Finally the doors opened and I managed to get inside and brace myself up against the wall. I was starting to sweat and the palms of my hands felt clammy. I felt dizzy and everything started to spin. I held on to the railing to try to stop myself from falling over or passing out. I felt as though I was going to throw up. I blinked my eyes several times to try to focus and then closed them for a brief moment. The upward motion of the elevator wasn't helping. I kept my eyes closed for a few moments, took a few deep breaths and tried to think about something pleasant and calming. I had this experience only one other time in my life and I remembered it clearly. My sister accidently shut the car door on my fingers as I was getting into the back seat of our station wagon. I saw stars and felt a rush of blood go through me like a rocket, a pain that shot through every nerve of my body. It was a feeling I will never forget. Now I was feeling the same type of rush but with no pain. After a few deep breaths the dizziness and sick feeling started to subside. Thankfully I was alone in the elevator. Maybe my blood pressure was elevated, or maybe I was feeling the full stress of the day. Whatever it was, it was subsiding. By the time I reached the third floor, I was better. It had come on quickly and left the same way. I cast it off as nothing to be concerned about unless it started to happen on a regular basis. I attributed it to the unusual day I was having. I decided that if there was something to worry about, at least I was in the right place.

I stepped off the elevator and headed for Section Fourteen. The hospital was exactly as many had described it to me: huge. A person could get lost for days in these corridors, wandering aimlessly despite how clearly the directions seemed.

The walk down the corridor to Mr. Tyler's room did me good. I felt like myself again by the time I approached his door, which had been left ajar. I walked in and saw him lying on the bed with his head against his pillow and a smile on his face. He looked peaceful and content with the world, as if nothing bad was happening and nothing could disturb his positive outlook. I only hoped that I would have the same outlook when I reached an elderly age. Mr. Tyler seemed to be the type who felt life was too short to worry about the small details. He seemed like a person that you could draw strength from. I realized I had gained respect for Mr. Tyler. I felt like I knew him well from hearing about the trials of his life and the loves and losses he experienced. There were many people who would not have been able to endure these things as he had and remain so joyful. He seemed to possess a secret about life, about hope that I couldn't quite describe. But it was a powerful part of who he was and it was evident when you were talking to him. I quietly made my way to the chair by the window. I sat down and decided to wait for him to wake up. And maybe I would tip my head back and close my eyes for a short nap myself. Having the quiet time would perhaps allow me to shed the events of this strange day. I closed my eyes and listened to the stirring of people in the corridor. I soon drifted into a shallow sleep. I could still hear voices and noises around me but at the same time, my body was resting and my mind was floating. A deep sleep came at last, sitting in that chair, waiting for Mr. Tyler to stir. I dreamed I was walking toward a building. I could feel my feet moving and the long coat I was wearing dragged on the ground as I moved. I felt like I was almost floating on top of air. I could feel my feet as I stepped on the ground, moving forward, walking toward another person. My hands hung slightly beyond the coat sleeves, and I flexed my fingers into a grip and then released them. My eyes were focused on a person standing before me, next to the building. My body stiffened as if I were walking into battle, one I would take on with brute force, fighting with my bare hands. I could hear my breathing, labored and deep. I was making aggressive strides toward this figure. The building became a moving slideshow, windows blurring past me with faces of people I had never seen before. There was a calm in my motion, a confidence that I would win this battle. A courageous victory was before me. The air swiped past my face, brushing my skin with grit and grime. I moved like a shadow, my long coat closing in behind me as I lunged into the dim existence, the gray emptiness beyond my reach. It was time to do battle and I could feel my body existing for that reason only; my mind set on one exact goal. The ghostly figure suddenly before me had no face, no smell, and I had no fear of it. I glided forward and my hands formed into fists, clenched for destruction. My whole life had existed for this very moment, this one moment to define all others. I heard voices, rustling, movement around me. The refusal to be distracted was strong. My eyes were open, focused, controlled. But the voices became stronger and I could feel my body slipping away from the power it felt before, and the voices from far away became closer. I woke up slouched in the chair by the window, mouth open, head tilted. I didn't know how long I had been sleeping. My eyes opened to see eyes looking at me. I tried to pull myself upright in my chair, shaking my head of the fog I was feeling. I wondered if I had been snoring.

"Sam, are you okay, son?" I heard Mr. Tyler asking me from behind the nurse who was looking down at me. She was making a diagnosis with her frown, trying to figure out if I was having some type of episode or seizure.

"I'm fine, Mr. Tyler, I must have dozed off for a minute there. Sorry if I snored or talked in my sleep. Did I talk in my sleep?" I looked around the room.

"No, I don't think you snored, son, but you were mumbling something, it didn't really sound like words. Were you having a bad dream?"

"I don't think it was a bad dream."

I felt like I was slurring my words. I glanced down at my hands, remembering the strength I felt, the sense of unbelievable power. I have never had that kind of dream before, seeing myself as a powerful character. I was strong and prepared for a battle I was determined to win. I felt strange, unable to fully gain my composure and become myself again. The nurse finally stepped back away from my chair and let me catch some air. I pulled myself up to a sitting position and cleared my throat. Redirecting all attention off myself, I asked, "Mr. Tyler, how are you feeling?"

"I'm feeling somewhat rested, my friend. Are you sure you are all right? You must have needed to sit and rest. Why I think you must have slept for at least an hour."

The nurse was still relatively close to me. She kept her eyes on me and I looked back at her. I knew what she was thinking. She wanted to take my blood pressure at that very moment, convinced that there was something very wrong with me. I looked away from her and turned my attention to Mr. Tyler.

"Oh, that's impossible, what time is it, anyway? I couldn't have slept that long, it only felt like a few minutes."

"No, no, it's been a while. I woke and saw you sitting with your head back, sleeping away."

I was determined to sway the attention off of me and my dream. "Well, I must have had to catch a short nap. I guess the excitement of the day caught up with me. Oh, and by the way, George is fine. He gave me no problems, greeted me at the door, and I had no trouble getting him to take his walk for me. He is a nice old dog, seems very content. It took me a little while to get back here because there was an accident right down the street from your house. Strangest thing."

"Oh, George is the best. He has been such a faithful companion to me. I hate that this has happened and I cannot be there for him. And thank you so much, Sam, for taking such good care of him while I am here. I am indebted to you, son."

He didn't ask about the accident, which I thought was odd, but perhaps he had his health on his mind and, of course, how George was doing took priority.

"So, do you think they are letting you go home today?"

In the back of my mind, I was really hoping he was going home and I could get back to normal everyday stuff.

"Well, I think they are waiting for test results before they decide. I feel tired but otherwise, fine."

He turned toward the window, looking away from me, maybe in an attempt to hide something that his eyes and face might tell me but that he didn't want me to know. His eyes were drawn and he looked tired despite the fact that he had been resting. And he looked bothered. Something was on his mind, I could tell.

"Mr. Tyler, is there something bothering you? Is it the hospital? Has something happened here that you are unhappy with? Because I can talk to someone if you want me to. I don't want you to be uncomfortable with anything here."

He looked at me as if he were surprised at my question and with the protective stance I was assuming. I had surprised myself when the words came out of my mouth. They didn't sound like me at all. I am the last one to take a stance. I usually step back and let others handle those uncomfortable things. I am not much of a fighter. What possessed me to say that? Must be in the spirit of the day. He did not answer me.

A new face came into the room, Mr. Tyler's doctor I presumed. He was tall, elderly, and prestigious looking. Probably very respected. He seemed confident and in charge. He had a smile on his face and his eyes were very prominent. I could tell he was someone who would look directly into your soul when he spoke to you. He made his way to the side of Mr. Tyler's bed and rested his hand on Mr. Tyler's shoulder as he began to speak.

"Mr. Tyler, how are you doing, my friend?"

"Dr. Jamison, I'm doing well, just a bit tired. Worried about old George, you know. Didn't expect to find myself in the hospital today but here I am."

"Well, I do need to speak with you a bit about what happened today. Is this a family member here with you, Abe?"

Abe, it suited him I thought to myself. Most people would think of Abraham Lincoln I guess. Not too many "Abes" around these days.

"This is Sam, he lives at my house. You can speak in front of him. He is helping me get back on my feet and any health issues you may need to speak with me about, I think it is safe to say with Sam in the room. So please, Dr. Jamison, what is it you need to share with me?"

It was interesting to me how Mr. Tyler never truly answered the question...was I family, friend, lawyer? He simply portrayed me as a trustworthy part of his life. I choked up at the thought that I was regarded as a confidant to such a gracious, kind gentleman who crossed my path through a newspaper advertisement. I had to admit, it felt good to be appreciated and respected as someone even a stranger could trust. It made me feel a little proud of myself. After all, there had not been many times when I had done something for someone else, other than Jake. Maybe I should work on this new part of me, this caring component of my personality I didn't even know existed until today.

"Alright, Abe, I will tell you what our findings have been so far. Through all the testing we have done, EKG and all else, we have found nothing wrong with your heart. Your blood pressure is a little high but nothing of concern for your age. Your heart rate is excellent, no unusual signs of stress, no blockage, no damage, nothing. We really have no explanation for what may have caused the pain in your chest to happen the way it did because quite honestly, all the things you described pointed toward a heart attack. We just cannot find anything that warrants that. Perhaps it was simply an anxiety attack. Is there anything that has come about recently that would make you feel anxious, Abe? Now, I have been your doctor for many years and you have been as healthy as a farm horse. I do not see a lot of people in as good health at your age as you are. I was really surprised when you came in with chest pains. But, I can tell you, I am glad to give you the news that we just didn't find anything."

I sat quietly in the background. Hearing this news prompted me to lean forward and rest my head in my hands. I was so relieved that this old man was going to be okay. Mr. Tyler responded to this news in a cheerful voice. I felt an overwhelming feeling of joy myself.

"Dr. Jamison, this is wonderful news," he said, and then I heard him whisper, "Thank you, Elle, for watching over me."

I was so moved at that moment, this man clearly felt the presence of his wife and was obviously still relying on her to watch over him and protect him. All this time I thought when he was looking out the window with a faraway look that he had lost touch with the real world, but in reality it was him simply focusing on the sweet face of his wife as he was trying to conjure whatever memories he could. I was sure he didn't go through one day without talking to her, feeling her presence with him. I didn't know if that was healthy or insane, but it was sweet that he never lost his desire to have her in his life. The room was silent as Dr. Jamison and I didn't know what to say at that moment. We waited patiently for Mr. Tyler to lead the conversation. I looked at him and smiled to reassure him I was as happy with this news as he was.

He looked back at me, lowered his head, closed his eyes, folded his trembling hands, and spoke again in a whisper, "Thank you for sending Sam to be with me."

I couldn't help the rush of emotion I felt. My eyes welled. This man had touched me in a way that even my own parents didn't. I didn't think of myself as an uncaring individual but up until now, there hadn't been a whole lot for me to become emotional about. My life was pretty routine and not much rocked me. Even moving to Boston didn't bring a tear to my eyes when I said goodbye to my parents or even Jake. But this was somehow different.

"Abe, I am glad things are working out this way for you, my friend. I have been your doctor for so many years, and it was disturbing to me that something might be wrong. I love sharing good news. Doctors don't always get to do that."

"Oh, Dr. Jamison, you have no idea. I am so grateful for such good news. Now I can just figure out what might have caused the stress. I truly don't have any idea. I am pretty easygoing, as you know. So, I will try to take it easy and keep doing what I am doing. Walking George a couple of times a day should give me the exercise I need. It does disturb me a bit, not knowing what may have caused this, but you know me, I won't give it another thought. Life is too short to worry about the unknown. Just live each day as best we can. Do you think I can go home today?"

"Well, Abe, I think we can release you."

Dr. Jamison turned and spoke to me for the first time since he came into the room. "Sam, do you think you can get our friend Abe here home safely and maybe keep an eye on him for a few days? We just want to make sure there is no recurrence to worry about. But I do have to say, he is as healthy as an old goat."

"Sure, I can get Mr. Tyler home and look after him for a bit until he gets his energy back and feels like himself again. It would be a pleasure. Should he take it easy for a few days or can he get back to his normal routine? I mean, I can walk George if he needs me to help. I don't want to push him back into doing too much too soon."

"Oh, Sam, I cannot bother you to do that," Mr. Tyler said. "You have your work. You just started a new job and just moved here. I am sure I will be fine, you don't need to worry about me."

I gave a look to Dr. Jamison. He had a smile on his face. He probably knew Mr. Tyler well enough to know that he would say those exact words. He didn't want to bother anyone with his needs. But I was not feeling comfortable with him being alone right now.

"Actually, Mr. Tyler, I think I will decide for you. I think I will stay with you for a few days, just to make sure you are strong enough and sleeping well enough to be back on your own. I have made my decision and I think that's what we are going to do. I will let you do your normal routine but I think I would feel better if I was there with you for the first few days. And if anything were to happen, you would not be alone. Yup, that's what I think we are going to do."

Mr. Tyler looked at me, nodded his head, and said, "Okay, if you feel that strongly about it, Sam. I think that is a good idea as well, just to make sure. After all, since we don't really know what caused this, maybe it would be good to be cautious for a few days."

Dr. Jamison seemed pleased with the decision. He nodded as if in agreement. He looked at me sternly, his eyes beaming right into my soul it seemed. "Are you a relative to Abe? I'm sorry, I don't recall."

"No, he's a friend." Mr. Tyler answered him before I could open my mouth. "The dear boy is a friend and he lives in the upstairs of my home. We share the same love of animals. He has a beagle named Bailey and as you know I have George. So we know each other and I am confident that Sam will be very capable of lending me a hand if I need it."

It was a quick response, almost as though he wanted to interject before I could mention that we had only known each other for two days. That would bring up questions in the good doctor's mind for sure. I wondered again why Mr. Tyler seemed so adamant that I be the one to care for him and his dog. Why had he called me as an emergency contact person? What was this old man up to? I couldn't help but have my suspicions. How and why was I chosen? Maybe the old guy just felt comfortable with me. We did both have the love for dogs and you can tell a great deal about a person who loves animals, right? I wanted to tell Mr. Tyler about the car accident and the strange story around that and see what he thought. But I didn't want to stress him about anything strange or different going on. I would feel pretty guilty if I was the cause of a relapse. I decided I would keep that story for another day or maybe not ever tell him. He didn't seem to be interested in it when I had mentioned it. Heck, I didn't even want to think about it. It was way too strange.

"What time do you think Mr. Tyler will be released?"

"As soon as I can get his discharge papers filled out and completed, he should be able to go home. Give me another hour or so and he'll be out of here. Sam, I will make sure I leave my pager number with you. Abe, I will leave some instructions for you to follow, just to take it easy and restrict your diet a bit. Let's keep you calm and on a bland diet for a week or so, just to make it easier for you. Sam, I trust you can help him out with that?"

"Yeah, I can do that. Whatever I can do to help."

"Alright then. Abe, I will see you in an hour and get you discharged. I am sure you are anxious to be back home again."

"Yes, yes I am, I miss George. He's a joy to be around. Wonderful companion."

Dr. Jamison shook my hand, thanked me for helping out at this time of need for Abe, and reminded me to call if I needed any help with anything.

Now the room became silent. I waited for Mr. Tyler to say something. It was an awkward moment between the two of us. He smiled at me and seemed to have no words. I felt compelled to sit back down and wait for the discharge papers. I wasn't sure why there was suddenly tension between us. Maybe he could sense I had questions about how I became such a big part of this situation. Impulsively, instead of sitting back down, I walked over to the side of the bed and put my arms around this little old man, reassuring him that I would be there for him if he needed me. I hugged him because I knew he was alone and lonely and probably worried about the strange health scare he had. As I pulled away, I saw tears rolling down from his tired eyes, maybe from the relief of knowing that someone would be there. Or maybe because he missed his Elle more now than ever. I suddenly realized I had promised Mr. Tyler I would stay with him but I didn't want to leave Bailey alone in a new setting.

"Do you think I could have Bailey come and stay with us? Maybe he would be good company for George? It would be easier for me to have him with me at your place instead of upstairs."

"Of course, of course, Bailey is more than welcome. Well then, I think we have worked out a very good plan.

And please, if you need to leave, you should do so. Do not hesitate to get your life back to normal."

"We will stay with you as long as you need us to."

Actually, I was looking forward to staying with Mr. Tyler. Maybe he could shed some light on the questions I had since this morning. which at this point seemed like days ago. I was embarking on new territory, stepping out of my comfort zone by putting another person's needs before my own. What on earth was happening to me?

six

"All changes, even the most longed for, have their melancholy; for what we leave behind us is a part of ourselves; we must die to one life before we can enter another."

~Anatole France~

The discharge papers came through in just about an hour as Dr. Jamison had promised. And with them there was a diet plan to follow and some low impact exercises to do every day. I had these explained to me since I was going to be his caregiver for a while. There were no other concerns for me to look for, as he was remarkably healthy for his age. He did have a slight limp and I still wondered what had caused it. I was sure I could slip that into a conversation at some point. I helped Mr. Tyler as much as I could with getting ready to leave. But he was very independent and graciously declined most of my help. He was a remarkable gentleman. They brought in a wheelchair, which was standard procedure for anyone leaving the hospital with the diagnosis he came in with. He sat patiently, waiting for me to bring the car around to the emergency exit. He was in great spirits as he said goodbye to the nurse who had tended to him the entire day. He showed such gratitude for all they had done for him and he gave them his blessing. They almost seemed as though they didn't want him to leave. Who could blame them? He was a joy to have around.

He slid into the front seat and I helped him buckle the seatbelt. His hands couldn't get the buckle to work. He caught me with his glance and said how sorry he was to be a burden. I told him to never speak of it again because he was no burden to me. The truth of the matter was, helping Mr. Tyler was helping me see what I was capable of. He thanked me again, not one to miss an opportunity to show his appreciation to anyone who helped him. Too bad he didn't have children, he would have been a great role model for a child. I was sure someday he would share with me the story as to why he and Elle never had any. They seemed to be the type of people who would want a household of kids running around. I didn't think I would ever have children. The best I could do was Bailey. That was about as much responsibility as I could handle on a permanent basis. But, Mr. Tyler, he was a special kind of person. Rare, I would say.

The drive home was quiet and I was watchful of every car on the road. I wanted to make sure I got Mr. Tyler home safe and sound after the day he just went through. Traffic was much slower now and I was relieved. I was not entirely familiar yet with the roads, even though I had made this drive several times now and knew my way. As I turned the corner to Mr. Tyler's house, I couldn't help but think back to the accident earlier in the day—the disappearance of the driver and the bizarre occurrences that took place. I pulled into the driveway and parked close to the porch steps so Mr. Tyler could get inside easily. I looked over and he had a smile of relief on his face to be home at last. Surprisingly George was barking. I could hear him as I opened my car door. Mr. Tyler gave a chuckle; it was a sound he missed.

"George old boy, I'm home. No need to bark."

Mr. Tyler had no problem unbuckling his seatbelt and opening the door to step out of the car.

"Sam, could you help me up these steps just this once. I don't quite have my feet under me yet."

"Sure, hold on, give me one second to get over there and give you a hand. No doubt you want to get inside and see George."

I helped Mr. Tyler out of the car, offering my arm for him to steady himself. He was eager to get inside and see his faithful George. I couldn't blame him. I felt the same way about Bailey. There is something to be said about the loyalty of "man's best friend." Whoever said that knew what they were talking about. I helped Mr. Tyler to the front door. He fumbled for his keys and only took a second to unlock the door. George was there, waiting for Mr. Tyler to greet him. Dogs are amazing creatures. Every greeting is as if you have been gone for years.

I helped Mr. Tyler to the living room couch and let him pet George and absorb the welcome home. George was so excited, I thought for sure he would need to go outside. But Mr. Tyler assured me, it was just the excitement of his coming home and that he would calm down within minutes. And he was right. After a few minutes, George was lying on the floor at Mr. Tyler's feet. It was exactly the greeting they both needed.

Mr. Tyler showed me the guest room where I would sleep. It was a small, comfortable room, and it was actually quite nice. It would be fine for a few days' stay. We were both beginning to feel tired from the long, unusual day. And Mr. Tyler was beginning to yawn. I could see his eyes were starting to look tired as well. We decided I would go get Bailey so that the two dogs could meet and become friends. They were both social so we thought they would get along just fine.

I made sure he was comfortable before I went upstairs to get Bailey and the few things I would need to stay at his house. He was preoccupied with George, giving him the attention all dogs want from their owner. Upstairs, Bailey was anxious to go out, so I brought him for a quick walk. We returned and I put some clothes in my overnight bag. It seemed funny to be packing the stuff I had just unpacked. Forty-eight hours, that's all it had been. I grabbed Bailey's dish and his food and my overnight bag, and we headed out the door. I figured if I forgot something I didn't have far to go to get it.

I put my things down on the porch outside Mr. Tyler's door so I could take Bailey in to meet George. I knew what the excitement would do, so I kept the leash on him. I opened the door and poked my head inside to make sure Mr. Tyler was still sitting there. And he was, George by his side.

"Mr. Tyler, I am going to bring Bailey in to meet George now. Is that okay?"

"Sure, bring him in, I am sure they will be fine."

I looked down at Bailey, gave him the "I am expecting you to behave" look and opened the door. He bounded in, went right to George, sniffed for a minute, sniffed Mr. Tyler, and walked back over to me and sat down. I guess this was going to be easier than I expected. I shut the door and walked over to the chair. Bailey sat right down at my feet.

I looked at Mr. Tyler, he looked at me and said, "Well, this seems like it will be okay, they don't seem to mind being in the same room with each other. Unusual for two male dogs."

"Yes, it does seem that they will get along just fine." We were both satisfied with how calmly they had accepted each other—no growling, no snarling, no hair raised on the back, nothing.

I went out to the porch and grabbed my bag. When I came back inside, the dogs were lying next to each other. The look on my face must have been an odd one because Mr. Tyler started laughing. I could not have asked for an easier transition. I took my bag into the guest bedroom. It was quiet, away from the front of the house. Mr. Tyler's room was between the kitchen and the guest room, which would make it easy for me in case he needed anything in the middle of the night. I was hoping Bailey would stay in the living room with George. I was assuming that George slept in the living room. Bailey always slept where he could monitor all the doors. He never slept in the bedroom with me. Even as a puppy, he wanted to be where every door was visible to him.

"Mr. Tyler, where does George usually sleep at night, in the living room or in your room?"

"He usually will sleep out here where he can keep an eye and ear on the outside traffic. He is pretty good at alarming me of any noises that don't sound quite right. Do you think Bailey will sleep out here with him?"

"Yes, I think they will be fine. I will leave my bedroom door open so I can hear them if they're moving around. I can bring Bailey into my room if I need to. But they seem to be comfortable with each other."

"Sam, I do so appreciate all that you have done for me today, getting to the hospital, taking care of George, you have truly helped me out and I appreciate everything. You have no idea how much comfort it gives me to know that I can count on you. After all, you just moved in and started a new job, and by the way, I can call your boss if you want me to and explain what happened today. I would just feel awful if they let you go because of today. Please go to work tomorrow and suggest to them that they call me so I can explain what happened and why you were called away. Let me do that for you."

"I have no intention of going to work tomorrow, Mr. Tyler. I thought about this and I truly feel you need me here for a few days, just to do some things for you and help you get your strength back. I would just sit and worry about you the entire time if I went to work. So, please do not give it another thought, I have already made up my mind. You need someone to help you."

"You have been such a blessing to me, Sam. Even though I have only known you for two days, it seems much longer than that. My goodness, so much has happened in these two days for you. You must be exhausted by now with all this excitement. I truly am so sorry for all the confusion and disruption."

"Mr. Tyler, if I can be honest with you...a few years ago I never would have thought of helping anyone other than myself. I probably would have let someone else deal with all of this. I am not sure what changed in me, but I have to say, I enjoy doing what I can for you. I feel like a better person today just to be able to help you instead of just helping myself."

I watched his face as I spoke. His eyes filled with tears and his expression softened. I knew he appreciated that I was with him. It must have been scary to be alone and worry about who is going to help you at a time like this. We were helping each other without even knowing it, without even planning it or thinking it through. It just happened that way. And that's the best kind of lesson, the one that just comes along when you least expect it. Before things could become too personal or emotional, I needed to redirect our conversation. After all, I can't remember the last time I got caught up in my own emotions.

"What do you say we fix ourselves something to eat and relax for the rest of the evening? I have had a long day and could use some time to relax."

"That sounds great," Mr. Tyler said.

"What can I fix you? I am no chef, my cooking skills are considered low to nonexistent. So you may need to coach me along. I do believe that if you give me a hand or at least some advice, we can have a gourmet meal tonight. Let's forget about that bland diet plan the doctor handed me and have a real meal. Are you in?"

"I sure am. Now that I think about it, I am very hungry. All those tests they ran on me today have made me hungry. I think there is some meat in the freezer, let's go check it out."

Much to my surprise, the freezer was full. Mr. Tyler was either a gentleman who prepares for a rainy day or he doesn't eat much but shops a lot. Either way, we had a lot to choose from.

"So, what do you want for dinner? Chicken, pork, beef, fish, sausage, you pick."

"I think chicken sounds pretty good. Can you talk me through a good recipe?"

"Of course, a few spices, some olive oil, and served over some pasta. That should do. How's that sound?"

"That sounds pretty good because I don't mind telling you it's been a long day. Do you have a microwave we can defrost this?"

"Yes, just a small one, but it should work okay."

"Do you like to cook, Mr. Tyler, or is it just something you have had to do since your wife, well, you know, has been gone ?"

"Oh, I love to cook. Even when Elle was here, we spent equal time in the kitchen. Didn't seem right to think I couldn't do my part. It was more meaningful to share in the chores than to expect one should solely be responsible. One day when you find that someone for yourself, you will understand what I mean."

I somehow knew he possessed a great deal of knowledge about relationships, successful relationships, and how to care about others more than yourself. I knew little about that. I had never really had a steady girlfriend. It just hadn't been a part of my life so far.

The kitchen was small but looked like it offered enough to cook a good meal. I wasn't sure how this was going to work so I just followed Mr. Tyler's lead.

"What do we need first?" I asked.

"Well, let's see if we can get this defrosted quickly. All of a sudden, I am starving as well."

Mr. Tyler was a very talented cook. Other than my mother and Jake's mom, I had never seen anyone work so well in the kitchen. He knew how to throw a bunch of stuff in a pan and somehow create a delicious meal. Over pasta was even better. No recipe, just threw everything together. Perfect. We ate as if we had not eaten in days. This was a gourmet meal to me. Bailey and George sat patiently at our feet, hoping something would be dropped to the floor.

I insisted Mr. Tyler take a seat when it came time to clean up. The kitchen was well organized and easy to put everything away right where Mr. Tyler had found it. It was the least I could do for him after such a long day.

We sat in the living room, full and content from dinner. The dogs had been fed and in a couple of hours I would take them out for their last walk of the day. Finally it felt like this day was really going to come to a close; the emergencies and unusual occurrences would be behind us. I wanted to sleep a long, restful sleep and wake up refreshed. I looked across the room at Mr. Tyler who was dozing, his chin bobbing off his chest. I hesitated to wake him but on the other hand, he should go to bed and get some sleep. It was after 8:00 p.m. It had been a long day for him. I watched him for a few minutes, hoping he would wake on his own. Then I heard him mumble something in his sleep. He shook his head as if telling someone "no" in a conversation. I didn't want to wake him. I was hoping to make some sense of what he was saying. This wasn't the first time he had mumbled under his breath, making me wonder if he was dreaming or if he was talking to Elle. He kept shaking his head "no," this time a little more agitated and with a little more intent. I felt I should wake him. I didn't want him to relapse in any way from the anxiety of a bad dream. I moved from my seat and walked over to touch him on the shoulder, but before I could get too close, he awoke, jolted his head back, and opened his eyes wide.

"Mr. Tyler, are you okay?"

"Oh, I must have dozed off for a second there. I am feeling a bit tired from such a long day. Perhaps it's time for me to go to bed and get a good night's sleep. Oh, wait, before I go, I want to talk to you about something. There's something you should know."

He sounded groggy and confused. The poor old man was tired.

As much as I would have liked to tell him about the accident and maybe have an answer as to why he chose me to come to the hospital, I didn't think it wise to do so tonight.

"No, no, you are extremely tired, Mr. Tyler and you definitely should go to bed. You need your rest after such a strenuous day. Whatever it is can wait. We can talk first thing in the morning over coffee. Now, let me help you up and get steady on your feet. You can get yourself ready for bed and I will take the dogs out for a final time tonight." I steadied him under his elbow as he pushed himself up off the sofa, putting all his weight on to me. I could tell he was quite unsteady and he wavered as he tried to stand on his own. I gave him a minute to gain his balance and make sure he was fully awake enough to walk.

"Yes, I think I will head to bed. Tomorrow is a new day and hopefully an uneventful one. And you're right, we can talk over coffee."

We both chuckled at the comment, after such a stressful day. He always seemed to have a sense of humor, even at a time when he couldn't quite focus on his thoughts.

"Do you need me to walk with you or do you think you are steady on your feet? I don't want you to lose your footing and take a tumble."

"Oh, I'm fine, Sam. Go ahead and take the dogs out for the evening. I will get myself to the bathroom and then into bed. And thank you again."

"Alright, if you're sure. Let me get them leashed up and out the door."

Mr. Tyler turned to make his way to his room as I walked across the room, both dogs watching my every step.

"Come on, Bailey, come on, George, let's get out for the last walk of the day."

They both jumped to their feet, anxious to stretch their legs one final time for the day. I leashed them both and hoped that walking them together would work out. Bailey had never shared walking with another dog or person. Out the door they went, tails wagging, pulling me behind. I barely made it down the porch steps without tripping as I forgot to turn the porch light on before heading out. But they seemed to know their way with no light to guide them. They walked side-by-side much to my surprise, as if they had been best friends for years. I was happy with that, no fighting, no power struggle, just a nice, calm walk. I could hear traffic down a block or so but it was pretty quiet on this block tonight. Then out of the corner of my eye, I saw movement. Someone was walking on the other side of the street, moving slowly and trying to go as unnoticed as they could. It was the same long coat I had been seeing for the last several days. If it hadn't been for them moving, I never would have noticed. It was clear this person was either watching me or watching Mr. Tyler's house. I decided it was time to find out. I pulled on the leashes to signal the dogs that we were moving across the street, but they resisted and tugged the other way. I pulled again and with a verbal command told them to come with me, but again they resisted. For some reason, they would not cross the street. George gave a small whine and moved himself to get behind me. I drew the leashes tight and gave them the command to stay and sit. As I stepped under the branches of a tree, keeping the dogs still and quiet, I was able to watch to see if this person looked over or just kept walking. I wanted to yell out so I could see the face, but I wondered if doing so would endanger the dogs or myself? The person kept walking at a quicker pace now, and it was obvious whoever it was did not want to speak to me. The urge to yell out was strong and the lack of bravery kept me quiet. In the shadow of the streetlight, I saw the person turn quickly to look back. The face appeared to be covered with the hood of the cloak—eerie, to say the least. I couldn't make out the features. This shadow of a person continued to walk away quickly and I decided to cross the street and follow at a safe distance. I pulled on the leashes of Bailey and George who were resisting with all their might. It was as though they felt something was not safe; they sensed uneasiness and wanted to keep their distance. I looked down at the dogs realizing the strong instincts they possessed, and I stopped pulling them. I stepped back on to the sidewalk and started in the direction of Mr. Tyler's house. They both needed to relieve themselves, and I stopped for a moment to give them the chance to do just that. I kept my eye on the figure, which was now disappearing into the darkness. I felt the hairs rise on the back of my neck as I wondered if this person was intentionally following me or stalking Mr. Tyler's home. It left an unsettled feeling in my gut. I knew there was something unusual going on with all the events of the day. Everything seemed a bit out of whack. The dogs were now pulling the leashes to head home, their tails tucked between their legs. They were spooked by this person or by something. They gave me all the warning signals they could and now they wanted nothing more than to get back inside where they felt safe. I too felt uneasy. I was keeping a watchful eye on my surroundings. I decided to make sure every door and every window was locked when I got back to the house. I may be twenty-eight years old, but deep down, I was a chicken about things that go bump in the night. And this was very creepy. I would have to talk to Mr. Tyler in the morning and ask if he has ever noticed that strange person before. After all, before today, he walked George by himself in the evening so he must have noticed something. Maybe there was a simple explanation. But for now, I couldn't get inside fast enough and lock the door behind me. This was sending chills up my spine. I just needed this day to be over.

Once back inside, I locked the door immediately and went from room to room making sure all the windows were locked and curtains drawn. The dogs lay back down next to each other. They too felt uncomfortable. I bent down to pet Bailey. This was a strange place to him and I wanted to reassure him I was there with him. George nudged my hand with his nose, looking for me to pet him, too. At least they had each other for comfort. I didn't hear any noise from Mr. Tyler's room. There was a faint light from under his door, probably a night-light for the old guy in case he needed to get up in the middle of the night. After what happened outside I didn't think I would get much sleep tonight. I thought about leaving a light on. Maybe I was making a mountain out of a molehill. Maybe this mystery person lived around here and didn't want to be bothered. Maybe I was just dreaming up some story in my mind. I really wished Jake were here. I remembered he never called me back from earlier. There was so little time this evening, I hadn't given it a second thought. I decided to give him a call again. Maybe I would feel more at ease if I heard from someone I knew. It was still early enough. I made my way to the guest room and grabbed my phone to call Jake. It rang four times and went to this voicemail. I left a message for him to call when he got the message. I really wanted to hear a friendly voice. Maybe Jake could take my mind off the phantom following me around. Mr. Tyler should be able to shed some light on this in the morning, I hoped. I walked back out to the living room, checking the lock on the door one more time and making sure all the windows were securely locked as well. It was then that I decided I would sack out on the couch next to the dogs, and leave the small lamp on the table in the hallway on. That way I would be able to see in case I needed to get up for any reason. I talked myself into sleeping with the dogs. After watching them cower outside, I wasn't sure who was more uncomfortable—them or me. But they say there is safety in numbers and that's what I was going to bank on tonight. I grabbed a pillow from the back room and a blanket off the bed and made myself comfortable on the couch. Hopefully I would wake earlier than Mr. Tyler and put everything back in the bedroom before he even got up. Either way, I was sleeping on the couch next to two dogs with the doors secured, windows locked, and curtains pulled. I wanted nothing more than to get some rest and think things through with a fresh start in the morning. I turned the lights off next to the couch and lay down, trying desperately to fall asleep. But my eyes were wide open, staring off into space, waiting to hear any unusual noise that goes bump in the night. I definitely was spooked. I was ashamed to admit it, but it was true. I couldn't remember the last time I had felt this uncomfortable. But I could say this—the last time I felt this way, my gut feelings were right. Something was wrong...very wrong.

seven

"There are two ways of meeting difficulties: you alter the dif-

ficulties, or you alter yourself to meet them."

~Phyllis Battome~

The sound of pouring rain woke me from a deep sleep. The light from the table lamp in the hallway was off. Except for the rain, all I could hear was the deep breathing of the two dogs lying side by side. It was pitch black, and I wondered if the storm was strong enough to knock out the power. I heard the low rumble of thunder. I lay still, trying to get my eyes to focus in the dark. I usually didn't have a problem sleeping through rainstorms, but tonight was different. It felt like only a few hours had passed since I fell asleep. I had no idea what time it was. As soon as I could see well enough, I would check on Mr. Tyler. I didn't want him to get up now without any lights on. I was clueless as to what his middle-of-the-night habits were. I didn't know where I could find a flashlight or even candles. I knew I had a flashlight in my apartment. After a day like yesterday, checking the weather status had not been on my mind. Otherwise, I would probably have brought my flashlight down with me, I heard a car go by and it gave the room a glimmer of light for a few seconds. Getting that few seconds of light gave me my bearings. I would have to make my way around the table in front of the sofa without tripping over anything. The dogs were awake now and making small movements with their feet as uneasiness settled over them. George gave a small whine. A quick flash of lightning followed within seconds by a rumble of thunder. The storm was getting closer, it sounded as though it was right over head. Another quick flash in the sky let me know the storm was close. I lay still for a few moments, waiting. Maybe if I closed my eyes I would drift back to sleep. I tried to relax and sink back on to the pillow when I heard a loud noise that seemed to come from somewhere outside the house. It startled the dogs. Bailey let out a low growl. That prompted George to stand up. With both dogs on alert, I thought it best to find my way to Mr. Tyler's room before they woke him. I heard Bailey give another growl and I tried to loudly whisper for him to be quiet. Then another noise, this time from the back of the house where the stairs were to my apartment. It sounded as though someone had fallen down the stairs.

"Ssshh, Bailey, it's okay," I said in a whisper so as not to alarm him. "It's okay, boy, be still now."

With no flashlight, I couldn't see to move around. I sat on the couch waiting for another noise and hoping a flash of lightning might give me enough light to see. The rain was coming down harder. Again, I heard the sound on the back stairs. I wasn't sure if Mr. Tyler had a back door to his living area that led outside. I didn't recall seeing a door. The lightning flashed again and this time I was able to see more clearly all the way through to the kitchen. I saw a door on the back wall that must lead outside underneath the staircase. I never thought to check that door when I secured the house. I was hoping it was locked. The noise was definitely coming from the back of the house. I decided to make my way to Mr. Tyler's room to wake him. He probably could tell me where to find a flashlight. The last thing I wanted to do was startle him. As I got up off the couch, Bailey got up, trying to get to me. George was lying down again and wasn't willing to get up quite as quickly. Bailey was at my side, seeing better in the dark than I was. I reached down to pet the top of his head, trying to assure him everything was all right. I wanted to diffuse his growl, which I knew would lead to a bark. He rubbed against me, making sure his scent was on me. "It's okay, boy, it's okay." The lightning flashed again, making my view of the room brighter. I stood up, keeping the vision of my path in my mind, and moved toward Mr. Tyler's room, hoping to keep from tripping over anything on my way. I made it to his bedroom door and reached for the doorknob. I turned it slowly in case he was still asleep. The lightning flashed again and lit up his room for an instant. I pushed the door open slowly, the old hinges creaking from years of use. He appeared to be sleeping soundly. Apparently, the sound of the pelting rain and crashing thunder had not ruined a good night's sleep for him. Unless...no I wouldn't entertain the thought that he had died in his sleep. Yesterday was bad enough. I couldn't give thought to today offering something worse. But yet, he slept without stirring through the noise from outside, the thunder, and the downpour. How could anyone sleep through so much? Bailey was at my side wondering what he should do. His motive was to follow me around, securing my safety and his own. George was now right behind him. He nudged me to make his presence known. With two dogs at my side, I tiptoed over to Mr. Tyler's bedside and tapped him on the shoulder. Just then the lightning flashed, making the walls glow for a brief moment. An eerie feeling swept over my whole body. I reached my hand out to nudge Mr. Tyler gently. As I touched his shoulder, I spoke his name in a whisper so as not to alarm him. He didn't respond.

"Mr. Tyler, I need you to wake up."

This time I said it with a little more urgency and nudged him a bit more firmly. Although he was covered with blankets, I could feel his body heat, which was a good sign.

I gave him another nudge, "Mr. Tyler, wake up. It's storming and the electricity is out. I need to know if you have a flashlight anywhere."

He stirred slightly and gave an under the breath grumble that someone who was waking involuntarily might give. I felt relieved to hear him groan.

"Mr. Tyler, I am sorry to wake you, but we are in the middle of a storm, the power is out, and I don't know where to find a flashlight or even some candles."

"Elle, is that you?" His voice was feeble

He spoke again, louder this time. "Elle, I am right here, dear. Please don't cry."

"Mr. Tyler, it's me, Sam. You need to wake up, Mr. Tyler, you're dreaming. I need to find a flashlight. It's storming outside."

Lightning bolts streaked across the walls, followed quickly by an intense rumble of thunder. I could see Mr. Tyler's face. The lightning flash illuminated his skin, draining any warmth that may have been there. He opened his eyes.

"What's going on, where am I?"

"Mr. Tyler, it's me, Sam. Don't be alarmed. I'm sorry to wake you, but we are having a severe storm, we've lost power, and I need to know if you have a flashlight somewhere. Do you have a flashlight, Mr. Tyler?""Sam who? I don't know who you are. Get away from me."

He flailed his arms to push me aside.

"Elle, it's okay, I am here to get you." He started to thrash with the covers in order to get out of bed.

I stepped back to let him awaken on his own. I had heard that people who were in a dream state or who were confused could become very difficult and sometimes violent. And they also could possess great strength. And even though this was a feeble little man, I did not want to take any chances. I would wait and let him gather his senses on his own. I heard George perk up when he heard Mr. Tyler speaking. Perhaps George could bring him to reality. I called George to come over to the bed. He hesitated, and like most dogs with good instincts, he sensed something was wrong. He sat by the side of the bed, his ears back, looking at me for reassurance. Mr. Tyler was trying to remove his covers, all the while grumbling under his breath. I could not make out a word he said. I watched as he slowly began to realize where he was, regained his sense of reality, and became less agitated. He shook his head as if to discard his clouded vision and clear his thinking. The thunder rumbled again, this time so loud I could swear it shook the whole house, and it jolted Mr. Tyler completely awake. He looked around as if dazed, trying to recognize where he was.

"Mr. Tyler, it's me, Sam, are you awake?"

"Sam, are you okay? What are you awake for, can't you sleep, dear boy?"

"Mr. Tyler, it's storming out pretty bad and we lost power. Do you have a flashlight somewhere in the house?"

"A flashlight, why yes, I have several. They are in the kitchen drawer across from the stove. Why is it so dark in here? I can't see too well. Let me get my glasses on so I can see you better, Sam."

"We lost power in the storm. It's been storming for a while now, Mr. Tyler. You were sleeping right through it. But I heard a sound outside, almost like someone falling down the back staircase. I need a flashlight to see my way around. Maybe I should go outside to find out what's going on."

"No Sam, I don't want you to go outside in this storm. Let's wait it out and once we get power back, we can investigate the noise. Give me a moment and I will get you that flashlight, but please stay inside where you are safe."

"I will stay inside if you are that concerned, I won't go out. But I will have to get a flashlight so we are not sitting here in the dark. You stay here, I don't want you to stumble over anything. I'll find my way to the kitchen, get the flashlight, then I will come back in here to get you. We can sit in the living room together until the lights come back on. I think that would be best. But for now, just stay here."

The crash of the thunder brought Bailey and George to my side, rubbing against me for comfort, both pacing the floor in panic. They too could feel something was wrong. I heard the crash of a tree limb coming down off in the distance. The lightning had struck that close. I could feel the hair on my arms stand straight up. I left George with Mr. Tyler, took Bailey by the collar and made my way through the darkness toward the kitchen. Other than the sporadic flashes of lightning, we walked on instinct only. I felt for the walls as I walked, trying to remember the layout of the house. I found the wall switch in the hallway. A few more steps and I was sure I would be close to the kitchen. I remembered the small table in the hallway, and I tried to envision where it was and how far it came out from the wall. One hand was out in front of me to guide me from any obstacle I didn't remember in my path, and the other was still holding Bailey's collar as tight as I could. He was walking unsteadily himself, keeping as close to me as possible. We finally made our way to the kitchen, using the wall as a guide. I ordered Bailey to stay as I moved into the kitchen. Another flash of lightning lit up the room. I saw the stove for an instant and knew that across from it should be the drawer I was looking for.

I heard Mr. Tyler yell from the bedroom.

"Sam, are you finding your way all right? Please be careful, I don't want you to hurt yourself. The drawer doesn't come out so easily, you have to jiggle it a bit. It's old, you know, just an old cupboard."

"I think I found it, Mr. Tyler. You stay where you are."

I heard another sound from outside, this time it was close enough for me to hear where it was coming from. It was right outside the back kitchen door. I wondered if it could be the person who rented on the other side of the house trying to get inside. But without a flashlight and something to protect myself with, I was not opening that door. Bailey gave a low growl as he too heard something outside the door. I ordered him to keep quiet. I stretched my hand out to feel for the drawer, running my hand along the front panel to find the knob. I grabbed it and gave it a good tug. Mr. Tyler was right, it was an old drawer, and it squeaked when I pulled it open. There were two flashlights inside, one felt heavier than the other. I assumed one had batteries and the other didn't. Finally, I would be able to see my way around. I clicked on the switch of the heavier flashlight. Nothing. The lighter flash-light was my only hope now. I reached in the drawer for it, pushed the switch up...nothing.

"Sam, I hear a noise outside. Someone is outside the back door. Sam, do you hear me?"

The lightning bounced its way from wall to wall follow-ing by a long roar of thunder. The storm seemed monstrous, directly over our heads, and so loud it drowned out every-thing. Suddenly, the kitchen door flew open. I could feel the rain pelting the house; I could smell it as it splashed up off the ground, its spray so intense it was hitting my face. The lightning offered a flash of an image—a dark figure, no face, it almost blended into the darkness of the house. Then everything was black again. The hand to my throat was strong and wet from the rain. I could smell leather. My hand let go of Bailey's collar. He was barking and growling, and suddenly my feet were out from under me. Everything was fading black and small patches of light flickered against my eyes. There was no face. My hand slipped off the leather as I tried to free the grip around my neck. Rain seemed to cover the kitchen floor. I couldn't breathe. The lightning flashed brief images that blurred against the walls. I could hear Bailey in the background, faint sounds of barking, growl-ing, and then nothing. I saw gray images, smears of shapes, a dark cloak. The lightning stopped, the thunder ceased, the barking was in the distance. I heard a faraway crash and a voice calling out. I heard my own screams for help. And then there was blackness. I felt nothing; I smelled nothing. The darkness enveloped me.

I opened my eyes and heard the rainfall, steady and force-ful. I could see the kitchen door was still open, gusts of wind blowing it back and forth, banging it up against the wall. Rain was splashing on to the kitchen floor. My face was stinging. My eyes felt swollen, and I could barely open them. I tried to move my head and felt an intense pain in my neck. I remembered the strong hands trying to take me out for a final count. Every movement was so painful. One thing was for sure: someone was serious about not wanting me in Mr. Tyler's apartment. Either it was me they wanted out of the way or it was Mr. Tyler. As I tried to lift my head off the floor, I felt faint. Getting up was going to be difficult, if not impossible. I held my head between my hands and felt the pain travel up my neck and around to the front of my eyes. I decided I had no choice but to move a little slower. At this point, I was thankful to be alive. I felt dizzy as I tried to sit myself up, my hand resting on the pieces of glass on the floor. I felt pressure in my temples and intense pain. I had no idea how long I had been lying there. I wondered if Bailey and George were okay. Where was Mr. Tyler? I wanted desperately to make sure everyone was okay, but I couldn't seem to get off the floor. What had happened? I remembered feeling for the flashlight in the drawer, but everything after that was a blur. I remember a figure coming at me with dark hands and no face. Was I in some sort of dream? I was beginning to think moving to Boston was the worst decision I had ever made. It's been all bad luck since I got here. I needed to at least sit up and try to take a look around me. The door was still banging back and forth, hitting the wall. The sound vibrated with each bang, adding to the severe headache I was already experiencing. The rain was still lashing against the patio wall just outside the door, whipping inside each time the wind kicked up. I moved my arm behind me in an attempt to lean on it to get myself up. The fear of someone trying to harm me or kill me kept creeping into my mind. But for now, I needed to get up off this floor, out of the rain and try to see if Mr. Tyler, George, and Bailey were safe. With my elbow under me, I pushed my body up, feeling the pain of the glass I was pressing into. Regardless of my pounding head and the urge to vomit, I struggled my way into a sitting position. I couldn't yell. My voice was gone, damaged from having two strong hands around me, choking the breath out of me. Finally, I was sitting up, blood running down my face. I tried to wipe it away, not noticing the blood on my hands and elbows was just as bad. My eyes felt swollen, almost shut. I needed to move quickly to avoid anyone coming back and finding me vulnerable on the floor. I feared for my life and for Bailey. I didn't know what might happen next. I was alone, I didn't know anyone, and I had no phone nearby to call for help. I sat on the floor for a moment, trying to get my thoughts clear. I couldn't see well enough to get a good look around the room. I wondered where the intruder was now. Something or someone must have scared them away because they had every opportunity to end my life. I was defenseless, couldn't see anything in the dark, and didn't know where I could find anything to use to defend myself. This whole thing was making no sense to me. As soon as I could make some sense of what happened to me, I would contact the police. I had to get myself to a phone or to my car. I brushed the rain off my face and I could taste blood. I felt the sting now and knew the pain and blood were coming from above my eyebrow. Maybe I hit the floor as I fell or got hit trying to defend myself. Everything was blurry to me; everything happened so quickly. I wiped my hand across my forehead and felt a piece of glass stuck in my skin. Hoping it was not too deep, I pulled it out carefully. My whole body was in pain. I realized I was not in good enough condition to help myself at all. I felt dizzy and nauseous. I felt myself collapsing back on to the floor. I then heard a voice, someone telling me to stay still. Someone telling me help was on the way. And everything went dark one more time.

eight

I saw Jake sitting with his mother next to her hospital bed. She was pale and gaunt, her eyes shallow in their sockets. She was holding Jake's hand, speaking to him softly, tears staining her face. The sorrow of her words, the last moments they would share together as mother and son. Jake's face was without expression, a faraway look in his eyes, maybe it was disbelief. He felt in his heart the moments would be few, and each breath she took could be the last. Both were struggling in their own world, both coming to a close in one way or another. Jake had suffered as a child when his parents divorced, and his father moved away. He often shared with me the hole in his heart, the crater that held no feelings at all. A life he once held on to dearly and with great trust was no longer in his grasp; his solid ground had shaken beneath him and everything was crashing around him. There were no words, no explanations that could give him back the security he once had in his heart and in his mind with his parents. It was the end of one strong tower and he would have to rebuild a new life, a consequence he did not want to bear. Jake's voice was shaky as he spoke in a whisper to his mother; a slight smile came across his lips to indicate he would be okay. She was leaving him and life was leaving her body. I wondered if life events were flashing through her mind: Jake as a young child, a young man, high school days, college days, intimate times between a mother and son that only they could understand and recall. She guided him through so many difficulties and decisions, questions about life and love. So many things that he didn't understand but she had answers to. And now, the foundation of his life was leaving him, the mother he wanted to see grow old and share her wisdom with his own family. I watched this scene with tears in my eyes as my friend, my confidant was letting go of someone he treasured and loved. My feet didn't move, my hands didn't touch his arm, my arm did not reach out around his shoulder, and my mouth did not move to speak. I stood beside him and it was as though he was completely unaware of my presence. I was in the shadows of this room, of this sad event. Each moment as a still shot, a picture show from years gone by. It was a scene from a movie, I could take out or add any frame I chose, readjust the ending, and cut out any moment I wanted. But this all seemed to fit together, final moments in a life, the peaceful ending to a story that reflected love and sacrifice. Removing any part would alter all meaning of this final moment. Each frame was to remain. I turned away from Jake, turned my back on this scene. I stepped into a dark corner, moving on to the next movie to watch, perhaps one of my own family, my own life. As I turned, I felt a hand on my arm, a tight grip stopping me. I didn't want to look into the face, I didn't want to see the eyes. I merely wanted to step away, to disregard the ending of Jake's story. I pulled to loosen the grip, to get my arm free, but the hand held me tighter. The voice was unrecognizable; it was low and deep, eerie but convincing. "Stay," was the only word spoken. I shivered as the fear traveled through my body. A quick turn allowed me to see briefly what would forever stick in my mind. The hand on my arm did not belong to Jake. The dark figure stood so close to me I could breathe it in. It was fear itself taking its stand next to me, grinding me to a halt, bolting my feet to the ground. I was facing my fears, my own dark abyss of failure, my inability to love someone other than myself. It smelled rank. It emitted fear and ugliness, gruesome dark pits of nothingness. It portrayed all the worthless moments of my life, the fruitless work and efforts. And I stood frozen, unwilling to look at my own life. I wanted to wake from this dream. But the shadow remained close to me. I felt it breathing behind me, creeping so close we could have been one. My body shuttered and the hair rose on my arms and the back of my neck. This moment felt like eternity. My entire body was frozen, experiencing the overwhelming awareness that something or someone else was in complete control of me. I wanted to move, to strike, to act out in some way. I closed my eyes, hoping, praying for it to disappear, giving every ounce of who I was in exchange for bravery. I needed one moment of bravery. I felt my breathing become short and labored. I felt a surge of emotions. Everything was on the verge of existing or dying. I felt myself choking when I wanted to speak. My throat was closing in on me. My mouth was dry, and my heart was pumping so fast I thought it would beat right through my chest. This moment would determine who I was going to be. This moment meant facing it all. I closed my eyes, sucked in as much air as I could without exploding my lungs, and forced my head to turn, my mouth to speak. My head turned to where Jake was standing and my eyes slowly opened to take in whatever view was before me. My hands were shaking, and I felt weak throughout my body. The room was empty, dark, no shadow, no Jake, no dying mother, no bed. The room was completely empty. My shoulders dropped. Was all of this real or had I dreamed it? Was I going crazy? My head was swirling. I felt faint, unsteady on my feet. Somewhere I could smell water, rain, and I could taste salt. My face felt wet and there was pain throughout my body. I felt panic rising in my chest. I couldn't breathe, and I felt as though I were choking. I felt myself slip to the floor. I could feel myself wilt and crumple like a heap of flesh and bones. I didn't feel pain from falling. I felt as though I was floating to the ground, something was softening the blow, bringing me down in slow motion. My hands became limp; there was nothing for me to hold on to or grab on my way down. My head was like a bobble, and I had no strength. My eyes were open but were only seeing darkness, floating gray clouds and forms. And then nothing...again.

nine

"True character stands the test of emergencies. Do not be mistaken, it is weakness from which the awakening is rude."

-Napoleon Bonaparte-

There was that smell again: sterilization, stethoscopes, and the smell of sick people, dying people. It consumed me. The smell of rubbing alcohol. I didn't feel awake. I could smell but could not see. Maybe it was for the best right now. I heard commotion around me, people moving about, voices talking but saying nothing to me. I felt alone in a room full of voices, sounds, and smells but no touch. I was in between knowing and not caring if I knew. My thoughts were jumbled. It was as if I was swimming, knowing that I was swimming, but having no arms or legs to help me move. The constant smell: dying people, sterilization. If I ever wished for sleep, it was now.

"What's his blood pressure look like? We need to keep a close eye on this."

"It's stabilizing. He was in pretty bad shape when we brought him in. I will check with Mr. Tyler."

"Claire, I want someone here in the room around the clock. This guy has really been worked over and we need to keep a constant eye on his condition. I want him in ICU until he takes a huge turn for the better. Has he said anything, mumbled anything that we can use to figure this out?"

"No, Brandon, nothing. We haven't seen anything like this in over a year. You remember the last time, don't you? I will tell you, it's not something I want to live through again. And if this is any indication, we are in for a long couple of weeks with this guy. Lord, give me strength."

"Claire, let's not draw any conclusions here, we'll just take this fella one day at a time. But right now, it's minute by minute. Let's get it together and do what we need to do. Let's get another IV drip going, I think he's going to need one. Claire, I want you to let me know if there is the slightest stir from this guy. Any movement—eyes, fingers, twitches, anything, you call me immediately. Any rolling of the eyes, a sniffle, anything, got it?'

"Yes, I will."

"Claire, look at me. It's our job to maintain everyone's frame of mind here, to stay as composed as we can. Now I understand we have a case here that has all the same similarities as last year and God knows I don't want to go through that again myself. But it's not our job to let these people get under our skin. We need to take care to him and prepare to work with him and Abraham, end of subject. I hope you understand me on this, Claire. Do not get personally involved!"

"You're right, Brandon, you're right. My gosh, it was just such a horrible thing last year. I will do what I can but really, I make no promises. If I can't see this through,

I am going to ask you to take me off this case, just so you know. We have seen this before and quite frankly, the last time almost did me in. You understand where I am coming from, right?"

"I want you to keep yourself in check. You are the best we have here and right now, this guy needs our best. You have a job to do so let's get it done professionally." He was almost pleading.

"Okay, I will do everything I can. I know what I have to do."

"Good, so I have made myself clear, right?"

"Yeah, yeah, very clear, Brandon, very clear."

The commotion was distracting. I couldn't tell if I was moving or they were moving but either way, it was tremendously annoying. I could smell rain mixed with rubbing alcohol, and neither was rousing good thoughts. My idea of who I was and what was happening eluded me. The only thing I knew was that there were odors here and they existed for a reason. The desire to see was so strong. I remained motionless, letting the change of smells come and go, trying to do it all calmly, and letting my body stay at rest. I drifted back to where comfort existed, back to sleep.

The voices around me were faint, the words slurred, running into each other. I could see images, movement, slight glimmers of light and then dark again. What had happened to me? I needed to wake up, to show signs of recovery. I needed to get back to Bailey. I needed to take care of him. I heard voices again, faint murmurs, images moving back and forth from where I was lying. I was forcing myself to move my mouth, to form words, for someone to take notice that I was trying to reach them, to speak. I thought maybe if I moved my finger even the slightest bit someone would notice. I tried to move my arm, raise an eyebrow, anything for them to notice. But it didn't appear I could do any of those things. I just needed to open my eyes. I couldn't do that either. I could still smell rain. I could feel it on my face, mixed with the taste of salt from a cut on my eye. I could see the bloodstains on my hand as I brushed the rain away from my forehead. The pain my body felt and someone trying to choke me, I remembered those things clearly. It was all coming back to me: the storm, the lightning, the power outage, and the total darkness of the house. I had been trying to wake Mr. Tyler. He was in his room but it was dark. He sent me to the kitchen to find a flashlight. The only light I had was from the flashes of lightning. I was sure I would trip and stumble over something in my path. Bailey was there and another dog but I couldn't think of his name. I was in charge, taking care of Mr. Tyler, sleeping in his house. I couldn't remember any more than that. My head was pounding, and I felt pain everywhere. I couldn't open my eyes. I just wanted someone to notice I was in here, awake, alive. I felt trapped in my own body, unable to communicate in any way. Suddenly, everything started to drift; the voices were distant, and I could barely hear them anymore. I felt warm and safe. The only thing appealing to me was sleep. I didn't know what day it was or if it was day or night. I only knew my body felt limp and exhausted, and that sleep would come and renew me.

"These cuts are bad, but I'm sure they will heal. We'll use the suave Mr. Tyler bought and keep clean bandages on them. Those cuts look pretty deep, too, and I would hate to take a chance of any infection setting in. The odd thing is that it doesn't look like a cut from a sharp knife, it looks like something more jagged."

"We'll just bandage it for now. The bleeding has stopped so I'm sure it's not too deep. We removed some glass from these other cuts, and I'm confident we got almost everything. Claire, wipe that clean for me and let's get these covered. And I agree with you, those wounds have a jagged cut instead of a sharp, straight line. We'll try to get more details later once he wakes up, if he wakes up. I want to keep him monitored. Any slight change, I want to know about it. Then we can start piecing this puzzle together. Let's just get him back on his feet."

"I want you in here with him. I intend to stay on hospital grounds. Just page me or you can call my cell. Either way, I won't be too far away. We won't have much time once he wakes up to do our part, so I cannot stress it enough. We have seen this before and we are well aware of how time is of the essence. Stay on your guard."

"Have you talked to Abraham?"

"No, I saw him when they brought Sam in, but not since then. I'm sure it won't be long before we do."

"Yes, you're probably right. If I see him or hear from him, I will let you know, Brandon. I thought we were done with this, but I was wrong. Should have left when I had the chance."

"Well, I'm glad you're here. You know what to do more than anyone else. Let's stay sharp on this one. We only get one chance to get it right. Let's not repeat Simon."

"Please don't say that name, it's just more than I want to remember. That never should have happened. There are memories I don't wish to stir, and many sleepless nights I've spent trying to forget. Please, let's not talk about him."

All I could see was the dark face, the gloved hand. I felt my throat tense up and my breathing became labored. The face was close to mine but it was dark, without eyes or features. I could feel the breath on my face. The rain was lashing at the door, lightning flashing across the walls. I felt my legs letting me fall, sinking on to the floor. I felt the sting on my shoulder, a hot, scalding tearing of my flesh. Then darkness. No sounds, no rain, no feeling. I could hear Bailey barking, fearing for his master, his instincts taking over. I tried to get up, to see. Suddenly I couldn't hear the barking, and I couldn't feel the rain or the wind. Darkness was everywhere. Pain surged through my body, and my face pressed against the wet floor. I faded into a deep tunnel, spiraling, spinning, falling.

ten

"Has he woken up yet?"

"No, Abraham, not yet. We haven't seen any movement either. The good thing is that his vital signs are all normal. We don't understand what is keeping him from coming out of it."

"He will, just give him a little longer. I want everyone to be ready. He's not like the others. We have some challenges ahead of us."

"Claire, how many people are working on this case right now?"

"So far, Brandon and I have been monitoring him. Brandon should be here any minute to talk to you. I don't think we need to involve anyone else, do you?"

"No, you two know what you're doing. I don't want anyone else on this."

"Abraham, are you okay? You look really tired. Did anything happen we should know about? I mean, it's important we don't have any surprises."

"No, nothing you need to know. We just need to focus on the next couple of days. No one can make any mistakes. I wasn't expecting a break in and him being attacked. It just means ramping my end up a little."

"I hear you, Abraham. We are in this together. Again."

"Don't worry, Claire, he's not Simon. That's not going to happen again. I promise you. We were all bothered with what happened and I know you took it harder than all of us. That's in the past." "Abraham, good to see you again, sir."

"Brandon, yes, good to see you. Tell me what your conclusions are on our Sam."

"He has some abrasions, but I don't think anything life threatening. He's been worked over pretty good, cuts here and there. Someone was gripping his neck pretty hard, I don't think to strangle him as much as to scare him. I think he mostly suffered abrasions, scrapes, and the choking on his neck definitely left some serious bruises. Nothing he will not heal from. The emotional trauma is most likely what's keeping him from coming around. It's just easier on the coping skills to stay where you feel safest. Abraham, it's good you got him in here when you did. But, either way, he has not woken yet, which is good. We did take vitals on him, his heart rate is elevated slightly, that's to be expected, and his blood work is normal. He took quite a blow to the head. That concerns me a bit. We won't know enough until he is awake.

"Yes, I am aware of that. I am sure he will be fine regardless. I have been with this young man for several days now. He is a fighter even though he does not feel that he is. I just needed a few more day to work with him so I could ease him into what's going on. This attack makes things a bit more difficult. So we will handle this with no mistakes. There is no margin for error. I want both of you to be aware of how strongly I will insist on this. No errors."

"Yes, we understand, Abraham, we are doing everything we can right now."

"We got him here, now we just need to concentrate on keeping him safe and so far, it's been quite a challenge."

I could hear mumblings and faint sounds that seemed miles away. I couldn't make out any words, just noise. My head was pounding. Several people were around me. The sounds were complicated now. It seemed like there was a roomful of people, more than I heard before. Lots of different tones, some were very low, men perhaps, others were quiet, maybe women. I would be patient and wait for them to notice that I was alive and I could hear them. Maybe I could sleep for a while. I would try to turn my thoughts to something pleasant. I felt completely alone. There was no one here who knew me well; no one to rescue me from this nightmare. I knew that all I could do was try to rest.

I felt my body relax as I drifted into a light sleep. For whatever reason, memories of my sister Hannah's Old Door Inn crept into my mind and into my dream. I could picture myself walking up to the door, and her greeting me with a warm sisterly hello and hug. It was a calm place, a wonderful place to go and relax. I missed seeing her and talking with her. She was a person who spoke quietly and always had so much common sense; something I lacked desperately. I respected her, the achievements she made in her life and how she has helped so many others. Why couldn't I be more like her? Why were we such different people but yet brother and sister? We came from the same parents but were completely opposite. Growing up, she was the one who always made sense of problems, and things didn't bother her the way they did me. I was the oddball of the family, quite honestly. Almost like I didn't belong. Even though she is three years younger than me, she exceeds me in wisdom. Hannah possesses an inner strength and drive that I witnessed in her at a young age. But she was also fun and crazy, and never seemed unhappy. We enjoyed the little things in life, and she could always talk me into doing something behind Mom and Dad's back. Not that she was bad; she just wanted to be adventurous. Her and I shared an experience once that started out as a typical bad decision made by two young kids. One talks the other into it and that changes things somehow. Hannah always wanted to ride my bike, always wanted to daredevil on the handlebars. This one act changed many things. I was young and she was insistent that she ride on my bike with me. I told her she would fall. I warned her that I might not be able to hold both of us at the same time. I warned her yet I let her ride with me anyway. I could have avoided her from falling and getting hurt. I just needed to stick to my gut feeling and tell her no. But she insisted so I let her try. She climbed on to the handlebars of my old beat-up bike and down the hill we went. The bike gained speed more quickly than I thought it would. I lost control, probably because I wasn't strong enough to hold her weight on the front of the bike and keep the bike from tipping. We went flying, Hannah first and then me. I saw her roll over and over, scraping her knees, hands, legs, and her forehead. I didn't know if she was dead or alive and at that very moment, I felt I was responsible for killing my sister. I too went flying, scraping my elbows, knees, head, and legs. I was bloody from head to toe. I scrambled to my feet and rushed over to Hannah, but she wasn't moving. I yelled her name, nudged her shoulder, insisted she get up. Nothing. I was terrified I'd killed her. I yelled for help, and the neighbors started to emerge from their homes. Thank goodness the first one to come to our aid was Mrs. Stauton. She had several children of her own, older than Hannah and me. She ran over and knelt down beside Hannah.

"Mrs. Stauton, she's not moving, I think I killed her. What am I going tell my mom and dad? I killed her. It was an accident. She wanted to ride on my handlebars and she insisted so I let her. It's all my fault Mrs. Stauton."

I couldn't help but panic. My little sister was lying there and it was my fault.

"Sam, slow down, dear, it's not your fault. It was an accident. Now, take a deep breath and let me go call an ambulance. You stay right here. She's not dead, she's breathing. You stay right here with her and I will go call an ambulance, okay?"

"Alright, but it's my fault. I wasn't supposed to let her ride on the handlebars, and it's all my fault."

"Sam!" Mrs. Stauton was shaking me by my shoulders now. "Sam, stop, she's not dead. She's hurt, but she's not dead. Now you need to stop and be quiet. Stop yelling and calm down. I need to go call an ambulance and you need to close your mouth and stop yelling. Do you understand me?"

"Yes, I understand. I'll be quiet."

I remember the tears running down my face and the blood running down from my eyebrow. I didn't even know how much I had hurt myself, I was just afraid for Hannah. Several other people from neighboring houses came out to see what happened and were trying to comfort me, telling me it was an accident and that these things happen. They assured me Hannah was breathing, and that she was just badly hurt and got knocked out. They kept telling me she was going to be okay. But, they didn't really know that for sure.

After just a matter of minutes, Mrs. Stauton came back outside.

"Okay, Sam, now listen to me, the ambulance is on its way. I told them she was badly hurt, but that she's breathing and that's a good thing. I also called your mom and she's on her way over. We are all going to stay quiet and calm and that means you are, too, okay? I don't want you blaming yourself for this. Now, are you okay, are you hurt badly anywhere? Do you need to be checked out at all? You have some blood running down from your eyebrow. Let me take a look at you."

I let her look at my eyebrow. It stung a little but not too badly. My elbows were all scraped and had bits of gravel stuck in the drying blood. My knees were both torn up and bloodied, but nothing a good alcohol pad wouldn't clean up. There was a long cut down my left leg, not too deep but bleeding a lot. It was running down to the top of my sneaker and settling in a puddle around my shoelaces. Mrs. Stauton assured me everything just needed to be cleaned up and bandaged and that nothing was serious.

My mom arrived in a matter of minutes. She pulled the car up to where we stood and flew out, leaving the driver's door open.

"Now, Clara, stay calm, she's okay, probably just had the wind knocked out of her. She's breathing, she's got a couple of good cuts and scrapes but she's okay."

"Beth, let me through to her. Thank you for being here so quickly, I just need to see her."

You could hear the ambulance sirens in the distance. They were getting closer. I was glad that someone who could handle life-threatening injuries was on their way. No offense to Mrs. Stauton, but she was not a professional. We needed professionals here to take care of my sister who I let get hurt. I didn't think I would ever forgive myself. My little sister was lying on the street, blood coming from her body and I was okay. It didn't seem fair. I should be the one who was hurt, I should be the one lying there, paying the price for my stupid mistake. But I wasn't, it was Hannah, just a little girl and it was all my fault.

"Sam, are you all right?" My mother was pulling me toward her, her arms reaching out to hold me. She was crying and worried, something I didn't see my mother do often. She gave me a hug, released me, and looked at me from an arm's length away. She held my shoulders in her hands, examining my face.

"Are you all right, Sam?"

In that moment, I knew for sure my mother loved me. She was worried and concerned for my welfare.

"Mom, I'm okay. It's Hannah, Mom. I'm sorry, I never should have let her ride on the handlebars. I told her no and she kept pushing me that it would be okay. I couldn't hold both of us. I tried, but I just couldn't do it. We were going downhill and I lost it, Mom. I'm sorry, it's all my fault."

The ambulance arrived, people moved out of the way, and my mom and I moved away from Hannah to give them room to tend to her. I heard them making comments like, "She's breathing, it's shallow, but she's breathing. Probably knocked the wind out of her. Let's get a brace around her neck as best we can. We don't want to move her unnecessarily just in case there is any damage to her spine."

To her spine? Oh my gosh, I had paralyzed my little sister! I looked up at Mom. "Is she going to be paralyzed?" I started to panic, I could feel it rising in my throat, my heart started to pound harder than ever before, tears running down my face. I felt as if I was going to fall over.

Mrs. Stauton came to my side and put her hand on my shoulder.

"Sam, they have to be careful moving her because they don't know what could be wrong. I am sure she will be just fine, but if they don't move her carefully, something could happen. Do you understand?"

My mom was at Hannah's side now. She was no longer concerned about me. I could see the look of worry on my mother's face. Her eyes were almost bulging out of their sockets and she no longer looked calm. She was staying as close to Hannah as they would let her, holding her tiny little hand, hoping it would give Hannah some comfort to feel her mother nearby. I was quite sure at that point that Hannah would never feel comfort in having me nearby her again. I felt hopelessly guilty. I was shaking and crying, and almost ready to throw up when I heard the voice of calm.

"Young man, is this your sister? Don't worry, she's okay, she was just knocked out cold but it looks like she's coming around a bit. Her heart rate is good and she's got some serious scrapes and cuts, but she's going to be fine. I am sure this was just an accident. I remember lots of bike accidents when I was a kid. Tumbles and torn-up elbows, you just live and learn. What's your name, son?"

"Samuel, Sam, I mean."

"Sam, are you all right? Do you have any cuts we need to take a look at?" He turned my arm in order to look at the scrape on my elbow and then checked the cut on my leg, which was still dripping blood down to my sneaker. He wiped it clean with an alcohol pad, which stung just as I thought it would, and he put a large bandage over it to stop the bleeding. He kept looking me in the eyes, catching me looking at him. He gave me a grin and I couldn't help but smile back. He did make me feel everything would be fine, and that Hannah would be okay.

They finally lifted Hannah on to the stretcher and loaded her into the ambulance. By now, she had come around and was trying to talk and wincing in pain, which was a good sign. Hannah was going to be okay. Mom thanked Mrs. Stauton again for coming to our aid and we got ourselves in the car to head to the hospital. This was when I knew what my mother really wanted to say would be said—when she had me alone.

"What on earth were you thinking of, Sam? Or weren't you thinking at all, young man? You both could have been hurt a lot more seriously. Do you understand you just lost all privileges to ride your bike for, oh, I don't know how long? How about forever?"

She continued to yell and lay down laws I knew she would never uphold. She was afraid and angry and when she felt those two things together, she said things she would normally not say. I wasn't quite sure when she was asking me questions if she wanted me to answer her or just sit there and listen. It was confusing. My leg was starting to throb from the cut, and I lost my focus on listening to my mother. She cursed me out for a good long time. I kept my eyes down for the most part, a little bit afraid to look at her. She really was in a rage of anger at me. I guess it was best for her to unload it all now and not later. Keeping it pent up could result in a pretty severe scolding. And then there would be Dad, oh yes, there would be Dad. So, I sat and listened, guilty as charged on all accounts, except one. I did try to tell Hannah it wouldn't work, that we would get hurt, and that actually did come true. The hospital was not as far away as I had originally thought. Of course, with the scolding going on the entire way, it made time go by quickly. Hannah was in the emergency room and we were on our way to be with her. Mom stopped at the nurse's desk to use the phone quickly to call Dad and explain where we were and what had happened. We were escorted into Hannah's examination room until the doctor could see her. She was lying on a hospital bed. There was a sterile smell and a sterile look; everything was white. Hannah was lying there, connected to a blood pressure monitor and oxygen. She was moving her head around, so obviously nothing severe happened there. Mom went to her, stood over her bed, and reached for her hand. Hannah pulled the oxygen mask off her face and asked Mom where I was. She turned and motioned for me to bring myself closer so Hannah could see me. Surprisingly, Hannah smiled at me and reached out her tiny hand to mine, which I held in return. And then she spoke these words that I would never forget.

"Sam, I am so sorry. You were right, it was a horrible idea and all of this is my fault. I never should have made you give me a ride. You knew better, but you did it because you wanted to make me happy. And I am very sorry. Please tell me you are okay. Are you hurt anywhere?"

The pressure valve released and the panic I was feeling for being the worst brother ever started to decrease. I saw a tear run out of the corner of Hannah's eye as she looked me square in the face. We would both share the responsibility of a bad decision, we both had injuries, and we both learned about each other that day. My sister was a big person. She had big shoulders and a bigger heart, and even at the age of seven could carry the weight of the consequences of poor choices. We smiled at each other, knowing when she was cleared to go home, we would soon be comparing who had the biggest scrape. The doctor came in before I could respond to Hannah. We just looked each other in the eye and knew that it was okay to not be okay.

The doctor said she was going to be okay. We were there for what seemed like hours. I sat in the corner and waited it out. Dad arrived forty minutes into the exam, gave me a hug, and assured me everything would be okay. He went to Hannah and gave her a kiss on the forehead, told her she was fine and would be going home soon. My mom and dad hugged, and my mother started to cry. Dad comforted her as she sobbed. It was her baby who had been injured, who would be scarred for life. What was I, chopped liver? From behind where Mom and Dad stood, I caught Hannah leaning over in order to see me, sticking her tongue out at me like she always did to make me laugh. She smiled at me and winked, and everything was back to normal. The afternoon went by slowly but we made it through. All of the tests run on Hannah were normal so she was cleared to go home.

"Mr. and Mrs. Wylkes, I have to tell you, this is an amazing little girl you have here. And Hannah, I think there must have been an angel watching over you today. You are one lucky little girl. You took a very hard hit to your head but you are going to be fine. It's a miracle she has no injuries whatsoever. I want you to watch her very closely for the next few weeks. I want to know anything that seems unusual or out of the ordinary for her."

Instructions were handed out to Mom and Dad. They were told what signs to look for that might indicate something was developing and they were instructed to bring her in immediately if that were the case. Hannah dutifully sat there between Mom and Dad, listening to all that could go wrong with her. And finally the moment arrived when we could go home. Thank goodness, because I was in need of a nap and my leg was throbbing; a good sign the healing had begun. So far, Dad had said very little to me, and I was waiting for the session to begin when I would hear about my lack of common sense and concern for Hannah. As we were walking Hannah to the car, she stopped, turned to my mother and asked her about the young girl at the scene of our accident. She wanted to know what her name was. I didn't recall a young girl at the scene. There was just Hannah, me, Mrs. Stauton, and several other adults. There were no other children. I was sure I would have noticed them.

"Mom, Dad, I want to tell you something that happened. It was scary at first but then everything began to make sense to me. I heard the conversations today between Sam and Mrs. Stauton. I know that everyone says I was knocked out cold, but I heard everything. I heard Sam worrying that I was dead, and Mom, I heard everything you said. Even though I couldn't move and everyone thought I was asleep or knocked out, I could hear everything and I knew everybody. It was like I was watching you watching me, do you know what I mean? If I were knocked out cold, I wouldn't remember anything or anybody. I heard Sam yelling for help and everyone saying I was knocked out cold and that I wasn't moving. Everything. Isn't that weird? And everything was white and foggy and blurry.

People kept moving toward me and away from me, just bits and pieces of them though. Some people I knew and some I had never seen before. I couldn't see their whole faces. Should I have died today? Is it a surprise that I could take a hit on the head like that and not die? I'm just asking. And that girl who I saw at the scene, Mom, she was in the hospital when they brought me in. She smiled at me but didn't say anything. How did she get there, Mom? Do you know who she is? Maybe all of this is because of God. Maybe she is my guardian angel. Mom, Dad! What do you think?"

That stopped Mom and Dad right where they were.

I found it odd this memory come back to me today and why is it making so much sense to me all of a sudden? I have spent years trying to make sense of that comment, of what she was saying and why she was excited about her visions. Why was she not afraid, I mean, she was just a kid, fearless of images in her mind that she couldn't explain, seeing people around her, some she knew, some she didn't. I never heard her say it was a dream. To her it was real, what she saw, what she heard, and how she felt. It was real.

We never spoke of that comment again, or of that day again, or of seeing people in white, blurry images—none of it, ever again. But today, finally, I understand the white, burry images, and being able to hear everything going on around me but having no ability to move. Today, I finally understand her.

eleven

"If you do not hope, you will not find what is beyond your hopes."

~St. Clement of Alexandra~

I felt myself waking up. I felt like I might be able to open my eyes. I wanted to see the faces of the people who had stood around me, talking about me, and taking care of me. I wondered how many days I had been here. How long had I been asleep? Now that I was awake, I intended to find out some answers.

"Sam, can you hear me? Wake up, son, you're at the hospital recovering. Can you hear me? It's Mr. Tyler, son. Open your eyes.

My eyelids were heavy, but the voice was someone I recognized. I felt dazed, and my vision was blurry but I could see the face. I needed a moment to refocus, get my wits about me. The voice kept repeating itself, telling me to open my eyes.

A few moments passed while my eyes were still focusing. Then I saw the familiar face, the face of a friend, and the only friend I had in Boston. Mr. Tyler stood over me and smiled as I looked directly into his eyes. I was glad to finally realize this was not a dream and that I was alive.

"Sam, there you are. Can you talk, son?"

"Mr. Tyler, yes, I can talk. What happened to me? Where am I?"

I spoke in-between clearing my throat.

"Mr. Tyler, why aren't you resting? You should not be up and around, you need your rest."

"Slow down, Sam, one question at a time. You're in the hospital, son. We had a break-in at the house and someone attacked you. But you are going to be fine. You have some pretty bad cuts and bruises here and there, but mostly, you got banged around pretty good. Nothing you can't heal from given a little time and rest. Do you have any blurry vision or headache?"

"Wait, who beat me up and for what reason? No, I don't have a headache and my vision is fine. Why would someone beat me up? Tell me what happened Mr. Tyler, because none of this makes any sense to me." I could envision bits of that night in my head. I saw it all clearly-the lightning flashes across the walls, the storm that was so intense, the wind and rain lashing at the house, the dark figure coming toward me, the wind howling so fiercely it shook the house.

"All in good time, Sam. Slow down. I will tell you everything, but for now, I want you to rest and feel assured that you have expert care from the best in their field. I would not put you in the hands of anyone who was not the very best at what they do. Trust me when I tell you, everything will be explained to you when you are fully capable physically and mentally. There is much to tell you, it's all going to be fine. We just need you to mend and then we can talk at great length."

"But, Mr. Tyler, who is the 'we' you are talking about? Can you at least tell me a little bit? What hospital is this?"

"Sam, this is my facility; I own and operate it. Please, let me explain things to you a little later. We are monitoring you and your injuries and that is what we need to focus on right now. Everything will be explained to you soon. Please rest and trust me, you are in extremely well trained and capable hands. Do you feel as if you could eat? Maybe some soup would be easy on your stomach. You need to have nourishment to get better. Do you have an appetite at all, Sam?"

"No, Mr. Tyler, I don't have much of an appetite right now."

I felt as though I was trapped in a nightmare. My thoughts were all over the place. The only thing for me to do at this point was to comply. I was at the mercy of those caring for me. My health and wellbeing were in their hands and there was little I could do to change that. I was hooked up to monitors and not going anywhere any time soon. I would have to be patient because it was the only option I had. I tried to study Mr. Tyler's face for a moment. He was reassuring me, and it was all I had at the moment to give me any peace of mind. His eyes were very bright blue, and they almost sparkled. They weren't the eyes of the tired Mr. Tyler I had met a few days ago. His face seemed to have fewer wrinkles and his hair didn't look so gray. He seemed younger and revived. His voice, however, was the same—soft, kind, and gentle but forthright. It dawned on me that I didn't really know this man well enough to trust him. I wondered how much of what he had told me was true. Were his stories just stories? Were they told to distract me for some reason? He looked down at me then, looked into my eyes.

"Your answers will come, Sam. Be patient and trust what I tell you. Sleep now and let your body heal. Everything will unfold. Trust me, please, trust me."

twelve

Waking...little did I know what it would mean to me. Little did I know what it really meant.

I awoke. The room was dim, and I decided it must be evening. I had no concept of time right now, just awake time and sleep time. And for brief periods in between when someone tried to speak softly without being noticed. In that time, I was not sure if I was awake or dreaming. But I felt safe, comfortable, watched over, and protected. From what, I was not sure. And for how long, I didn't know. But it was comforting.

"Ah, Sam, you are waking up finally. Tell me how you are feeling, son?"

It made no sense to me. Why was Mr. Tyler here? Why wasn't he home resting from his heart attack? He was in no condition to be here watching after me.

"Rested," I replied. "Simply rested. What are you doing here, Mr. Tyler?"

"Good, that's very good. That's a sign of a deep sleep, the kind that rejuvenates the body and the mind. Excellent, Sam, I am happy to hear that. Now, let's see if we can get you to eat something. I brought you a nice bowl of soup. It's good to start with some fluids first and we can add more as you like."

He moved the tray table closer to me and motioned the nurse to help him get me to a sitting position. They got a few pillows propped behind me and I was finally ready for soup. I was connected to one monitor and an IV but once I was eating and stable in all my vitals, those would be removed.

"Do you think you are able to eat this on your own? I mean do you have the strength? It's been several days now since you have used your arms to do much of anything. You've been worked over pretty good and I understand you may have a lot of aches and pains you didn't think could ever exist. I will be here to help you, so please just ask."

"Why are you here, Mr. Tyler? What's going on?"

"Go ahead and eat, and we'll talk in a few minutes."

The food smelled wonderful. I didn't realize how hungry I was until it was right before me. Even though it was just soup, it smelled like a gourmet meal. I was ready to dig in as my body was craving nutrition. The first attempt didn't go so well. I spilled soup down the front of the hospital gown and on to the blanket tucked up around me. I couldn't move my arm the way I had hoped. Mr. Tyler was right; I had less mobility than I thought.

"Oh, I'm sorry for the spill. Maybe it will take a few times for me to get this right. Let's try that again."

I dipped the spoon into the bowl and slowly moved my arm toward my mouth, this time with success. I closed my eyes and savored the taste. It truly was delicious. So as not to eat too quickly, I took a moment before I dove in for the next spoonful. I never realized how much joy there was in eating a spoonful of soup. And I never realized how encouraging it was to be able to do just the simplest movement. Mr. Tyler sat patiently watching me draw each spoonful to my mouth. It only took me a matter of minutes to finish the small bowl and a slice of bread. That was enough for now. I was sure if the soup did not give me any complications, solid food might be on my list of things to look forward to this evening. Simple pleasures started to take on new meaning.

"So, Mr. Tyler, are you going to enlighten me with what's going on or are you going to continue to tell me to sleep and you will tell me everything later? Even though I may be in rough shape physically, I mentally need to understand what is happening here and why it's happening to me."

"I understand, and you have been patient. But before I sit down with you, we need to evaluate your condition a bit more. Let's get some vitals stabilized and a few of these tubes out of your arms and then we can talk. Claire, be a dear and let's get his vitals record. He may be ready to be on his own. Let me know what your findings are so we can get Sam back on his feet again."

"Got it, Mr. Tyler. Okay, Sam, let's get your blood pressure taken and check your pulse. Before you know it, you will be yourself again, okay? You are in good hands here, rest assured on that. Don't be anxious about anything, just know that Mr. Tyler will explain everything to you as soon as you are somewhat healing and on the mend."

"What's your name again?"

"Claire."

"How long have you worked in Mr. Tyler's hospital? What's the name of this hospital, if you don't mind me asking?"

"I have worked here for a long time, Sam. Mr. Tyler is a wonderful man and has taken care of many folks like you. This hospital is not like any other. He will explain that to you when the time is right. There's really no name for it, we just call it Mr. Tyler's facility. I know you have lots of questions, Sam. Just be patient and he really will clear up all your fears about what happened and where you are. But, where you are going, now, that's up to you!"

She smiled at me, a sweet smile. She had soft features, small cheekbones, and light brown eyes. Her voice was gentle and soothing. I couldn't help but believe what she was saying. She was a bit mesmerizing when she looked directly at me. She could not have been more than her late twenties, so I had to wonder what she considered a long time.

"So, how long is a long time, Claire?"

Just then Brandon walked in to my room. He was interested in knowing the vitals and how I measured up as far as removing any intravenous equipment.

"Claire, how do his vitals look? Abraham wants to know if we can cut these lifelines on our friend here."

"His blood pressure is actually pretty good, Brandon, and in one minute I will have the results of his heart rate. I just need to look at that printout. Other than that, Sam is looking to be on the mend. Hard to keep a good one down, right?"

A good what? What did she mean by that? I had become very suspicious since I moved to Boston because so many things were not making sense to me. A week ago, I was as calm as a clam about everything, but that feeling had since eluded me. Too many questions to be answered. I felt as if my whole life had been turned around and I was not sure how. And if I was in the hospital, shouldn't someone be asking me if I wanted to contact my parents or my family? That alone was a bit odd.

The final decision was made. I was doing well enough to have tubes and drips removed. My blood pressure was down and holding, and my heart rate was right where it needed to be, considering. My mending was on its way. My shoulder was sore, but there were no strains or breaks. No internal injuries, which was a miracle according to Brandon who whispered to Claire about how lucky I was.

And before I knew it, Claire had left the room. I never got to ask her how many years she had worked here. But I had a feeling it would have been an answer that made me question everything even more.

The room was quiet. Everyone had left to do whatever it was they did at this hospital. For a moment, I felt as if this was all just a dream. Nothing made sense to me and no one was giving me answers, so I must have been dreaming. Things like this didn't happen to me. My life was uneventful and boring. So far, living in Boston had been anything but that.

I must have dozed off. The room was lit by a warm glow. It was quiet. I couldn't hear anyone moving around as they had during the day. I looked around and in the corner sitting in a chair was Mr. Tyler. He was just sitting there looking at me, almost as if he was waiting for me to wake up. He didn't speak right away.

"Ah, Sam, you are awake. I wanted to let you sleep because it's the best medicine for you right now. I was just reading and staying quiet so I wouldn't disturb you."

"What time is it, Mr. Tyler? What day of the week is it? How long have I been here?

"It is 7:30 at night and it is Friday. You have been here for four days, recuperating with the aid of my excellent staff. You were attacked while in my home the other night. Do you remember that, Sam?"

"I remember most of it, I guess. Listen, Mr. Tyler, I've got a lot of questions, lots of stuff that just doesn't make any sense to me and I feel that..."

"Sam, I ask you to let me explain things to you as clearly as I can and without further frustration to you. I know you have been very confused and things are a bit unusual, but trust me, you will understand everything perfectly fine by just listening to me. Are you willing to do that?"

"I guess I have no choice, Mr. Tyler. I am here, injured, without answers, confused. I really have no choice but to trust you. You have given me little reason to, but nevertheless, I will listen to your explanation. So, what do you say we start talking?"

This was the moment I had been waiting for since I arrived in Boston. I had a strange, creepy feeling that there were things out of the ordinary. And now I was finally going to get my answers.

thirteen

I have always been a person who likes to listen to some-one's story. I always thought you could learn a lot from hearing another's perspective and how it measures up to your own. Sometimes, there's great value in taking the time to do just that. You never know who may say something that can change your life, or adjust how you see things and live every day. My life was about to become adjusted even more, immeasurably adjusted. What we don't understand is the concept of how ready we need to be at all times. Life changes quickly, substantially, and for some, forever.

Mr. Tyler sat across from me in what looked like a very comfortable chair; a chair that you could settle into for per-haps hours. A long-conversation chair. Strangely, I didn't remember seeing the chair there earlier. Maybe it had been brought into the room as I slept. I was pretty confident it wasn't there before. They were preparing for a long sit.

Claire and Brandon stepped into the room with Mr. Tyler. They stood against the wall, quietly. It dawned on me that they didn't have formal titles in front of their personal names, like "Dr." or "Nurse" . Just Claire and Brandon. I was trusting these people with my life. I was ready to hear explanations.

"Sam, Claire and Brandon have been working with me for several years. We know each other very well and can offer you a great deal of comfort if you have reservations regarding what I am about to tell you. They have dealt with others who have come into my hospital facility to receive the attention you are receiving. So, please be comfortable with them here today. They are here to help you, nothing more than that. You were beat up pretty bad, not as bad as some who have come through these doors, but still pretty bad. So it's important for us to get you on the mend before we say too much. You body needs to be healed and your mind clear. So, please tell me, are you feeling better? Are you in any great pain or do you feel that the pain you are feeling is manageable? It's a vitally important part to this process so you need to be truthful in your answer to me."

"Mr. Tyler, I feel fine, not as much pain as I had yesterday. My mind feels clear and I am very anxious for some answers. So, if you don't mind, let's get on with this. I think you have stalled long enough. What on earth is going on here?"

"I will admit that all of what has happened seems a bit strange. But let me try to explain as much as I can without raising any further questions in your mind. We operate within a system of people who we call 'Keepers.' Their sole purpose is to possess and protect an item, which I will talk more about later. Keepers are chosen at various times in their lives and are, I should say, protected and watched until the day comes when they take on their role independent of others. They are coached, trained, and given every tool they will possibly need in order to maintain a Keeper's secure lifestyle. I cannot divulge names of people who have been involved in this because they are living a protected life. And as a Keeper, it is my responsibility to maintain the secrecy of who they are at all times. You, Sam, well, I chose you to be a Keeper. And I am responsible for you. And I know that raises a great deal of questions in your mind. But first, let me ask you a question that will aid you to gain some perspective. First and foremost, I need to ask you what you feel your spiritual beliefs are. Do you feel you believe in God?"

I hesitated, unsure of the question's importance and definitely unsure of what my answer might be. I thought back to Hannah, her question about God, something never really discussed in my home.

"Yeah, I guess I do. I don't know, maybe not. I haven't really ever thought much about it. I don't remember practicing church or faith growing up. What's that got to do with any of this? Does my faith or lack of it have anything to do with getting beat up? Am I about to get a Bible lesson here because I have to tell you, I am not up for anyone preaching or Bible thumping to me right now. Especially how I need to get 'right with God.' Come on, what's going on?"

"Everything I am going to explain to you makes it necessary for me to ask you where you are as far as faith. It's important that I know what you think and believe."

The conversation my sister Hannah had with Mom and Dad when she was hurt during our bicycle accident was really the only time God was brought up. She made mention of God after we left the hospital. Why has that story all of a sudden become so memorable to me? I hadn't thought about that in so many years. Why would it creep into my mind now? The look on my parents' faces told me there was a discomfort level, and they definitely didn't want to comment. How are these things important?

"Mr. Tyler, you just need to spit this story out. I am a patient person, but the last couple of days have tried that patience like crazy. I don't really know you very well so what does whether or not I have faith in God have to do with any of this? And on top of that, strange things have happened over the last few days and I just want to know what I am supposed to think of all this."

"Alright, let me start at the beginning."

He sighed, looked down at his hands folded on his lap, and began.

"You must have heard of Moses from the Bible, right? Every kid, I would expect, has heard some story from the Bible. You must remember the story of how Moses parted the Red Sea, God spoke with him, empowered him through his faith and had things asked of him that seemed unlikely for someone of simple measure. You must have heard of the story of him and his staff, the miracles performed in front of Pharaoh, the plagues that God brought forth, the Staff that became a serpent before Moses' eyes and how Moses, with the help of his brother, Aaron, did God's bidding to release their people from the bondage and affliction of Egypt? Through these miracles performed by Moses and his Staff, God's people were free. Do you recall any of these stories from the Bible?"

"I guess over time I have heard bits and pieces, but nothing like a formal teaching or classroom at church, nothing like that. I went to church with Jake and his mom sometimes, but that's about it. Who cares about all that? What's does that have to do with me?"

"Well, it's got plenty to do with you. So, please listen to me carefully."

Was this guy crazy? Maybe when he lost his wife, he lost his grip on what's real. I decided to be cautious, but hear him out. I was beginning to feel panic and a surge of uncertainty was starting to swell in the pit of my stomach. None of this felt quite right.

"Alright, let me start from after Moses performed all the miracles," Mr. Tyler said.

He looked into my eyes and held my look for a brief moment. He then looked away and drew a deep breath. And so the story began.

" Listen carefully Sam. As the years passed by, after Moses had died, the Staff was passed down through generations of Israelites and remained safe in their possession, never losing its significance. In 70 AD Roman legions camped outside of the walls of Jerusalem and in five months, they battered down the walls and completely destroyed the city. During this time, the Jews had many historical artifacts of great significance that they needed to safely remove from the city in order to maintain possession. There were several secret tunnels or passages that the Jews could use to accomplish removing these artifacts and keep them protected. It was at this time that a group of Jewish Christians, with the help of the religious leaders, the Pharisees, removed the Staff of Moses, one of the artifacts. It was turned over to the Christians, who smuggled it from Jerusalem and fled to Pella. And it was this group of Christians that developed a secret group of chosen men and women to keep the Staff concealed. This group is what is now known as the Keepers. They believed they could keep it safe. And it was in fact kept safe and hidden for centuries. Over time, as many years passed, it remained concealed and eventually landed into the hands of a gentleman by the name of Arthur Sprank. As individuals or groups tried for many years to steal the Staff in hopes of destroying it and its significances, there was one group in particular who continued to grow in numbers and strength. They were given the name Invaders. Their sole purpose and dedication was to find the Staff of Moses and destroy it. Knowing this, Arthur Sprank produced four duplicate Staffs for a total of five, one being the original. This was done to confuse the Invaders and lead them on a wild, relentless hunt. A hunt the Keepers vow will never succeed. Believers alike feel the time is near, the time when more of the truth of God's word will reveal itself. And the Invaders have become urgent in their search. The Staffs have been passed from person to person, those who were chosen by the original five, and have continued being passed for years. And these people are aggressively sought after and hunted if they are suspected of possessing one of the Staffs. Each original Keeper has over the years chosen a future Keeper and the number has grown. Before Arthur died, he designed cases that had no Staff inside, a ploy to confuse the Invaders even more and throw them off track. One person has the original Staff in their possession, but they are unaware of it. All Keepers are people just like you and me, going to work every day and living their lives just like everyone else. You wouldn't know if you were sitting next to a Keeper. So after years and years, the Staffs continue to be circulated to different folks who were chosen carefully as ones who can blend into society easily, but be faithful to their mission. The Invaders are designed to do just one thing and that is to find a Keeper and take the Staff if they possess one. And it is vital to the preservation of the Staff and for the safety of a Keeper that they are protected at all cost. Life as a Keeper is like living with a new identity. You watch every move you make at all times, knowing you could be hunted for the Staff in your possession. That's the importance of leading an inconspicuous lifestyle. But the importance of what you are doing is priceless and a responsibility you will never forget. You are a part of maintaining the safety of the Staff, which will eventually be back into the right hands. It was the tool God chose to send signs of who he is, of his authority and power over every person and everything. His power was delivered through this Staff, through Moses and Aaron.

I looked at Mr. Tyler's face in pure amazement, unsure of everything he just told me. The story seemed unreal, but truly amazing. I had more questions now than I had before. So, what he was trying to tell me was that I had been chosen to protect a Staff, which would eventually make its way back into the right hands of someone who knows of its full potential, whoever that might be. And that there were many others who had taken on this responsibility the same as me and they live for the rest of their lives being sought after or even hunted down. And I was to accept this as true and take my place in the long line of the chosen "Keepers" as Mr. Tyler calls them. Now I understood why I was hunted down and attacked. Someone thinks I and Mr. Tyler have the Staff in our possession. Well, what would make someone think that? The company I keep? My honest face? Did I look too average, which ultimately puts me in a pool of those connected to such a possession? Was this guy crazy?

"Sam, I realize this sounds outlandish to you, I mean, someone telling you this must be crazy out of their mind. And I understand because I've known others in your shoes. They were newly chosen Keeper, listening to the same story, the same unrealistic existence, always looking over their shoulder, and then to top it off, they were expected to find a future Keeper. Really, they were in the same position that you are now. The only difference is that they had read the Bible many times in life and I myself am a believer. I knew of Moses, I knew of those in the Bible, and I know of what will come. So much of what I thought to be a privilege to me must be a nuisance to you since you teeter on the edge as a nonbeliever. It all sounds so ridiculous, doesn't it?"

"Wow, Mr. Tyler, I don't know what to think. I mean, I don't want to insult you or anything, but are you making this up? Have I hit my head or am I dreaming? None of this is something I am interested in. I just want to get out of here and go home. Maybe even back to Cleveland. Boston has not been very inviting to me so far. So, if you can medically release me, I would appreciate it. And, are you a doctor? I mean, how did all this happen? How did I end up in a hospital owned by you? I feel more confused now than before. Do you know who got the best of me here, who worked me over?"

"It was an Invader, no doubt in my mind. Somehow, and I'm not sure, but they were tracking me and found you as well. It's difficult to explain right now, but I am convinced somehow they figured out I was trying to bring you on board and were coming after both of us. I felt you would be safer staying with me, especially since I didn't have the time to explain everything to you and allow you the time to accept this position or walk away. There were Invaders around. I noticed them a few days before you moved in. I had to do something to get you into a safe area as quickly as I could. I faked being ill and having to go to the hospital. That way I could get you away from the office atmosphere where you would have been out in the open. So, bringing you into the hospital would throw them off a bit. It was all predesigned, I admit it. I had no other choice. I put people in locations to keep an eye on you until I could find a way to have you with me. I am sorry, Sam. I completely understand your lack of trust in me, now that you know the truth. But I had no other choice. I'm sorry, Sam, I truly am. I didn't see that coming and I should have. But right now, I have to do what's best for you."

"You mean to tell me, my being here was predesigned by you and on top of that, you suspected someone was following me and you didn't offer an explanation at that time? You let me wander through this charade, opening myself up to danger? And none of this is my choice? This is nuts, you just have to let me get out of here. I need to get back to my apartment with my dog. And by the way, where is Bailey? I have a responsibility to him and no one is probably taking care of him at all. And where is my cell phone?

I felt angry, I felt lied to and misled. I knew none of these people and I truly didn't wish to know any of them beyond today. It was seldom that I let anything bring me to this point of anger, but there's a time when someone pulls the wool over your eyes and you really can't help yourself.

"Sam, there are people who would prefer you leave this place and ignore everything I just told you. And believe me, they are banking on the fact that you will become angry and frustrated and walk away. They are looking for you to do just that. And I can assure you, unless you stay, they will be bringing more harm your way than you can imagine. They will strike you at your weakest point—your family, your dog, your job. They will stop at nothing to get information from you to get their hands on this artifact. Sam, you must understand how important it is for you to examine all of these things before you decide to let your immediate reaction drive your final decision. There were lots of folks depending on you to do the right thing. And they are still depending on me to do the right thing. And that is to teach you as much as I can in order for you to carry out what has been given to you. You have been considered for several years. You were not chosen randomly at the last minute, someone we just came upon. A great deal of time and effort has gone into you so far. Please, take a few days to think about this. I know you will do the right thing for the right reason. It is upsetting to you right now because you don't understand everything."

"What don't I understand, Mr. Tyler? It seems I am being held captive in order to carry out a responsibility that I don't even want to be a part of, and I certainly don't understand what you mean by being watched for several years. How long have you been watching me? I have to tell you, I am feeling lied to and forced to do something against my will. This is sounding more and more like something I don't want to be a part of. Can you blame me?"

"Sam, I do understand how you feel. Let me tell you the story. I was married to Elle going on eleven years and we lived in the same house as I do now. I remember it was early summer and we started to notice someone constantly walking past our house, day after day. It was odd to us and we were going to register a complaint with the police or at least make them aware that it appeared someone was stalking our home. Well, on that very same day that we had talked about it, Elle had gone over to see a friend at the hospital. I wasn't feeling well, so I stayed home. Someone knocked at the door. I didn't think anything of it because no one had ever come to the door that I felt I needed to be in question of so I opened it. This tall man with a hooded coat and a facemask pushed his way in, shoved me up against the wall, threatened to hurt me and Elle if I didn't back down and forget about the mission. I had no idea what he was talking about and I told him just that. I was terrified, especially since Elle was going to be home soon and I didn't want her to be in any danger. I tried to rip his facemask off. We wrestled for a few minutes and finally he let me go. Before he left, he turned and told me I had been warned and the next time, I wouldn't be so lucky. I had no idea what this guy was talking about. I was so shaken, I ran to the door and threw up on the lawn. I didn't want Elle to see me this way and I knew she would be home at any time. I regained my composure knowing I would have to tell her what happened. How would I describe what just took place? I didn't even understand it myself, so there was no way I would be able to convey this to someone else. I wondered if I should call the police and register an assault in my home or just stay quiet. I couldn't fathom why this person was threatening me or why I was being watched. How was I to avoid another attack? Did they perhaps have me confused with someone else? I felt this was some kind of joke, that maybe someone I worked with was trying to pull a prank and I was at the center of it. I had no idea what I was watching for or who I was looking for. I was expecting Elle any minute, and I didn't know what I was going to tell her."

"Mr. Tyler, please, I understand you are lonely and you are living out some kind of fantasy story here, but I am not interested. I just want to get my clothes, my cell phone, and go home to Bailey. I feel okay and I think I can go ahead and leave. I really thank you for helping me get back on my feet. Someone just broke into your house and I happened to take the brunt of the attack. Thank goodness you were spared. But right now, I just need to walk away from everything that has happened since I came to Boston."

"Sam, I just ask you to stay the night, get some rest and think this through carefully and thoroughly. This is a big decision and many are going to be affected by what you decide. You are right, I cannot make you do anything; the decision is entirely up to you. But all I ask is that you take into regard what I have shared with you and ponder this before you make a decision. Please stay and get a good night's sleep. And if you still want to leave tomorrow, I will not stop you. I beg of you to consider what I am asking. Will you at least do that? You don't have to listen to the rest of my story, but please just stay the night and consider what I have told you."

I looked into his eyes. Urgency had replaced the calm I saw before. His deep, serious look penetrated me. At best, I would give it some thought overnight.

In an attempt to avoid being rude, I politely asked everyone to leave. Although my outward excuse was weariness and feeling overwhelmed, I truly was angry and couldn't quite wrap my mind around this insane story or what was being asked of me.

Mr. Tyler left, as did Claire and Brandon. I sat alone trying to knit together the bits and pieces of each story told to me. I welcomed the quiet. I felt an immense amount of anxiety welling up inside of me as I recalled each setting and the unusual situations as explained to me. The more I thought, the more I wanted to leave, get Bailey, and head back to Cleveland. I feared my ambitions in Boston were not going to be everything I had hoped they would be. I had been here six days and everything fell apart from day one. I missed the familiar routine of my life, getting together with my family occasionally, talking with Jake, and working at the dead-end job I had. Yes, I even missed that. I felt it would do me no harm to relocate back in Cleveland and try to put this experience behind me. Bailey would be happier and so would I.

In the midst of pondering the earlier events and enjoying the quiet, the door opened slowly.

"Knock, knock." Claire poked her head through the open door. "Can I come in and talk with you for a bit or would you rather not?"

Claire was a very nice person, soft spoken, kind, and caring. She took care of me for the most part, along with bandaging and re-bandaging my wounds with great gentleness. I liked her instantly.

"Of course, Claire, come on in. I was just trying to relax a bit and fall asleep. Big day for me tomorrow. I think I have decided that Boston is not for me and Bailey and I are going to head back to Cleveland. Boston just hasn't been very kind. Even though it's only been six days, I am pretty convinced I don't belong here. But, I'm rambling."

She came in sheepishly, almost uncomfortable to be in the room alone with me. She was very quiet and tender-footed.

"No, Sam, you are not rambling. You have had a lot happen to you. It's okay to talk about these things and actually it's the best type of medicine for you. Is there anything you want to talk about? I've been told I'm a pretty good listener!"

She giggled, trying to lighten the mood from earlier events. She was very sweet and sincere, and maybe she was just the person I could get some answers from.

My shoulder had started to ache, even though they discovered there were no breaks. My whole body actually was feeling a lot of aches and pains in places I didn't even know I had. Maybe it was stress.

"Claire, would it be possible to get something for the pain? It's starting to act up again. I think I took something about five hours ago. I don't need much, just something to ease it up a bit and allow me to relax and get some sleep tonight."

"Oh, yeah, Sam, let me get something for you. I will only take a minute. Be right back."

"Wait, Claire, was there something you came in here for, something you wanted to ask me or tell me?"

"Not really, Sam, nothing in particular. I just thought you might want to talk about some of the things that Abraham said to you today. He gave you a lot of information all at once and sometimes people have questions. That's all, I just wanted to know if there was anything you might want to talk about."

"You mean there's been more people in here who have heard this same story? I'm not the first person who has gone through this?"

All of a sudden I was interested in finding out more about this mystery life that Mr. Tyler had described to me. Like living the life of an undercover agent or something weird like that, always looking over your shoulder, wondering when you will be hunted.

"Well, Abraham, or Mr. Tyler to you, he is something, a special kind of guy for sure. I have utmost respect and admiration for that man. He has done great things in his life and has seen many trials and losses. He has led a life of service to others and has done it without giving it a second thought. He is a true God-fearing man, and I know if I had a problem, he would be the one I would call on. Just a really great man."

"How long have you known Mr. Tyler or Abraham? What should I call him? I just don't want to be uncomfortable with all this so let's get our names straight. I'll just call him Abraham like you do. How's that?"

"I have known Abraham for almost six years now. He opened this private facility about twelve years ago, and he only takes in special and unique situations. And it is completely run on private funding. No government monies change hands here. He hires all personnel and staff himself. As you have probably guessed, we are a tight group. We have some common knowledge of the secrecy that must be maintained for particular people who are brought in here such as you. Abraham would never tolerate people working in his facility who were not trustworthy. He opened it shortly after his wife went missing. I heard she was a remarkable woman with a big heart, and that she loved helping children and others. It was such a terrible time in his life. Opening the hospital helped him to redirect himself into helping others instead of being alone in his sadness. And many have benefited from what he does."

"How old are you, Claire? If you have known Abraham for six years and you have a nursing degree that must have taken what, four years, that makes you at least twenty-eight years old if you started nursing school at eighteen. Am I right?"

She laughed at my desire to discover her age. After all, from what I've been told, it's taboo to ask a woman her age. But if you guess it, most likely there will be a sign on the woman's face telling you that you hit it right on the money. But not Claire. I couldn't read her at all.

"Well, Sam, I am twenty-eight years old. But, I didn't start school until I was twenty. My nursing degree only took me two years, not four. And I did all of my intern training right here at Abraham's facility. He wanted me to learn from who he considered the best in their field and I accepted the offer."

"How did you meet him, I mean, was he screening graduates from local colleges?"

"My mother was a nurse in the hospital over on South Crescent. It was a small hospital at the time, and she met Abraham when he was brought in for an injury."

"So, what kind of injury are we talking about? Something like what happened to me? Tell me the truth, Claire, what's going on here?"

"Well, you remember Abraham told you about the break-in at their home and how that put a scare into him, right? Well, he finally told Elle; he needed to be honest with her. But I guess curiosity got the best of them and they decided to do a little digging. One night they had gone to the library to research the newspapers for reports on home break-ins, gang activity, arrests, or local tidbits that might give them some answers about the night of their break-in. They looked for police reports, complaints from citizens, and things like that. They found nothing, not one piece of information to go on. So after several hours of searching, they decided to start for home. The rain had started to come down pretty good. They were only a few blocks away and had stopped at a stoplight. From out of nowhere, someone in a black cloak stepped out in front of them, came around to the driver's side of the car, grabbed Abraham by the neck, and threw him down to the ground. The stranger started hitting him and Abraham fought back. Elle locked the doors of the car and blew the horn. It was the only way she could think of to draw attention from anyone nearby or driving by. The person in the cloak stood up, pointed his finger at Elle in the car, walked up to the door, and banged on the window. And then as quickly as he had appeared, he was gone. Abraham was lying on the road bleeding, his eyes all swollen, his lips swollen and split, and a couple of his ribs broken. Elle unlocked the door and quickly helped Abraham to his feet and back into the car. She got him to a hospital right away. She knew he was in a lot of pain, and she was terrified for him and for whatever those people wanted of him. When they got to the hospital, Elle took him through emergency and they immediately called Nurse Habers, my mother. She took Abraham into an examination room and tended to his abrasions and cuts. She was one of the staff at the hospital who worked with any cases that came through classified. On top of his obvious abrasions, he had a dislocated knee-cap. They would have to keep him for several days to get his knee taken care of, so they accommodated Elle to sleep in the room next to Abraham.

"Is Mr. Tyler a Keeper?"

"That's not for me to say. But I can tell you this. The number of protectors far outweighs the number of Invaders. You have no idea, Sam, how large this is. Like Abraham told you, there are five Staffs placed through-out the country in order to protect the original. Each one is moved around at undisclosed times and locations. Someone is actually the Keeper of the real one according to Mr. Spank's plan. He was the one who organized and implemented this whole idea and because so many have become involved, the Staff is being greatly protected."

"Claire, did you come in here to convince me to go along with Abraham and what he is asking of me?"

"No, I came in here to see if you were okay. If you recall, you were the one who asked me, right?"

She smiled very sweetly at me. She knew she was right. I had been the one who initiated the conversation. But I was glad I did ask because the story peaked my interest and she provided some of the answers that were weighing heavily on my mind.

"I have one question for you, Sam, if you wouldn't mind answering it for me. I don't want to pry."

"No, that's fine, go ahead and ask."

"Have you been having dreams?"

"What dreams are you talking about?"

"You know, the ones where you are a fighter, you have this incredible power. Have you had those dreams yet?"

I didn't know what to say. How did she know about the dreams? I didn't tell anyone, not even Mr. Tyler. I sat up in my bed and looked at Claire, who was looking intently at me.

"Claire, how do you know about the dreams? The only way you would know about that is if I told you. And you and I both know I haven't shared that with anyone."

"Sam, there have been several others who have had dreams. They have been here, beat up, hurt, almost dead. They have shared with Abraham that they have had a dream of extreme power, strong hands, the faceless figure.

I wanted to know if you had a dream because it sets you apart, Sam, it actually means something. You will have to talk with Abraham about it, and he will be able to tell you. But I think I should go now and leave you to get some sleep. It's been a grueling day for you. I realize there has been a lot for you to take in, but a good night's sleep can do miracles." She got up from the chair next to my bed and turned to the door.

"Claire, are you ever in danger because of the things you know?"

"No, Abraham takes good care of us here. We have a purpose and we are always watched over. Get some rest, Sam. Tomorrow is another day. Do you still need the painkillers?"

I had a feeling that she was not being completely honest, and that her answer was designed to give me peace of mind. Once people became involved with the Staff, it seemed they were no longer out of harm's way.

"Actually, I think I will skip the painkillers for now. But thanks, Claire, you did answer some questions that I had."

She left as quietly as she came, and I was alone with my thoughts once more.

fourteen

Somehow, I knew sleep would not come easy, and that hours would go by before I would find rest. So many thoughts traveled across my mind and none of what was shared with me made sense. None of the stories knit together in a way for me to feel convicted enough to stay. And for the most part, it all seemed purely unbelievable. I tried to close my eyes and let the dealings of the day roll off my shoulders. I knew it was going to take more than that. I kept thinking back to the question Claire had asked me, the one regarding the dream. How had she known about that dream? She described it in a way that made it seem as though she had experienced it herself. Was Claire actually a Keeper? Is that how she knew so much? And if that was the case, was Brandon also a Keeper? How many others that I have come into contact with so far were Keepers? What, for God's sake, did these dreams mean? My headache was starting to get stronger and I knew sleep was not coming soon. I looked down at myself, the sling now removed and the bandages that were still everywhere covering cuts and scrapes. I questioned if I could clear my mind of the past days' events and settle myself enough to sleep. I felt the need to get out of bed and move around. I decided a quick walk might stimulate my mind and body enough to achieve a positive mindset once again. And quite honestly, who was there to stop me? I lifted my head and shoulders off the pillow. The soreness in my neck was excruciating, but I was determined to get up. After all, I wanted to go home tomorrow, and there was no better time than now to show everyone I could get up and move around by myself. I managed to get myself into a sitting position. All I needed to do was swing my feet and legs around and stand up. It sounded simple but the pain in my back, shoulders, and legs quickly reminded me of how sore my body really was. But I was persistent that I could do this. I wouldn't be going home if I couldn't pull myself together and take a little bit of pain. I needed to do this for Bailey. He must be wondering where I was, and whether I was ever coming back to take him out for a walk or spend time with him again. Mr. Tyler didn't reassure me as to who was taking care of him. I needed to get back to Bailey. He was my responsibility. If I could put a little pressure on my legs and stand up on my own, I was pretty sure I could walk. I just needed to take one step at a time. My lower back was pretty stiff, but I thought standing would actually make it feel better. I was wrong. My legs buckled under me and down I went to my knees. I didn't have the strength I thought I had. After the beating I took, I wasn't so sure I would ever feel like myself again. Claire was right, I was in no shape to get out of this bed and go home. I would have to get that through my thick skull and just submit to being taken care of. I turned and looked over my right shoulder. Not too far from me was the buzzer so nicely placed in order to get help if I needed it. And now I needed it. I felt embarrassed and angry. I had never in my entire life been unable to take care of myself. Here I sat, weak and too sore to even get on my own two feet to take a step. I reluctantly grabbed for the buzzer and gave it a good push. Exasperated, I hung my head to my chest and waited patiently for an able-bodied person to help me back on to the bed.

Claire came into the room, running, and almost out of breath. She looked at me with panic in her eyes and came to my side within seconds.

"Sam, what happened? Please don't tell me you are so stubborn that you actually tried to get out of this bed by yourself. Do you not understand the extent of your injuries, that you do not have the strength yet? Good God, Sam, you need to take it easy for a while. You're in no condition to test your strength. Stubborn people make my job so difficult. I need you to start listening and stop fighting. You will do more harm to yourself if you insist on doing things your way."

She put both hands under my arms and lifted with all her strength. She was not a big woman, but she was surprisingly strong. She lifted me back on to the bed, helped me swing my legs around, and brought the covers back up around me. I had a feeling she was not very happy with me at that very moment. And I was making her job difficult. I was ignoring everything everyone was telling me. I tried to look into her eyes, which by now were filled with tears. I had upset her enough to make her cry.

"Claire, I'm sorry. Please, please don't cry. I don't know how to handle people who cry. I'm not good at consoling so please, don't be upset. I won't foolishly try to get up on my own again. I thought I could handle it, and I was wrong. You were right, I am stubborn and I have had no consideration for anything anyone has said to me. Call me stubborn, but please, don't cry."

I was pleading with her to keep her emotions hidden just for my own selfish reasons. I never could handle anyone being upset to the point of tears. Not that it happened often and for that, I am thankful. But when I was faced with it, I crumbled.

"Sam, you have something before you that has been in the making for a lot of years. It's important that you consider listening to what Abraham is saying to you because what he is telling you is true. Look at yourself. You're all beat up, you can't even get out of bed, for crying out loud, and you question what Abraham is telling you. You think someone doesn't like you and beat you up because they know you well enough after two days of living in Boston? Does that really make sense to you? Who in Boston knows you well enough to take a dislike to you and beat the living crap out of you? Can you give me a good answer to that because if you can, I will walk away and never bring this up to you again! Really, Sam, I fear for you. Stubborn behavior can be very harmful if it motivates you in the wrong way and right now, you are endangering yourself and others around you because you think you have all the answers. And I am telling you, you have no answers and nothing you are thinking is correct. In the morning, Abraham is going to be back in here, he is going to be looking for an answer from you, and you know what, you better have a good one. You better be able to take care of yourself because he won't be able to protect you if you keep fighting the fact that you are a Keeper. You were chosen and you cannot escape it unharmed. Do you understand what I am saying to you? I have tried to give you a calm rendition of how life is going to be from now on, but if you want to be so stubborn, then I cannot help you and Abraham cannot protect you. That's something you can think about before morning. Now, if you need anything more for your pain, let me know now. I will get something for you and make sure you are comfortable. But if you try to get out of bed again on your own and fall, you will stay there the rest of the night. I have given you fair warning. Stubborn acts will bring consequences you will not want to face, but nevertheless, they will happen. And they will be whatever you choose them to be."

Claire was pretty upset and I was sure there wasn't much other than "Yes, ma'am" that I could say to satisfy her. She was quiet and reserved on the outside, but get her upset and you better watch your step. And I had pushed too far and ignored too much.

"Some pain reliever would be fine and that should be about all I need. Claire, you have to understand..."

She cut my sentence off as though my words meant nothing to her. "Sam, no more talk from you. But I will tell you one more thing. There was someone else who was just as skeptical and stubborn as you. He was in worse shape than you when he came here. We talked and reasoned with him until we were blue in the face, but he refused to hear anything we had to say. He was a chosen Keeper and he turned a blind eye to it. After a week of healing and talking, he got up and walked out the doors of this hospital. Six days later, he was found dead over by the ballpark. He made his decision, and it cost him his life. And there was nothing we could do to help him or bring him back. To this day we don't know if he was killed by an Invader or if it was some other person, but what we do know is that he made a choice and we couldn't do anything about it. We took a long time to get past our failure in convincing him that what we were saying was the truth. Since that time, we have had to keep a perspective that sometimes there will be those who won't want to know the truth, won't want to understand how deeply we care and how hard we work to maintain protection for a Keeper. Ultimately, the choice has to be yours. Once you accept your task, you are always protected, and there are many who keep you in their sight at all times. There are those who watch for Invaders and divert them from getting near you. But you have to choose; we will not do it for you. And with that, I'm going to get your pain medicine and perhaps you can get some rest."

She turned and walked out of the room. Her sincerity and certainty were strong in her words, in her demeanor, and most of all in her eyes. I couldn't get past her eyes and how she looked directly into my face and didn't blink, didn't look away. She meant what she said, and she had a passion in her words that made me wonder if what was being said to me actually was the truth. No one had ever spoken to me with such vigor and sternness as she did. She believed in what she was telling me and I could see she feared for me if I turned away from this responsibility. She came back in quietly with two small pills in her hand and a glass of water. She watched me closely as I swallowed them down and drank the entire glass of water. She turned and said good night and closed the door. I didn't know if she was still angry or upset but I did know she was serious. Sleep would be short if at all for this night. There was much for me to think about and lots for me to consider. Tonight would decide many things for me, and none that I was sure would make me comfortable one way or another. But, I had a decision to make and I needed sleep in order to think clearly and be sharp-minded. Tomorrow I would question Mr. Tyler. I

would dig for more answers and more meaning and then perhaps the questions would stop coming and I could peaceably
make a decision. But for now, I needed rest. Much needed rest.

I awoke suddenly. The room was dark and it felt cold. I
had an eerie sense that someone was in the room with me.
With one eye barely open, I scanned the room slowly, hoping the eerie feeling was only a dream. The room had only
one window, which wasn't allowing in much light. I felt
sure I was being watched. I had this feeling before, when
I had the dream, the one where I felt sheer strength surging through my body. My room was filled with shadows—
dark, black evil swirling around me, engulfing my bed. I
could almost breathe it in, the sense of fear. I didn't want
to feel that dream again. I didn't want to feel that strength,
that supreme power and flawless bravery. But I was back
there, the dark cloak draped around me, the room moving,
shadows lurking nearby. My senses were alive. Before my
eyes appeared an apparition, an evil face. It came charg-
ing at me, stopping inches from my eyes, its face dark, its
eyes sunken and black. It screamed words at me I could
not understand, didn't want to understand. I froze, my
hands gripping the sides of the bed. The strength in my
body seemed to fade. The confidence of my superpower
dissipated, eluded me when I needed it most. The figure
was plunging back and forth, each time getting closer
and closer to my face, looking me directly in the eyes. Its
intimidation was working; my fear welled up in my throat.
I was unable to move. The dark image was laughing at me
with its cracked, swollen lips spread across rotted teeth.
I loosened my grip on the side of the bed and brought
my left hand around to take whatever hit I could. My fist
was tight. All my energy was going into this punch, which

would hopefully send this evil force away to reconsider its return. The hit was powerful; it jolted the dark figure's face away from me, its slime splattering on my bed. It's sallow skin fell off its disfigured skull, slipping off the bones that made up its structure. I was horrified. My heart felt as if it would pound right out of my body. The eyes stared at me, looked through me. I lifted my other fisted hand off the side of the bed and raised it up with every ounce of power left in me. I hoped one more hit would take it down. Then it screamed, the sound shaking the walls and resonating everywhere. My fist landed on the rotten flesh, stripping it off the grisly stank bones of what once appeared to be the face of a man. I began to scream too, not knowing what else to do. Rotted flesh fell to my bed, decay oozed from the face and dripped down on me. It gave one last yell, showing its power and evil intent. With every ounce of energy left in me, I yelled at the figure, challenging its power over me. The figure pulled away from me, shrinking into its cloak and denouncing its position to overtake me. As quickly as it came, it left. I felt sweat rolling down my face and my breathing was labored. I scanned the room, looking for any evidence of a return. I sat straight up in my bed now, readying myself for another attack. All that was left was the smell of fear. My blood was pulsating at a rate that I feared my body couldn't possibly sustain. I fell back on to the pillow and blackness overtook me. The room was silent and my breathing began to return to normal. The last thing I remember was breathing calmly, my eyes closed, hands at my side, no energy left in my body to move.

What hell did I get myself into?

fifteen

The light switched on. I could feel it on my face.

"Sam, wake up, you were dreaming. Wake up, you've had a bad dream."

My eyes felt heavy and my body ached. I could barely see who was standing before me. Everything was a blur as I tried to focus on the image leaning over me. The voice was familiar but it seemed farther away than my bedside.

"Sam, it's Mr. Tyler, boy, wake up. You were having a nightmare of some sort, thrashing and yelling out loud. Come on, wake up."

My eyes began to focus and I could make out the face. Yes, it was Mr. Tyler. Thank goodness, a familiar person.

"Mr. Tyler, what happened to me? Was I dreaming or did something really come into my room and threaten me? You have to help me understand all this or it's going to drive me crazy. Who are these people and what do they want with me?"

I was panicking. I could feel my heart racing again and my breathing was labored as before. This must be how an anxiety attack feels.

"Well, let's get you fully awake, boy, so we can talk rationally. I think you will be able to understand better. Claire, let's get Sam a drink of cold water. He and I can sit and talk for a bit, I'm sure he will feel better then."

Claire left and returned quickly with a glass of water, which I drank down willingly. Mr. Tyler sat in the chair next to the bed, waiting for me to gain control of my senses. I felt exhausted but wide awake. The emotional roller-coaster of the last few days had taken its toll on me, and I felt worn down as if I might collapse from exhaustion. The cold water tasted good and it helped me feel more awake. I looked at them both. Their faces showed signs of deep concern. Claire's eyes were wide open with either wonder or fear, I couldn't really tell. I asked what time it was. It felt like the middle of the night. I wondered when Claire and Mr. Tyler slept or if they ever went home. Or was this their home? But Mr. Tyler had a home where he was my landlord. Nothing made sense.

Mr. Tyler spoke calmly and quietly, trying to reassure me that all was okay, and that I just needed to tell him what happened. He wanted to know what the dream was about, and he said every detail mattered so I wasn't to leave anything out. He said because it was fresh in my mind, this was the best time to talk about it.

"Mr. Tyler, I'm not so sure I want to relive this dream, I mean, it was evil, something you would see in a movie. There is no way any of this could be real. Maybe it's just a subconscious reaction to everything that has happened since I've been here. You have to admit, life has not gone smoothly and maybe I'm just overwhelmed and it's all coming out in some horrifying dream."

"Tell me your dream, from the very beginning to the end. Don't leave out anything, every little detail matters, it all means something, I assure you."

The details of the dream came back precisely as though I was still experiencing it. I could feel the rush of blood surging into my temples. I felt my blood pressure rising as I described the darkness, the feeling of power, doom, strength, and the relentless need to survive. It was a dark and grim experience, one I did not wish to live through a second time. The cloaked demon that twice now had entered my dreams disturbed me so badly that this time, I wanted someone to know. Mr. Tyler could answer my questions for me. I was sure he had some clue as to why this dream recurred. It was so real, it seemed as though this creature, this being was right in the room with me. And that's the part that disturbed me the most. Mr. Tyler listened closely, writing down short, quick scribbles as I spoke. Claire stood by his side, her eyes wide with fear as she too listened to my dream. When I finished talking, Mr. Tyler continued to write. Claire continued to look at me with a horrified stare, almost without blinking. The room became quiet. I looked from Mr. Tyler's face to Claire's face.

"Sam, I want you to look at me and focus on what I am about to tell you. When I told you that being chosen as a Keeper is a serious undertaking, I did not use the term loosely. Invaders are not just seeping into your thoughts or as you would think, your dreams, they are surfacing now into the real world. The intruder at my home the night you were attacked, do you recall any particular thing about that person? The height, for instance, or a scent of any kind, such as smoke or car fumes or anything of that sort? Were there teeth missing? Did it have long hair maybe, or tattoos? Is there anything that you can recall? It is critical that you try to remember every little detail."

"Mr. Tyler, I was attacked in the dark, the lights were out, it was storming, and the flashes of lightning were all I really had to see anything at all. I don't recall any markings or distinctive qualities. The only thing I remember was that he was extremely strong and it was all I could do just to get his grip off me. To this day I do not know how I overcame that attack. I mean that person had power. The kind of power that average people don't have."

"Alright, yes, I suppose it would be hard to notice anything with the lights out. This person was clothed in black, right?"

"Yes, that I can tell you. As a matter of fact, his face was all black. I don't know, it looked like face paint, it was so dark. Or maybe a mask. But it was definitely black. And I didn't notice if there was any smell, you know like paint would smell." I could hear panic rising in my voice, I could feel it in my chest. "Mr. Tyler, I just can't remember."

"Alright son, you have tried hard to give me whatever details you can remember and I won't press you. Now, about tonight, you were alone in this room, lights were off and you were trying to fall asleep. And other than the bruises and marks on your knuckles, you actually did fall asleep, is that right?"

"Mr. Tyler, I really do believe I fell asleep. I remember Claire leaving the room. It was quiet and I felt tired. It has been such a long day, all I wanted to do was go to sleep for a while and wake up with all of this gone. I don't know for sure if I was awake or asleep because honestly, it's all a big nightmare. Meeting you, coming here to Boston, everything except Bailey has been a big disaster. I need you to provide me with some answers, some type of sensible direction here because I am on the edge of losing it. I mean like getting up out of this bed and getting a cab, finding my dog, and leaving this city. So, please, Mr. Tyler, please help me with finding an answer here. Because so far, all you have really done is make matters worse. Your answers give me no comfort, they make no sense, and I am one sentence away from calling you all crazy and out of your God forsaken minds. Now tell me, who was in my room tonight? If someone from this place you call a hospital was in here trying to scare me or hurt me, I have the right to know. And I think I have been patient enough."

"These dreams have happened before to other people we have dealt with. It's the battle between the desire to stay where you are in life or face those inner fears in an effort to step out of your comfort zone. Inner fear and insecurity can look ugly and limit everything you choose to do. You are the only one who can face it and overcome it. I'm here to walk you through this process, but you need to be willing. That decision I cannot make for you. Truth is Sam, there was no one in this room tonight, just you. There's a time when you need to settle within yourself the path you take. It is my hope for you these dreams go away and for you to make the right decision"

sixteen

"Don't you ever wonder maybe if you took a left turn instead
of a right you could be someone different?"

~Unknown~

This group of people made it very easy for me to want to leave Boston for good and never look back.

" Right now, let's refocus on what is before you. You have been selected to be a Keeper and that is something that is not going to go away. You have to choose your path. You can either be under the watch and protection of the Keepers or you can go out on your own and take the chance of being caught up eventually with an Invader. I cannot guarantee your safety, as much as I would like to. I have the Staff and its safety to be concerned about at all times. Please understand if I sound uncaring or blunt, but you do realize that your decision needs to be made soon as I feel there is an Invader at your heels, and I am endangering others here. We cannot keep you here without putting all other factors into motion. I would have to move you to a hospital without our protective boundaries and staff. At this point, we are all at risk. So, please, Sam, make a decision. I will leave you alone for a while and when I return, you will need to give me your answer."

He said nothing more about the dream, leaving me to understand that I simply had a nightmare in which I lunged at an imaginary figure to defend myself. I sat with my mouth open, gazing into the faces of these people who I was trusting with my life. I thought of all the risks and life-threatening events that would probably be before me and how worth it all was to ensure the safety and authenticity of the one true Staff that was in someone's hands at this very moment. It could be in my hands without my knowledge. I would need to conduct myself as though I knew nothing about it or its whereabouts. All of these things would become the life I would lead and my life would never be the same again. Perhaps that wouldn't be so bad after all. Maybe this was exactly what I needed to do to bring purpose and meaning to my life. This could be the exact thing I had been looking for. Maybe after all these years of wondering what I would amount to in my life the answer was finally before me and I needed to make the choice of all choices. I didn't know if I should feel cursed or blessed. I didn't know how to make this decision. I didn't know if I was being fooled or if this was real. I didn't know the answer to any of these questions. But I did know how odd it was that these things would start to happen on the day I came to Boston, and that Mr. Tyler had been a consistent figure in everything that had happened and he was the ringleader of all these people in this particular hospital. Was I ignoring the inevitable? Was this going to happen one way or another? Mr. Tyler, Claire, and Brandon all seemed to think so. Why couldn't I believe it? What was making me so skeptical? I felt that I should have faith in what Mr. Tyler was telling me, that perhaps he really was who he said he was, that I had been chosen as a Keeper, and that I had a responsibility to do whatever was asked of me. Was this the path my life was to take, my purpose, designed for me? I didn't have the answers to any of these questions beyond the shadow of a doubt, but I did feel something tugging at my gut, something I didn't understand completely. Perhaps it was time for me to move forward and take a leap of faith.

"I need everyone to leave my room. I have things I want to think about and if everyone could leave, it would give me a chance to do that."

All eyes turned on me. I could sense that I had said something they were not expecting.

Mr. Tyler finally spoke. "Okay, we will leave you to your thoughts. Take all the time you need, think it through thoroughly. We will be nearby, just call for us if you need anything." His eyebrow lifted as his eyes met Claire's, questioning what might be in store for all of them. This decision weighed very heavily on Mr. Tyler I could tell, but it was my decision and I was tired of being on the fence regarding what to do.

"Thanks, I just need to take some time to myself and make a decision. Not having any direction with all of this is going to drive me insane. Please give me some time and I will let you know."

I realized there was no kindness in my voice, just the insistence that I be left alone to think and make a final decision. Where was Jake when I needed him? He had helped me make every critical decision in my life. He would be able to give me the perspective I had been unable to give myself. I needed to give Mr. Tyler an answer. I sat in the bed alone with my thoughts. I was terrified.

seventeen

It seemed like time stood still. This was a decision that would shape the rest of my life. How would my friends react to me if I decided to be a Keeper? Would I even have friends anymore? Would there be anyone I could trust? Would Jake still be my friend? Would my family see me differently? They wouldn't be able to know what I was doing. I would never be able to tell anyone. I would be living a double life, keeping my distance as best I could without giving any explanations. Keeping secret communications with people who guard me against the Invaders. Would I always be looking over my shoulder, wondering if my life was in danger? Was this the life I really wanted? I could walk away and never have to worry about this again, never hear about Mr. Tyler and his mission, his secret mission. He could move on and find the next victim to fulfill this so-called "protection of the Staff" supposedly used by some guys in the Bible. I had gone through all this crud, nothing that I chose to go through, in order to fulfill someone's crazy story—a story that I wasn't even sure I believed.

On the other hand, what if everything Mr. Tyler said was true? What if I was chosen? Had I been watched, monitored, shaped, and protected for years to finally reach this moment in my life when I would take the reins and accept what was expected of me? I was being asked to do this out of sheer faith and obedience. Was all of this predesigned to climax on this very night? What I wanted more than anything was someone to verify that the step I needed to take was the right one. I needed someone besides Mr. Tyler to give me some type of indicator that I was supposed to live out this mission that he so strongly and so thoroughly said had been designed for me. I was too scared to make this life-changing decision for myself. I never made decisions myself. I've always had someone else to confirm that it was the best thing and the right thing. When I decided to move to Boston, it was Jake who encouraged me more than anyone. He thought I would have so much more success in my career if I moved away from what I was familiar with, that I would be a better person for becoming independent and that I would have so many things in life that I could accomplish if I didn't live near my family. He really inspired me to move away from my parents and siblings and become my own person. I needed someone to push me then and I needed someone to push me now. Maybe it was time to make a change in myself, in the way I make choices, in the things I do and don't do. Maybe I should trust in what Mr. Tyler was telling me and believe that he was being truthful. Maybe it was me who had the problem and that was why I had little success in what I had been doing in life. This could be the chance I had been waiting for to do something that counts, to make a change and make a difference. Suppose this was all true, this stuff that Mr. Tyler had been saying to me, that Claire had been saying to me. Suppose I took the leap of faith and said why not. I kept thinking of what my sister Hannah would say or do. She would rationalize between the two concepts of having the willingness to try or the stubbornness of doing nothing at all. Lying in this bed all banged up, bruised, and beaten was a clear indicator that someone wanted to hurt me and I needed to believe that Mr. Tyler knew what was going on from firsthand experience. It made no sense that someone would do this for something that didn't matter at the end of the day. It's too farfetched to be some game to play with someone's life. I could read it in Mr. Tyler's face, the serious look in his eyes. And even when he talked about his Elle, he possessed a serious, sincere look. My head was spinning with everything to consider, every small detail swirling around up there, and me trying to make sense of it all. I just needed to rest my eyes, tip my head back, and wait for the answer to come to me. This was honestly the first major decision I had ever had to make on my own that altered my life. And I was failing miserably at it. Back and forth with no direction and no decision made. Mr. Tyler was expecting answers soon. I was expecting an answer of myself. Too much had happened in a few days' time. The normal life that I was accustomed to was gone. All that was left was what would come from making this one decision.

The door opened slightly, letting in the light from the hallway. It was Claire.

"Sam, is it okay if I come in for just one moment?"

"Sure, Claire, come in, it's fine. I'm not doing anything but deciding the rest of my life here." I said it jokingly, but

I'm not sure Claire quite understood my sense of humor, which could be dry and misplaced at times.

She came over to the side of my bed and sat down gently.

"Sam, I know you asked for time alone, but I so strongly feel as though I should say just one thing to you. So, here it goes. We all have to make decisions in our lives, some that only impact ourselves, and some that impact other people. You happen to have a decision to make that impacts both. But if there has ever been a time in your life that the decision you make is for the good of something else and you have before you the chance to make a difference that will bring hope and light to others, you most definitely should make that decision. It may seem like a small thing to you, I mean, without having Biblical knowledge or faith this all seems silly and without direction. But let me assure you, you will not be without faith for long. This is a time when you have to take that leap of faith and the rest will come. You will want to fight with everything you have to protect and deliver the Staff you will be responsible for and the mission you have been entrusted with. I believe that deep down inside you lies a man with great strength and great ambition to do the right thing, the honorable thing. You have to decide on this night that you will let that part of you become prominent and allow it to guide you. Suppressing through self-doubt has been your style for years, an easy way around making tough choices. You have leaned on others to make decisions and then you ride their coattails. But not this time. This time, you have to be the one to lead, the one to choose, the one that rises above. You have guts and you have belief underneath this wallowing exterior, this easy-going facade you present to the world. If you don't stand for something, you fall for anything, I'm sure you have heard that phrase. And that, my friend, is no way to live your life. It shows weakness and lame dexterity. I know you think this is none of my business, that this is your choice in the matter. But, my mother was once a part of this. She stood her ground, she gave until she could not give any more, and she was honorable and a pure example of self-sacrifice for the bigger picture. Stop thinking about how this affects only you and start considering how it affects so many others. Think about the impact you can make at a higher level. You will always come across the unknown, that's just part of life. But, when someone who knows so much with such a convicted spirit comes along and puts before you a task, it's something you need to pay attention to."

She spoke with such sternness, such earnest that I couldn't help but stare into her eyes as she invoked to me her passion for this cause. She knew little about me, yet pegged me in every aspect of falling short to take on meaningful behavior. I wasn't someone who chose the difficult path. I always chose the path that someone else had plowed for me. She was right. This was a decision not only for me but for others. I had to find the strength within myself to step outside my comfort zone. And that thought alone scared me. It forced me to see that I needed to grow as a person, become less self-absorbed, and become accountable for something besides my dog.

"Claire, how do you not be afraid of a decision? How do you make choices when you have no knowledge of what you are doing? How do you do that and not have fear?"

"There is always fear, Sam, in anything that is new and untraveled. But the reward is that you did it anyway, that you drove yourself to press on and move forward when you didn't know every inch of the road ahead. That's when you move by faith. The unseen things will always be there, but the challenge is to not let that fear stand in your way. Don't take the path of a coward when you could take the path of courage. Failing only happens when you choose to do nothing in the face of uncertainty. Don't be that person any longer. You are wasting your life by doing things that in the bigger picture make no difference. Finally you have something in your path that will make a difference and for whatever reason, you are struggling with it and dissecting it to be meaningless. You have to choose, Sam, it's no longer an option to wait. I know you asked for time to think, but I feel you are thinking with tunnel vision so I felt I should say something. So, now I will leave you alone."

She chuckled as she stood up, perhaps uncomfortable that she said so much or possibly offended me. She didn't make eye contact as she left the room. She stopped at the door and without turning back, said one more thing.

"Sam, I was pretty uncomfortable coming in here and saying what I said, but it's not always about being comfortable. Sometimes it's necessary to say what needs to be said instead of what we would like to hear. But that's not who I am anymore. I would rather put myself out there and be unpopular with you than say absolutely nothing and let you just ride out the storm with ease. I stepped outside my comfort zone for you, not for me. That's what it takes sometimes, just so you know." And with that, she shut the door behind her and the light from the hallway disappeared. I was alone again. How could a coward like me face the dangers ahead? How could I do anything that was being asked of me? I fell silent with my thoughts in the darkened room.

Hours passed and then I slept—a deep, dreamless sleep that allowed my body to heal. I awoke with the answer.

eighteen

"No sensible decision can be made any longer without taking into account not only the world as it is, but the world as it will be."

~Isaac Asimov~

"Mr. Tyler, I need you to come in here! I need to talk to you!" I yelled as loud as I could.

The words coming out of my mouth were strong, confident, energized, even joyful.

After a moment, the door opened and Mr. Tyler practically flew to my side, an anxious look on his face, his eyes so wide open you could have seen into his soul.

"What is it, Sam? Are you alright?"

And for the first time in my life, I felt as though someone else had entered my thoughts and my body. I felt as though the old Sam had left and the new Sam was emerging..

"I don't know what happened overnight, but I woke with a conviction in the pit of my stomach to move forward. I don't know what's coming in my life, but if I don't look to this change, I will only regret not trying. I've made a decision and my decision is to have you tell me everything I need to know, Mr. Tyler. Tell me what you need from me because I want to be a Keeper, I want to be the best one I can be. And without you guiding me, I will stumble for sure and I will disappoint. So, please, if you will, tell me everything I need to know."

His face exploded with a smile from ear to ear, his eyes brimmed with tears and a look of pride came over his face that only a father would cast upon a son. He didn't hesitate one moment before he said, "Let's get a good hot breakfast and then we will begin at the beginning."

nineteen

"Take the first step in faith. You don't have to see the whole staircase, just take the first step."

~Dr. Martin Luther King Jr.~

I didn't know what I was about to embark on, but I wasn't scared. I felt a new energy, like I was seeing for the first time, hearing words for the first time. And I can honestly say, I felt alive for the first time. There was something inside of me that had changed in that quiet time, lying alone in that bed with just my thoughts. For the first time I prayed to God to change my heart, to clear my mind of doubt and fear, and to give me the strength and bravery to make a decision that would change who I had been and where I was going. And to allow me to take on this quest, this challenge, and do it to the best of my ability. I prayed for the knowledge and wisdom to finally step up to the plate and be strong for a reason that only a few would ever understand. I realized that up until now, I had done nothing but drag myself through life without dreams, without purpose, and without self-respect. I wanted those things, but never wanted to pursue them for myself. I wanted it all dropped at my doorstep through someone else's labor and

I would just reap the reward. But this time, I would earn it because I possessed a passion to make it work and to better the world in whatever way I could. And if that meant standing for something and believing in something I could not see, then so be it. It would take faith and knowledge to accomplish even the smallest step but I was willing to try. Failure only comes from the lack of trying and I was tired of being that person. I was tired of being tired.

"Before we begin, Mr. Tyler, can I talk to Claire alone?"

"Sure, let me find her."

A few minutes passed while he searched for her. I sat alone, thinking about my decision, trying not to let my mind drift. This was going to be a big change for me.

"Hi Sam, Mr. Tyler said you were looking for me. Are you okay?"

"Claire, yes, I'm fine. Come over here and sit down for a minute. I want to share something with you."

She approached me slowly, not sure what to expect from someone who had been so irrational for the last several days. I didn't blame her.

"Claire, I want to tell you that I am going to move forward with being a Keeper. I thought about everything you said and it started to make sense to me. So, I thank you for your words of honesty and encouragement to nudge me when I needed to be nudged and for giving me the things to think about at a time when I really didn't want to think at all. I am hoping this decision will change me, I know slowly at first, but I am willing to step up and try. I don't want to embarrass you in any way, but thank you, you helped me through a really difficult decision."

She listened carefully and looked me straight in the eyes, which honestly made me uncomfortable because

I am accustomed to letting my eyes wander in order to never let anyone see through me. I had so much to learn and so many things to change. I purposely looked directly at her as I explained my decision and how I had arrived at it, trusting that she would be happy with my choice.

"Sam, this decision is something you made because you wanted to change for yourself, not for me. It's important that you see that through your own eyes, not mine or Mr. Tyler's. This is not about pleasing him or me or anyone for that matter. It's about doing the right thing at any cost because your effort will produce a positive outcome. You are being obedient to your beliefs. Doing the right thing has nothing to do with the people who helped you through it. Please put no focus on me. You chose the right path for the right reasons for you. I stand for God and for all those who are believers and followers in the Bible, those who are obedient to his direction and to his orders. People made choices because they had faith. When you learn about the significance of the Staff, that it was an instrument to show God's power and domain, you will understand why it is so imperative that those who are chosen now to bring it to a safe place are under a protection, and those who are working together to provide that protection are willing to be the barrier from what may try to harm you. So remember, this is not something you choose to do to please others, it is something you do out of obedience. Preserving the truth, remember that."

Again, I sat in awe of her words, her strength and conviction. She chose right from wrong even in the face of adversity.

"I understand what you are saying, Claire. So, thank you for giving me the insight and the vision of a new direction and a new purpose. I guess I feel gratitude in what you were willing to share with me at the time I needed to hear it. So, I move forward."

She turned and left the room. I wasn't sure how much I would see of Claire after that day, after that conversation. But, honestly, I did hope to see her again, not so much because of the Staff, but because I liked who she was. I wondered what she meant when she spoke of preserving the truth. I decided I needed to find the truth first.

Mr. Tyler came back in looking much less stressed. I supposed I had given him the good news he had been waiting for. I was anxious to begin talking with him. I had made a decision and now I needed to be true to my word. The times in my life that I had questioned the most were times when I needed to make decisions. They were always the times when I searched out someone else to decide for me. And thinking back, those were times when I had less respect for myself than others. In the last few hours I had realized that I had never moved forward with anything important. I had been stuck in the same rut, spinning my wheels. The things that had happened to me over the last several days were things that allowed me to open my eyes to something of great change. And now that I could see that clearly, I was ready to step up and say it was time for change. I was ready to change how I had lived my life and ready to make a difference in something beside just myself.

"How are you feeling, Sam? How is your shoulder? Do you feel you are gaining your strength back?"

"My shoulder is feeling much better and I feel I have some strength back. I'm doing okay, Mr. Tyler, thank you for asking. How are you feeling about things? You look to be relieved about my decision. I know that it's been a difficult couple of days for you with all the events and all the resistance I have given you. But, if I can tell you honestly, it's been quite a bit for me to grasp, understand and accept. It is by an act of faith that I have decided to move forward to try to do as you have asked. As anxious as you have been about this, I am equally anxious, perhaps for other reasons. But I will hear you out and move into the responsibility you have for me. So, how and when did I actually become a blink on someone's radar?"

"It was years ago. There are people that have connected you in ways you do not know of. Some things I cannot share with you in order to provide continued protection to them. And I understand that does not offer you much comfort, but it is vital that some information, such as places, times, and names remain privileged for now. I would like to talk to you now about what we need to do for you to move forward with the concentration on how to blend into society and what to look for that will keep you several steps ahead of Invaders. If they know who you are and what you are protecting, trust me, they will become ruthless in their search for you to take the Staff for themselves. You will have to learn who is for you and who is against you. You will have to learn the signs, the patterns, and how to be watchful on a constant basis. You have to learn how to be self-reliant and how to count on your intuition. There are people who will be counting on you, who will eventually cross paths with you, and your confidentiality will be priceless during those times."

"Sounds like the life of a double agent or a spy. Sounds like you basically have no life at all but to always be hiding behind what appears to others as a normal life and a normal existence."

"Pretty much, yes. That's about what it will be like. Your family will know nothing, your friends will know nothing, your employer will know nothing. There will be other Keepers and they will be your best and closest friends, the ones you will trust and rely on. But the price you pay now will bring you rewards later, just remember that. It's not about the here and now, it's about what comes down the road and being a part of something bigger than yourself. What you do will bring an end result in something that you cannot even fathom. You are preventing people from taking away something that is Biblically priceless, an item used by one of God's chosen to lead his people. It gives me goose bumps just to think about having that responsibility and how we affect the outcome. I thrive on that piece of knowledge alone. It's an honor to do this work. You understand that, don't you?"

"I do and I am sure that as I learn more, it will become more and more apparent to me. So, let's begin. I have wasted enough time and energy on deciding. I am ready to move forward."

twenty

"He knows not his own strength that hath not met adversity."

~Ben Jonson~

The hours went by while he talked, I listened; he taught, I learned. Mr. Tyler was a man who truly believed in everything he was telling me, and it inspired me to take a deeper look at myself. He explained the need for me to have my own faith and my own understanding of what is true. He could only plant the seeds and share the knowledge he had gained over the years, but the true faith could only come from within me. He shared his wisdom at a level I could understand. He talked for hours, relating back to times in his life when he had questions and needed answers, when he had his own doubts and reservations about moving forward. He talked about how difficult it was sometimes and how he sometimes needed to dig his heels in deeper and run on faith. It was a strenuous time for him and important for him to keep his responsibilities as a Keeper away from Elle as much as possible. He didn't want her to be involved in any danger that might come her way because of it. They never spoke of that night, as he lay in the hospital, healing from a beating given to him by the Invaders. To this day he is unsure if Elle was taken to send a message. He stressed to me the importance of keeping my life private as much as possible. At times in our conversation, I couldn't help but feel overwhelmed, something that had happened to me all my life. I always ran from anything that created that feeling in me. That was the reason I could never embrace anything that required me to step outside of my comfort zone. And even though this journey was one that I knew nothing about, I felt encouraged. I felt that I could make a difference in my life and to a greater cause.

Time passed and Mr. Tyler tried to get as much into one day as possible, feeding me everything he could think of that would benefit me initially. I caught myself wondering about Bailey and Jake. I knew they were being left out of all of this and I wondered how I would incorporate the life I had been leading into this new, secret existence. How would I blend it all in a way that would work and would appear normal to others? I hoped it would eventually all come together. After all, I hadn't seen anything unusual about Mr. Tyler's life when I first met him. He seemed to be just a normal, elderly man, living in a house where he once lived with his wife and was now renting space in order to survive financially. But now I find out that I had been hand-selected years ago, and my finding his particular apartment was predesigned in some way. I was supposed to come to Boston and I was supposed to be the one he called from the hospital in order for him to keep me within sight. He knew that at some point I would be introduced to this life that was before me. Mr. Tyler had everything prearranged. We talked well past lunchtime and we realized that it had to be close to dinner as our stomachs were growling and hunger pains were setting in. Claire and Brandon had not come around all day. It was just Mr. Tyler and me. My shoulder had not bothered me all day, so my body must be starting to heal itself. Either that or I was so concentrated on listening that my body's aches and pains were secondary. I suspected that eventually everything would be explained and I would understand it all thoroughly. But right now, I needed to eat.

"Mr. Tyler, I think it's time we stop and have something to eat. We've been talking all day. It must be time for dinner around here. Where is everyone anyway? I haven't heard any sounds from outside this room since you came back in this morning."

"Yes, I suppose it is time to eat something. The staff has been busy with other things but they are around. Let's go see if we can find something for dinner. Are you feeling up to a walk? You've been sitting here all day listening, you must be exhausted and tired of hearing my voice."

He was joking but in actuality I was tired and I needed food and something to drink. I'm sure it would do me good to get out of bed. A good stretch of the legs and muscles would feel good. I hoped I would be able to hold my own weight on my legs this time instead of collapsing as I did before.

"I think getting up and taking a short walk sounds pretty good, Mr. Tyler. Where can I find some clothes to throw on? And one other thing, what are your thoughts on my leaving here? I'm starting to feel better and could probably go back home, don't you think?"

"I think you are on the mend, Sam, but not completely recovered enough to leave here. Let's give it some time, maybe another day or so and you will be good enough to leave our supervision. But until then, I took the liberty of going to your apartment and finding you some clothes to wear, knowing of course that you were going to want to wear something a bit more comfortable and fitting than the hospital garb you are wearing. We also have been taking care of Bailey for you. He is in very capable hands."

I was a little surprised that Mr. Tyler had gone to my apartment to get clothes for me. I thanked him for doing that. The last few days had been unsettling and having something that belonged to me would at least provide some comfort. I asked him where my cell phone was and if it was safe. I told him I had placed a few calls to a friend and was anxious to hear back from him. He didn't appear too eager to hand it over to me but his explanation was sufficient for now.

"We have your phone in my office, Sam, where it is safe. That's very private property and I wanted to make sure no one tampered with something that contains so many phone numbers and addresses. You know, it's important for us to remember in these days of technology how we truly have no regard for all the private information we take with us into the social arena every day, out into a world we all know is not as safe as one would think. Everyone you contact with your cell phone is susceptible to anyone gaining that information but yet we trust when we give our information to friends and family that they are guarding it with their lives. And for the most part, that's not the case at all. Also, we had to run a check on the people you called, just to be sure we can eliminate them as Invaders. You can't trust anyone Sam. But, I'm rambling. I am keeping your phone in a safe place in my office. Maybe until you are back on your feet that would be a good place to keep it. Are you all right with that?"

"And where is Bailey?"

"Bailey is being taken care of by a dear friend of mine who is also watching George for me. He is in good company and capable hands. I wanted to make sure he was with someone who would take him for walks, feed him correctly, and give him proper attention. Not to worry, I have your friend in secure hands."

"You really think of everything, don't you, Mr. Tyler? I mean, it's like you did everything just as you planned to and nothing happened by chance. That's not the case, is it, Mr. Tyler? You didn't have anything to do with this attack on me, did you?"

"No, son, I had nothing to do with this attack. If anything I have been doing everything in my power to keep you alive and well so we could groom you for the position of Keeper as you were chosen for. I would do everything possible to keep you safe and on the right track. It is crucial for our mission."

I realized by asking that question I was feeling somewhat suspicious of Mr. Tyler. I was hoping that with each passing day, the suspicion would disintegrate and trust would replace my fears. Even though I had decided to be the Keeper I was chosen to be, it didn't mean that some reservations would not exist in my mind. They say time will tell and I guess time will tell if that is true or not.

twenty one

Changing into my own clothes made me feel like a brand new person, even if it was just a shirt and pants. I felt that I was on the mend, finally. Whatever happened to me during that time alone in the dark, thinking, trying to reach a decision, impacted me in such a way that my body had started to recover from the trauma. And my mind was starting to heal, to recharge, so to say. Once I made the choice, it empowered me. I felt a release of energy throughout my body that gave me the desire to take charge. It was something I had never felt before and I liked it.

The hunger pains were getting stronger. I realized my appetite was coming back. Mr. Tyler poked his head around the corner.

"Are you decent?"

"Yeah, I'm changed. It feels great to be in clothes again. My body is still a little bit sore, but I managed." I chuckled and he showed his approval by grinning at me.

"Oh, I understand. I've had many hospitals stays that just couldn't get over fast enough, and it always felt great to put on a pair of comfortable blue jeans again. What do you say we try to find some food around here? Let's get you up and moving around a bit."

"Absolutely. My stomach was just telling me the same thing."

I was having light, comical conversation with Mr. Tyler, something that had not happened since we met. I was hoping these types of conversations would happen more often. It just felt better to laugh than to worry. He patted me on the shoulder, a sign of camaraderie and trust. He acted very fatherly toward me. He had recognized my lack of direction and ambition, and he was trying to shape and mold me. And I accepted it since I was looking for direction.

"There's a cafeteria downstairs. Couldn't build a facility without having something to eat readily available, now could I?"

"I would say not. And I could eat half a cow right now. How many people actually work here, Mr. Tyler? I mean, you have a complete setup for taking blood samples, X-rays and MRIs, you operate on people, and there's a cafeteria. It's a pretty extensive facility. It must take quite a few people to run a place like this."

"Well, yeah, there's about thirty of us here on staff. We are not operational around the clock. We only accommodate, as you are well aware, the particular folks who come our way. Some of the Keepers come in for checkups and wellness stuff, you know, medications, broken bones, things of that nature. They are safe here. We have our security operating at all times. You will always find the building under surveillance no matter what. The site needs to be secure for staff and patients. There's too much risk for them as they know more than the average nurse or doctor would know. They know things about the clients who come through the doors and for that reason alone, they are under watchful eyes. It's a risk they are willing to take for the Keepers' security and welfare. There is much at stake, Sam, in who you are and who you know. And the staff knows we all work to protect each other. It's necessary to make the program work and be safe while doing so. I know you have some reservations about all of this, son, and quite honestly, I did too. But, as you learn more about your position here, your questions will all be answered. It just takes time and faith. Trust me. I've got your back now and I'll have your back as long as I am physically able to do so."

"Thank you, Mr. Tyler. I know I have been skeptical and ornery and have acted like a brat, but it's a lot to take in and believe."

"No apologies necessary. I understand completely, that's why I am willing to take the time. Someone did that for me, gave me the time to understand the ropes and to gain confidence in myself and the cause. It all takes time and patience. But remember one thing: the more you begin to understand, the more valuable you become to an Invader. They do not want the Staff protected. They do not want it to be put back into the hands of the appropriate ones. They have been battling with the truths of the Bible, trying to disprove its accuracy. They claim all believers are ignorant, and their one major goal is to stamp out anything that could substantiate what we consider truth. They are angry, threatening people and work with great discretion and secrecy, but for evil. We have had to learn many of their methods and thought processes in order to know how to protect ourselves. You, too, will learn these things and it will become second nature to you before long. You will know what to look for. Listening and watching are good tools for learning. Keep your eyes and ears open at all times."

At the end of the hallway, we turned right and continued for a short distance until we came to a set of double doors. Mr. Tyler opened the doors and that's when the magnificent aroma hit me like a tractor-trailer. The wonderful smell of fresh baked bread permeated the entire room. I thought I had died and gone to heaven. Stations for sandwiches, entrees, desserts, pasta, and drinks. I was so hungry I could hardly contain myself. I was sure my eyes were larger than my stomach, but I didn't care. I just wanted to dive into everything I saw.

"Oh man, Mr. Tyler, you know how to eat and eat well. Is all of this done according to your wishes or did some other genius come up with it? Because I have to tell you, I need to pat the guy on the back who came up with all this food. Where should we begin?"

I heard Mr. Tyler chuckle and another pat on my shoulder followed.

"Let's go see how much we can put on one plate, shall we? All of a sudden, I'm feeling pretty hungry myself."

We walked to one end of the counter, got ourselves plates, and proceeded to fill them with anything and everything. There were meats, vegetables, breads, desserts, salads, everything to please a hungry appetite. It was a hungry man's paradise. And I intended to try as much as I could in one sitting. My plate overflowed. Mr. Tyler continued to chuckle behind me, relishing the fact that I had regained my appetite, which was a good sign of healing and mental improvement. He opted for a reasonable plateful. He had tried everything before and knew what to go for. I was willing to give everything a good shot and a thorough analysis. We sat at a round, comfortable table set with a tablecloth and silverware. This was a cafeteria with class.

I ate and Mr. Tyler talked. I looked up at him occasionally, nodding in agreement and acknowledgement, but was more interested in filling my stomach than anything else. He talked of bravery and of taking on a battle that few knew about. He said all of the people that have made the choice have never regretted it. They began the mission one type of person and came out the other end soldiers with some scars, but lots of self-respect and honor. It required putting on the full armor, the armor of knowledge and belief. He said that it sometimes happened over a long period of time, but it had never failed a person yet. He said it was a duty and an honor to be a Keeper and it was something to always be proud of and be willing to die for. At those words, our eyes met. For some reason those words went through my heart and into the pit of my stomach. I laid down my fork, sat back in my chair, cleared my throat, and tried to utter the few words I had to say.

"I have never in my life thought I would be faced with believing in something so strongly that I would be willing to die for it, Mr. Tyler. I have always thought I would die for my family or for my friend Jake, or for Bailey, but I never thought I would actually be facing it for real. And I won't know until I am face-to-face with my own death whether I can carry through with it. I know that sounds cowardly but honestly, until that very moment, how do you really know you would die for a cause?"

"You believe it in your heart and you prepare yourself mentally that it would take your last breath to let anyone take away your right to honor what you believe in. That's how you know, Sam, that's how you know!"

As much as I wanted to man-up at that very moment, I felt tears well up in my eyes. I tried to blink them back and act casual, but they began to spill on to my cheeks and down my face. I looked at Mr. Tyler and tears were streaming down his face, too. The words hit home, and it finally dawned on me how sincere and strong this man really was. I thought back to a few days ago when I had met him for the first time. He seemed like a simple, meek man who lived alone after losing his wife and rented out his home to make ends meet. I remember thinking that I would have to check in on him from time to time because he was alone and so frail. I had planned to help him out around the house and make sure he was all right. Little did I know how strong and self-reliant this man was. He had the strength and wisdom of a dozen men and more integrity than most. I felt guilty that I had judged and doubted him before. I thought he was tricking me into joining a cult with some twisted little game he was playing because he was a lonely, ill man. But now I saw him differently. Now I could see right through to the heart of this man, the years of fighting for a cause he so deeply believed in. He had accepted a mission that he would see through until his last breath. Why else would he take me under his wing this way? Why would he bother with every small detail and involve so many others? It had to be true that I was chosen and brought here to begin my mission. Nothing else made sense to me. Everything else was too farfetched. I had no proof of any of this, just this man sitting in front of me with tears streaming down his face and the look of sincerity in his eyes. That was all I needed right now.

We looked away from each other, drying our eyes as privately and inconspicuously as possible. Neither of us succeeded. We gave a gentlemen's agreement through a nod of the head, a sign that said we understood each other's feelings, and let it go at that. We continued to eat in silence. I realized for the first time that deep down inside of me, I was growing in strength, which was something I needed to do. I was finally reaching the point where it was what I wanted to do.

The rest of the day flew by. I had a good amount of things to ponder and consider. I knew as soon as I was on the mend that I would be expected to begin my mission—a life changing mission, to say the least. I didn't know if I was ready, but I would give it the best shot that I could. I wished Jake were around to talk to and bounce some ideas off. But I knew I should be thinking independently. Leaning on someone all the time had to become a thing of the past. I could not bring innocent people into my mission. I needed to protect them from those who wanted to harm me. I understood now why Mr. Tyler took my phone and kept me from seeing Bailey. They are links to my past, to the life I was leading of dependency, and he knew I would continue to use those things. I had to admit, it was very tempting. I needed to keep my mind on what was ahead of me and how I was going to live a double life. Protecting my friends and family from harm was critical to me if this was going to be my path. I mentioned to Mr. Tyler if I should contact Jake and my parents to let them know I was doing okay. If I didn't contact them, they would suspect something was wrong. Wouldn't it be better to detour them from suspecting anything? He hesitated, but agreed.

We parted ways for a while. Mr. Tyler had to follow up on some last minute information he had received. I didn't ask and he didn't share. I sat alone in my room for the first time since my decision. It gave me time to absorb some of the changes that were about to come my way. I tipped my head back and closed my eyes. I needed some rest if just for a few minutes.

My old life was behind me, my new venture was before me, and I was more alone than I knew.

twenty two

"You gain strength, courage, and confidence by every experience in which you really stop to look fear in the face. You must do the thing which you think you cannot do."

~Eleanor Roosevelt~

I awoke. It felt as though I had shut my eyes for only a few minutes. The noise was loud and I bolted into an upright position, fully awake. Another loud crash, this time it was more than something falling from a desk to the floor. Just outside my door there were scuffling noises, things crashing to the floor as if on purpose. I couldn't think straight. Should I leave my room where I felt safe or go out into the hallway to see what was happening? Was anyone in danger? Mr. Tyler? Claire? I didn't hear any voices or screaming, just scuffles and the sound of things hitting the floor. I panicked, unable to move my feet. I couldn't grasp what was happening just a few feet away from me. I couldn't decide how to deal with something that could be life-threatening. What could I do? Call out to someone, open the door and take a look, offer some type of help? And what kind of help would I be to someone battling for safety when I would probably just add to the panic?

I quickly realized that I was offering no assistance what-so-ever, and that there were probably people who needed my help. It was necessary for me to put myself out there to help in whatever way I could. I was not being brave or helpful by staying in my room wasting valuable time. I opened the door ready to take on anyone who stood in my way in my effort to maintain everyone's safety. What I found surprised me.

There in front of me on a desk right outside my door was a recording device, the tape running its course. Mr. Tyler was standing next to the desk, a disappointed look on his face. Claire was standing next to him with the same look on her face.

"You realize by coming out here you put yourself in harm's way? we could all be dead by now, waiting for your help?" Those were piercing words to hear. My feet froze as I stood in the doorway, my eyes downcast to the floor. I didn't know if I felt anger at being tricked or anger at myself for failing the test. I knew beyond a shadow of a doubt I was going to have to swallow my pride and be ready for correction. I knew they thought that I only cared about my own curiosity and not the safety of the team. I could feel the words coming.

"Give me your thoughts, Sam. What did you think was happening here?"

"I heard noises that sounded threatening and I couldn't decide if I should risk being injured by helping those I knew were in danger. I know I failed. I know you are going to tell me to consider first my own safety as a Keeper. If I fail, the mission fails. You can just let me have it right now."

"Do you think that is what you should do when you know danger is at your doorstep? Is that keeping in mind the safety of the Staff you were chosen to protect at all cost? Sometimes you have to think through the whole picture and your part in the mission. There may be others in danger, that's true. And there may be some who will endanger their lives for a cause. What do you think would happen if you made the choice to protect those who are trying to protect you for a greater cause?"

"So what you are saying is that there may be times when people are in danger but they are fighting for their lives in order to protect me so that I can fulfill my mission? That's a lot to swallow and accept. It goes against the human grain to stand by and let others fall into danger and perhaps death so you can succeed in your mission, don't you think? It seems like a selfish act, that what you are doing is more important than human life."

"People who are 'in the know' of what you are doing have already decided they would sacrifice their safety for what they believe in. They have one job to do. They realize you need to be protected and watched in order for the mission to be accomplished. Otherwise, what is it that we are all truly standing for? We all believe that there is a Staff that was once in the hands of Aaron and Moses, the Staff through which the Lord delivered his power, signs to the Pharaohs, to those who challenged God's authority. The Staff is believed to bring truth to those who have no faith. It is imperative that we keep it safe and deliver it into those rightful hands once more. That's your mission, Sam. It's not your mission to save lives or keep others from danger. You were selected for a purpose and it's necessary for you to focus and have your mission at the forefront of all the things you do, all the places you go, and all the people you come across. You will be the one who has to step aside and let others do their work. Don't look back. Remember those who fought for what they believed in. Complete your mission and bring forth the truth we are all waiting to see unfold, and know the Defenders were right in everything they did for that reason alone. Do you understand how strong you will need to be, how difficult at times it may be for you to make those split-second decisions? You will have to let this type of life become second nature to you. Always protect the Staff, no matter what the cost. Are you starting to see the intensity of what you were chosen for?"

I looked at Claire's face as Mr. Tyler spoke. I got the instinctive feeling that Claire had lost someone in the exact same circumstances Mr. Tyler was talking about. What I wondered was what Claire really did here? I was hoping I could talk to her again privately. I watch her face and sometimes I see sadness. Claire has a connection in all of this besides being a nurse at a hospital for special cases and secret medical attention. She knew more and I was hoping to get that story out of her at some point. I turned my attention back to Mr. Tyler and what he was telling me. A sinking feeling started to creep into my gut telling me I had not made the right choice.

"Mr. Tyler, I see what you are saying. As mind boggling as this all seems, I do understand. The mission comes before anything or anyone, got it. My instincts right now tell me differently, but the reality of it all is that if you cannot change how you think, you will be the injured man and all others before you will have sacrificed in vain. Mind control, keep your focus, never let them see you sweat, stay strong and powerful, but fit into everyday life as seamlessly as possible. Am I right?"

"Absolutely, you are right. And as discouraged as you may feel right now, you are going to live and breathe that every day from this point forward. The Keeper has a responsibility to deal with whatever comes along, to get the job done, to press on and never look back. Keep looking forward. It's like the military in some ways. It does make you harsh in some ways. But in reality, you have to stand for something or you fall for anything. And that's just the bare facts of it all. I don't want anyone to die for me. I don't want harm to come to anyone at my expense or because of my mistake or weakness. But if they are going to choose to put their life on the line for me, I better know what I am doing, and I better have faith in my purpose. I better darn well believe that they are living out their purpose. I better have a clear understanding of how it all fits together. I better do whatever it takes for me to get it right and do it with honor, dignity, and unfaltering faith."

I understood the importance of commitment, teamwork, and strength. But was I the one to do this? Did others falter in believing in themselves as much as I was? Did I make a hasty decision to do this without knowing exactly what it would entail? I felt shaken. I really was losing my sense of solid ground. Those people who had taken the responsibility and accomplished a normal life sounded like they were characters in a story. But to have the reality of it right at my feet caused me to hesitate. I didn't realize the discipline it was going to take would be so overwhelming for someone like me. I began to question myself and I knew that if I continued questioning, I would pull myself out of this plan. Mr. Tyler's plan, Claire's plan, Brandon's plan, and now my plan. I needed to keep a level head and just look forward. Somewhere in this master plan, I would need to know how I was chosen and what all of this was based on. Someday, I would know the truth.

"You know, Mr. Tyler, it's hard for me to accept that you want me to take care of only myself because I guess I have done that all my life. I assumed that was something I needed to change. But now I need to look at it from a different perspective. I do understand everything you are saying, but I ask that you give me a little bit of time to absorb it. I am sure I will be able to do everything you are asking me to do."

Again, I looked at Claire as I spoke, wanting to see her reaction and whether she would look at me directly. She didn't. She kept her look elsewhere and made no eye contact with me at all.

"Just remember, Sam, so much is relying on your ability to focus, keep your eye on the prize at all times, and get the Staff into proper hands."

"When do I get to know who's who and where everybody is located? I should know that, right? I mean, if I need help, I would search them out?"

"No, their safety is just as important as your own. You don't get to know any more about them than they do about you, you understand what I'm trying to say? It's vital that everyone's identity remains as secret as possible. If you were, God forbid, captured and they tried to get other's names from you, well, trust me, they would probably succeed, and I would guess that they would have no further use for your life. You have to understand, Sam, these people have no sense of decency for others' lives and what pain they may cause. They are scoundrels and lowlifes with no concern for you or anyone else. They will do anything to never have to hear the name God again. Please understand how strong they are in their belief. As soon as the Staff is in the proper hands, we can then prove beyond the shadow of a doubt that miracles were performed, no magic, no gimmicks, just miracles. And I hope I am still alive to know about it. Oh, what a wonderful day it will be."

The look on his face was euphoric, a look of pure and complete joy. He tipped his head back with his eyes closed and I knew he was praising God. I didn't know if that was something I could ever understand, but I knew I had met a man who believed strongly and with every ounce of his being. He wasn't afraid to show it, speak of it, or live it. He was a believer and he would do whatever it took to see this mission through to the end. If I didn't believe in God, I could at least believe in Mr. Tyler and his strength to carry on and endure. He was inspiring and for whatever reason, I was captivated with him. I wanted to do whatever I could to see this man smile and be happy. Maybe it was because he lost his sister so young. Or maybe it was because he lost his Elle. He was left to live alone and take on the remaining journey of his life without her, without family, but with a purpose. He was driven. He was always steering in one direction. I wanted to be that way and maybe he was the example I had been searching for all this time. I felt so compelled to do what he needed me to do, to finish the race with success and prove what he believed in so dearly and wholeheartedly. I wanted to be like him and if I couldn't, at best, I would do what I could to please him. And that would have to be good enough, at least for now.

"Well, Mr. Tyler, I can see how much this means to you." I shuffled my feet, trying not to get too mushy or personal, but sincere enough so he knew he could count on me from now on. "I'm going to give it my best. I will keep my focus and aim for the success that we are all working for." I looked at Mr. Tyler and Claire, trying to get a good feel from the looks on their faces. I had a feeling they had heard this before and something somewhere went very wrong. I would have to find that out later, perhaps from Claire. Maybe Brandon would be willing to share this deep, dark secret that was keeping the somber look on Claire's face every time the subject came up. It must be quite a secret, that's for sure.

"Now, let's get back to work, we have been taking up too much time with some silly experiment. But as long as you get the idea, Sam, it was worth the little bit of time we spent. Let's talk about how you will live, where you will live, and what is expected of you. I am sure by now you are confused about how you will manage your personal life and still earn an honest living and blend into society as much as possible. It's not as difficult as you might think. You just need to make a few adjustments along the way. Things you would normally do are not things that are acceptable in order to stay, how would you say, on the down-low."

I chuckled to hear an elderly man use such a modern term. It did put a smile on my face, which was something I had not done a lot of in the past several days. Despite the seriousness of this mission, he managed to keep a sense of humor and was actually quite a comical individual. I did enjoy talking to him. He was a great storyteller and had so many life experiences. He simply captivated me for whatever reason. Keeping my life on the down-low was not going to take much exertion. I led a boring day-to-day existence. I blended in quite well and, for the most part, had little to do with others. Perhaps that was another reason I was chosen—I simply wouldn't take much rework in the social category. It was pretty much Bailey and me now. Even when I lived in Cleveland, my life had been uneventful. I took my leads from Jake and actually spent very little time with my family. I really didn't fit in anywhere very well, so I just drifted from one thing to the next. I didn't feel I had much to offer. I was just an average person with an average life. No wonder I was chosen, I was a boring, bland person with nothing much for anyone to worry about. No one would ever think I was doing anything remotely dangerous or life-threatening. I guess it made sense to choose people as Keepers whose lives were uneventful. I fit that perfectly. All I really had was Bailey, and my parents even tried to talk me out of that. And now, I had to wonder why they did. I was the introverted type, so having a dog was not such a bad thing. But my parents were pretty upset that I got Bailey, and they even tried to get me to take him back. I wondered why. I would have to ask these questions of Mr. Tyler another time. He was pretty concentrated on telling me everything I needed to know.

The time passed quickly. Mr. Tyler chose his words wisely and they began to impact me as he spoke. Not buying on credit would keep me off the grid. Using cash whenever possible was an important step. If I needed to stay at a hotel, I should stay at one that took cash. I should pay cash at the grocery store and for clothing. I should limit my computer use because it leaves a trail. And most of all, I couldn't be naive. My name is associated with everything I do and someone who knows how to find me will see it. Even though the Invaders may not know my name, or at least I would hope not, I should use it very seldom.

I shouldn't talk about my family or where I was from. I should make up a story about myself and move around. I could use a nickname if I felt more comfortable. Using my true name could be a big mistake. When I sign my name I should make sure it is not legible, it should be sloppy so the letters cannot be recognized. I should never go to the same grocery store, and never have a pattern about the things I do. I shouldn't go for a walk or to the gym at the same time every day. I should never do the predictable, and I always need to be aware of that. I should go to different restaurants, never frequent the same one, and always pay with cash. If I have to cash my paycheck, I should go to different banks instead of the same one all the time because it's harder to track. And I should never cash my check on the same day every week. People look for patterns and the same sequences of events. I have to fool them. I need to keep a journal and write down dates and things I do so I can always go back and change my patterns. I shouldn't rely on my memory, it will fail me when I'm trying to remember every little move I made. I should try to move and not live in the same place year after year. I should find somewhere that allows me to rent monthly or for three months at a time. Usually folks who rent rooms out of their homes, like Mr. Tyler does, are the ones who are the most flexible. They understand transitional living and can be more forgiving. I need to blend in with the crowd, and go where there are usually lots of people. I should never go somewhere remote alone; I need stay to where there are a lot of people and lots of traffic. I have to blend, I cannot stand out. I shouldn't wear clothes that are different. They should be common clothes, blue jeans, dark-colored shirts, dark-colored jackets, ski hats, things that make me unnoticeable. I should always change things, either the time of day I do things, who I talk to, what they call me—change is very important in that respect.

Mr. Tyler said that some of these things I was already doing because I didn't really like to stand out in a crowd. My cell phone was a problem because it was not private and could be traced, listened to, and tracked down to where I live and where I go every day. I should turn it off when I go somewhere different so I cannot be located. I should be very conscientious of technology, it's only good when used by someone who is a good person, but honestly, in the wrong hands, my entire life can and will be exposed. I should only use my phone if I'm in dire need to do so. There is a device they can put on my phone to make tracking difficult, but he will get back to that later.

The list went on and on. I should have taken notes, but as Mr. Tyler said, things in writing in the wrong hands could be dangerous to me. Keeping a journal of my events and what I did and when was about all I needed. Everything else should be shredded and kept away from anyone who could get a hold of it. The more he talked, the worse the vision of my life became. Keep to myself, but not so much that I appear to be a strange person. Keep socialization to a minimum and never talk about myself. Always bring the conversation around to talk about them. Have a job where I work independently so there is little socializing and chit-chat about what I'm doing after work. Having a girlfriend is okay, but she can't know me extremely well until I know first how much I can trust her. Mr. Tyler dated Elle for three years before he asked her to marry him. And he was not a Keeper at the time. These were all things I needed to remember in order to stay protected. I should take a martial arts class, so that if I did have any confrontations, I could take care of myself. I should do whatever it takes to keep people from talking about me, gossiping. I should make the effort to stay out of touch with my family, and not visit them as often as I would like. If anyone at all is on to me, my family will be at risk.

He talked for a few hours and I listened as best I could. Everything was crucial and I didn't want to make any mistakes. The impression I got was that my life was to be that of a loner. And under no circumstances was I to take the Staff in my possession for granted, I was never to open the case, never tamper with its lock, and whatever I did, never, ever show it to anyone. I was never to bring it up in conversation and I had to keep it in an inconspicuous place at all times. But if I needed to move quickly, I should make sure it was the first thing I took. I was never to leave my journal behind. Mr. Tyler said my journal and the Staff were the two most important things to have on me at all times when faced with any emergency. He said I should always be aware, sleep with one eye open, and always face the door at night. When I went to work, I should leave the Staff behind in my apartment. I should make sure my landlord knows to never give out information about me, no matter who they say they are or how well they say they know me. I should ensure that my life remain private. I should trust no one and not believe anything I hear. I should always keep my eyes and mind on being watchful. I should try to watch the world news, the local news, and keep myself on track with what's going on around me. Local arrests, gang involvement, dumped bodies, abductions; those were things to keep a mental note about, even journal it if it helps. He said it would become second nature to me after a while, a way of life. But in the beginning, everything would make me nervous and everyone would be a suspect. He said that eventually I would be able to identify the things that were normal and those that were not. Life would settle down and I would feel more natural.

He spoke for about an hour more. Don't forget this, do without that, don't live here, never do that, it was mind-boggling. But when all was said and done, I knew for sure he did not miss a thing. He told me everything he could think of. It was getting very late. It had been a long day for both of us. I was so tired, but my mind was running, making mental notes of everything he told me. None of it was written down because in the wrong hands, that could be a big mistake. Mr. Tyler looked exhausted. He had been a Keeper for many years and I was sure with everything he was managing, he probably had lots of restless nights. But he also possessed a sense of peace about the danger he lived with. He explained to me that we all have a day chosen for us, a day when we would be gone, and we would not live one day longer than God intended for us to live. So, in reality, each day we have was a gift and a new day to do whatever good we could, and we should live it as our last, and never expect more than that very day. He spoke those words to me with such deep belief, as matter-of-factly as anyone could speak. I trusted this old man with his wisdom and grateful heart, his hard work and diligence that brought blessings and knowledge to many others. He was a threat to those who had no belief, but quite a comfort to those who knew him. And that was where he found his solace, his peace. He knew who he was and what he was here for. He never seemed to question anything he was doing or why he was doing it. He just trusted his God and remained faithful.

We said our good nights and I closed my door to go to bed. The light shone under my door, and I knew there was always someone there, watching and protecting me. It gave me great comfort to know that. For outside this building, I would soon be a hunted man. And I found no comfort in that.

My eyes were heavy. I lay down without changing my clothes and hoped for pleasant dreams or no dreams at all, just a restful sleep. If I did dream, perhaps it could be about sailing, feeling the fresh cool air on my face, and the sunshine beating down to warm the day. Gliding along with no cares in the world. Sleep at last.

I never did call Jake or my parents.....

twenty three

"To exist is to change, to change is to mature, to mature is to go on creating oneself endlessly."
~Henri Bergson~

My eyes opened suddenly. The room seemed unusually dark and an unsettled feeling crept up the back of my neck. For the last few days the light from the workstation shone under my door and illuminated my room. But tonight it was off. I didn't know if someone purposely turned it off, maybe to give me a better chance to sleep. I wanted to think of the best-case scenario, but it disturbed me for some reason. Something woke me abruptly and I was usually a pretty sound sleeper. It seemed too quiet. Something had disturbed my sense of peacefulness. Something just felt wrong. I lay still, remembering what Mr. Tyler had said about keeping myself safe for the sake of the big picture. I felt very uneasy. My instincts were telling me to just stay put and be calm and quiet. Was it just my imagination? I had listened to so many scary things over the past twenty-four hours, maybe I was just imagining that something was wrong. Maybe living the life of a man on the run was a little more than my mind could deal with. Was I going to wake up every time I heard a bump in the night? Was my imagination going to start running my life?

I lay still for what seemed like an hour, but in reality was probably only a matter of minutes. It remained dark and quiet. I didn't hear the hum of the computers or other equipment operating. It was unusually quiet. My eyes were bulging almost out of their sockets. I could feel the pressure starting to build from tension and the task of trying to see in the dark. I wondered if this was another one of Mr. Tyler's tests. Maybe I would find out in a few minutes that staying in my room, quiet and still, had been the right thing to do. Perhaps Mr. Tyler would come through my door any minute now to congratulate me on my lack of engagement. He would pat me on the back for making the right decision. Another test completed.

It had started to rain. I could hear the of raindrops against the window in my room. Hopefully it would just be a shower, not a storm. The thought of a storm did not sit well with me. No lightning yet, just the rain. I lay still, thinking out my options as Mr. Tyler taught me. Keep myself safe above all things, which was a difficult concept to swallow, but Mr. Tyler stressed that it was most important. I couldn't help thinking of Bailey and Jake and if they were worried about me. Because, frankly, I was pretty worried about myself right now.

Within a few minutes the rain had started to come down harder. My eyes strained to see as I lay in the dark, curious about what may be happening outside my door. I decided that my curiosity would soon get the best of me and I would get up and see for myself that everything was fine and that my imagination had just been running wild. In some ways, it was starting to scare me, the changes I had already gone through, the paranoia that was seeping into my world and my thoughts. I didn't want to be someone who never had a positive thought about anything and who looked at everything in the world as horrible and life-threatening. Somehow I needed to learn how to balance all that I was taking on without letting my thoughts get out of control. Would this new life redesign me in ways that I was unprepared for? As I lay there, questions kept popping into my mind and doubts started to take hold, again. I didn't want to have these reservations. I had already committed.

The rain pelting at the window brought back memories of that horrible night at Mr. Tyler's. I didn't want to recall that night ever again. But as I listened to the rain come down, it was all that I could think of. I heard the roll of thunder in the distance. Small streaks of lightning started to flash through the blinds and I began to feel myself freeze from the bad memories. I felt the urgent need to find another person, to find someone who could calm my nerves and let me know everything was all right. There was still no light or sound from the other side of the door. Just nothing...

I pulled myself up to a sitting position. I knew the light switch was across the room, a straight shot from the bed. My shoulder ached a bit but not enough to stop me from getting up and moving around. I swung my legs over the edge and my feet touched the floor. I rotated my shoulder to loosen the stiff muscles a bit. My healing had happened quickly. Whatever Mr. Tyler was prescribing was certainly working. I had never healed from anything so quickly in my life.

I sat on the side of my bed, making sure this was the right decision. Mr. Tyler would not think this was wise, but I couldn't sit any longer and wonder. I knew something wasn't quite right.

It was only a few steps from the bed to the door. I was hoping a flash of lightning would give me the visual I needed to make my way over there. I stood up and began moving. I reached out for the light switch on the wall and pushed the lever up. To my surprise, the lights did not come on. I questioned whether the lights being off had anything to do with the storm outside, but it didn't seem close enough to have done that kind of damage. Now I was confident that something was amiss and that someone had purposely turned the lights off. A feeling of total fear went through my body. Where was everyone? I could feel the panic starting to rise in my chest and into my throat. I knew I was in danger, the pit of my stomach was telling me so. I tried to breathe deeply and slowly. There was something going on in the building. I needed to make a decision fast. Should I stay in my room or go out? I could be the only person in this building alive right now and it was because of me that others lives were at risk. It was because of me that they could all be injured or dead. How would I live with that?

My panic was mounting. I was having trouble taking a deep breath and thinking clearly. I needed to close my eyes and resist the panic. Think, Sam, think. Think back to what Mr. Tyler told you to do. First thing was to stay calm and think through every scenario carefully. Put safety first. Even though I was not a Keeper yet, I still needed to make sure I kept myself from harm.

Suddenly I heard sounds on the other side of the door. It sounded like the scuffling of feet somewhere in the hallway. I realized that whoever was out there was coming to hurt me. I was a target. I knew my life was on the line, and the others' lives as well.

Panic consumed me. I knew I was supposed to keep calm and keep my wits about me. I had to think fast and come up with a plan. I was wasting other people's time as well. I needed to do something and I prayed it would be the right thing.

As I turned away from the door, I heard movement directly on the other side. They were within inches of me. The doorknob began to turn. I lunged at the door as hard as I could, trying to detain and hold back whoever was on the other side. But the person on the other side was much stronger than I was. The door pushed back at me. Someone was coming into the room. It was total darkness and I couldn't see anything. The rain was coming down harder and the storm was right above us now. My adrenaline was pumping. I could feel my heart beating so fast I was sure it would beat right out of my chest. My eyes were open wide and my whole body was on alert. I needed to feel the strength I had felt in my dream.

Panic took over. I knew I was at the mercy of someone whose only plan was to make it impossible for me to complete my mission. And at that very moment, the door pushed open, causing me to fall onto the floor. My intruder stood before me.

twenty four

"Never be frightened! Be fearless! There is no room for fear. Fear is death, fear is sin, fear is hell, fear is adharma and fear is disloyalty. All delusions emanate from this evil called fear."

~Sant Sri Asaramji Bapu~

Where was I going to find the courage that I needed in the next split second to do the right thing? If there was a God, I decided that he needed to help me now. And for that split second, I closed my eyes and prayed.

And with my eyes closed, I heard a voice. It was a voice I had heard before, small and soft yet urgent in its message.

"Sam, it's me, it's me. Don't panic, quick, we need to get out of here!"

I opened my eyes and as the lightning flashed, I looked into the face of familiarity. It was Claire!

"What? Oh my God..."

"Ssshh, be quiet. No time to give you answers. We need to get out of here. I've got Abraham, he's been badly hurt."

The lightning flashed again. I could see Mr. Tyler. He was holding his side and blood trickled down his face. Claire spoke quickly in a whisper I could barely hear. Lightning suddenly lit up the entire room. I could see her face was smeared with blood. Her hair was in disarray. Mr. Tyler was badly hurt, beaten, I could tell from the way he moved. They were insistent that I follow them.

"Claire, what the hell happened?"

"There's no time, Sam, we need to get you out of here. Don't ask questions, just follow us. This windows comes out and that's exactly what we're going to do."

I heard Mr. Tyler give a groan and almost collapse in pain. It looked as if he had no intentions of going any farther.

"You two go without me, I will only slow you down. I'm hurt badly. Please, go without me. Claire, you understand me and I need you to follow through for me. Now both of you, get out of here before it's too late for all of us. Go, get out of here. Claire, do as I say. Get out. Take Sam with you and make sure you get him to safety."

The lightning flashed again and I looked into Claire's face. We were not prepared for this moment. We had a split second to make a decision. We both knew what the other was thinking and we acted quickly.

"I'm not leaving him here, I'm just not leaving him here. He goes with us. He's not hurt so bad that we cannot get him somewhere safe. We will take our chances, but he's not being left behind! He has done everything for us so far and I intend to do what I can for him. Do you understand me? He comes with us."

My sudden outburst surprised Claire. She looked directly into my face but gave me no argument. She knew I would not leave Mr. Tyler behind. She knew it was a decision she was going to lose if she argued with me. She knew in her heart it was the right thing to do. I could read her face. I saw it in her eyes. Mr. Tyler would have to live with our decision.

"You're coming with us, Mr. Tyler, no argument. Claire, show me how this window comes out. And tell me how much time we have."

She moved quickly and said, "Come here."

By the light from the flash of the lightning, we walked to the window. Claire was hurt but still able to move about with ease.

"The top piece pushes out. These latches release the window from the inside. Here, feel."

She guided my hand over the latch. I felt where the release catch was.

"We only have a few minutes to get this thing out of our way and get moving. There is a vehicle stashed in the shed right across from the back door. Keys are on the visor. Now help me get this window moved. There are suction cups hidden under your bed. They press on the window and pull it toward you. Once we pull it away, we can lower it to the floor. Make sure you don't break the glass until we have left this room. We got them detained down the hall, but that will only last a few minutes. We got caught off guard. I'll fill you in later. Let's get this window down."

I fell to the floor and reached under my bed where I found several suction cups on a small shelf. I had been in this room for several days and never knew I could have made a great escape at any time! With the suction cups in hand, I stood up and handed one over to Claire. I turned and looked to see Mr. Tyler slumping to the floor. I quickly turned to help him.

"Sam, let him go for now. Get this window out, we'll go back to him."

"Claire, he's hurt bad, we need to help him and stop the bleeding."

Claire turned and made her way to me.

"You listen to me, Sam, and you listen good. Mr. Tyler is going to be fine. I need your attention on this window so we can get everybody out of here safely. Now, I have no time or patience to hear anything else you have to say. Get over here and help me take this window out or there will be no saving anybody. This is not the time to have an indecisive attitude."

I turned away from Mr. Tyler, who had fallen to the floor, blood oozing from his side. I pressed the suction cup to the window and Claire unlatched it. It gave a quick jolt and moved away easily. The window was heavier than I had thought, but I was working with an adrenaline rush that would allow me to move cars if I needed to. I set the window on the floor, leaning it up against the side of the bed. Claire had already turned her attention to getting Mr. Tyler on his feet.The lightning continued to light our way."Sam, in the drawer of the table next to the bathroom is a box with a handle on the top, way in the back. Go get it!"

I ran to the small table next to the bathroom and put my hand in as far back as I could reach. There it was, the box she was talking about. I grabbed it and made my way over to the open window.

"Come on, help me get Mr. Tyler through here. Be careful not to grab his side, he's been hurt badly but I think he will be able to make it to the car."

All the time she was giving me instructions, I could hear Mr. Tyler muttering how he needed to be left behind or else we would be too late in our escape. The rain was now coming into the room through the open window, lashing at us as we helped Mr. Tyler through, trying our best not to cause any more pain for him. I heard voices coming down the hall, someone was yelling to hurry up. They were coming for us and were only a matter of seconds away from my room.

"Sam, push your bed up against the door. Do it! Now! They will be detained for a few more minutes. Grab the box! I've got Mr. Tyler, just get the bed pushed over there."

Mr. Tyler was groaning in agony, barely able to move his legs on his own.

I grabbed the bed by the headboard and pushed it over in front of the door as hard as I could, moving the glass first. The noise would definitely be heard and they would know we were escaping the room in whatever way we could. That was bound to give them even more incentive to move quickly and do whatever they needed to do.

"Hurry up, Sam, get over here. Climb out carefully and as quietly as you can. They already know we are up to something. Hurry up. Crawl out backwards, grab the window by the suctions cups and release them. With glass everywhere, they will have to get through it, it may buy us some time. I have Mr. Tyler. We can make it to the car and get out of here. Hurry up!"

I felt panic but I made it out the window. I turned back to grab the suction cups and release the glass so it would break over the entire floor. They had not gotten through the door yet, but I could hear them right outside. I realized at that moment that I had been saved. The only thing left to do was make it to the shed. I handed the box to Claire and picked up Mr. Tyler. I carefully placed him over my shoulder and carried him as best I could. We had no time to help him walk. He was right, he would slow us down. But that didn't mean I couldn't carry him! He groaned even louder and I knew I was hurting him by carrying him that way. But it was between pain or death and I chose pain. Mr. Tyler deserved to come with us. I would not let him die at the hands of the Invaders he had been running from for so long. Claire ran in the direction of the shed with the box in her hand. Mr. Tyler and I were only a few steps behind her. As the lightning flashed, I turned quickly to see the door fly open in my room. They had pushed the bed out of the way and made their way in. They would now be at our heels. Moving quickly was imperative to our survival. Claire yelled out for me to hurry and not look back. And then I heard the shot. In front of me, Claire went down on her knees. My mind was in survival mode. I wasn't sure what I was thinking or if I was thinking at all. I just reacted and made a decision to grab Claire and carry her to safety. With Mr. Tyler over my one shoulder, I reached down, grabbed Claire by the waist, and pulled her up to me. She was cradled in my arm, blood coming from her shoulder. I kept running toward the shed, which was now only a few feet away. No one would ever believe I carried two people, one in each arm, through pelting rain with gunshots behind me. I couldn't even believe I was doing it. I ran with all the power I could find in my legs, desperate to get safely to the car. It would be our only chance of survival. More gunshots were fired. They were clearly using the lightning to their advantage. Every streak made us a more visible target. The shed was in front of me. I had made it. With only moments left, the car in reach, the door handle visible, I heard a shot and felt a sharp, searing pain in my shoulder. I felt my energy faltering. It crossed my mind that I might not make it, but I knew no one would make it if I didn't continue on. My shoulder was on fire. I eased Claire up alongside the car, holding her with my knee.

"Claire, I've been shot. Hang on, I'm going to open the door and get you inside. If you can, move over so I can get Mr. Tyler in next to you. Claire, do you hear me?" I felt I could barely breathe. I was in no better condition than they were.

Her voice was faint and she was almost incoherent from the pain. She uttered something under her breath and I prayed she had heard what I said.

"I need you to slide over as much as you can, you understand me? Slide over so I can put Mr. Tyler in the car. I promise you, Claire, I will get us out of here if you just do as I say. Please, Claire, hear me!"

"I hear you, Sam, I hear you. Please hurry, Sam, they are coming. Don't let them get to us. God, please help us."

She was so faint in her answer I could barely hear her. Her breathing seemed labored. My shoulder was numb, I was fumbling as I moved myself along, but I was determined we would all make it. I got her in the car and she moved over as I had told her. I slid Mr. Tyler off my shoulder as gently as I could. Pain was searing through my body and I felt close to giving up. Mr. Tyler had passed out from pain, but was still breathing. I slammed the door shut and grabbed for the driver's side door. My knees buckled and I tried to reach for the door handle as I fell to the ground. The rain was relentless and the thunder rumbled so close it made the ground shake. I pulled myself up by the handle of the car and opened the door. With all my might, I climbed into the front seat behind the steering wheel. Completely covered with rain, mud, and blood, I pulled myself into a sitting position. I felt faint from the pain. I heard Claire yell from the back seat, her voice wavering in and out.

"Grab the key, Sam, the key in the visor. Grab the key! Sam, hurry up!"

I opened my eyes, the pain was beyond tolerable. I reached my hand up, shaking and bloody, to the visor and tipped it down. The keys fell and I moved my hand to catch them. They landed on the floor below me, between the gas pedal and the console. I took a deep breath and leaned myself forward to reach for the key. The pain was excruciating. I stretched my hand a bit farther and grabbed the key between two fingers. I couldn't help but pray under my breath for God to please help me through this, to please not let me die like this.

Everything seemed to be happening in slow motion. I had no thoughts, just pain. My body was a blur. I heard a low roar from somewhere. I knew I was alive, but felt as though I was close to dying. I was floating. It was comforting, relaxing, but there was pain. I had memories of others with me, small flashes of images that reminded me that I was not alone. Perhaps this dream would remain forever. I felt peaceful. There were sounds coming from somewhere, but they weren't from me. I couldn't recall who the others were, if they were alive, or if they too were floating between life and death. I realized I could feel my legs and my stomach ached. I felt like I might vomit. The haze in my head was clearing. There was someone next to me, another body. Were we both dead? Were we between heaven and earth? Suddenly the surge of pain from my shoulder went through my entire body, causing me to tense every muscle. And at that moment, I knew I needed to retch. I forced my body forward, crying out in pain and letting my stomach empty. It was at this moment that I knew I was alive. I couldn't move without feeling the pain, the extreme burning sensation went through my whole body. And pain meant life. I tried to open my eyes. I had no energy. I couldn't tell if I was dreaming or if I was awake. The pain was so severe I wanted to throw up again. I could feel the warmth and pain coming from my shoulder. I had been shot. That was a reality. I could hear groans coming from somewhere. I felt faint. I wanted to stay awake. I didn't want to fall.

I awoke and could feel the sense of motion. My mind was still hazy. I couldn't see. I didn't know where I was. The only thing I felt was motion. I couldn't feel my shoulder. I knew I had rested for a while, but I couldn't tell for how long. I had the feeling that I was out of danger. I lifted my head in an effort to see around me. My chin had rested on my chest, draped so low it's a wonder I could breathe. The only sound I could identify was a low hum, a constant sound, the sound of a motor. I tried with great difficulty to remember what had happened. I wanted to lift my head, to look around me, but my body wouldn't allow it. I felt as though I had been through war, and that war had won! For a brief moment as I was able to turn my head slightly and I could see another body next to. My vision was blurry, but there was a shape next to me. I had no idea who it was. Perhaps I was dreaming. I tried with great effort to open my eyes, as painful as it was, but there was something wrong, something was preventing me from opening them. I tried to raise my hand to touch my face, but I couldn't even do that. I wanted to open my eyes. I wanted to see who or what was next to me and where we were going. But nothing. I collapsed from exhaustion and pain, not knowing what would happen to me, or Claire, or Mr. Tyler. But this I did know. I was alive at least for now because of those who made the choice to save me and I did the same for them.

twenty five

My body was calm, warm, relaxed. My eyes wanted to open but resisted the temptation. I just needed to let this feeling be a part of me for now. I needed more than anything to let everything go and just allow my body to be still. There was no pain, no stress, no noise, no movement. I felt warm and calm. I wanted to remain here for as long as I could. Everything was serene and I was alone without any cares without anybody or anything to worry about.

I'm not sure how much time passed or how long I had been in this state. But it was interrupted by noise coming from nearby. I could hear mumbling, murmurs, commotion. There were voices trying to bring me out of the full slumber I so badly wanted and needed.

"Sam, wake up, Sam, you need to wake up. You are not in danger, you are safe. Wake up, Sam. You are with friends."

I understood the words, but struggled to do what was being said. I would need to force myself to leave such a warm, consoling place and go back to the dangerous world I had been in before. As hard as I tried, I couldn't really recall much about that world right now, but it was there, somewhere deep in my memory. I knew it was a place I didn't want to visit anymore. Waking up would mean being in that world again. But this voice insisted, it was urgent, it needed me to wake up. I wondered who the voice belonged to. It was not familiar to me, but it did say I was safe. Perhaps I should take the chance and wake up. Maybe it would be okay. I knew once I opened my eyes there would be no turning back. I would never be back in the comfort of where I was right now. Never again. Never.

Those words ran through my head over and over.

"Sam, please wake up. It's time, we need you to wake up. Everything will be fine, you are with friends, people who care about you. It's time to wake up, Sam. You need to come out of this, wake up, Sam!"

The voice was urgent. It needed my response. I needed to wake up, open my eyes, and come back to reality whether I wanted to or not. People here needed me, I had a job to do, and I was necessary. I needed to come back to the cold and unknown and leave the warm, peaceful place I was in. I knew I was needed and I had to make that choice.

Time passed. The voices had ceased asking me to awaken. Maybe they gave up on me and would turn to someone else. Maybe they realized I could do no good for anyone, not now, not ever. I wondered if I had died. Maybe everything was over for me and I was just trying to hang on to whatever last memory I had of life on earth.

Everything sooner or later would fade away. After all, if I were alive, I would have moved by now, I would have opened my eyes. I would be awake. I would be looking for Claire and Mr. Tyler. I would be doing everything I could to make sure they were okay and back on track. I would be worried about Bailey and Jake and my family. They were what had kept me going all these years. My family and my friends. But I was not a part of that life anymore. I couldn't open my eyes. It was over and I would need to accept that I was separated from everything I once knew and would now be on my own. Who was going to take care of Bailey for me? I was his whole world. How could I let him down? How could I let my family down? They would never understand. My family would never know that I tried to do something meaningful, respectable, and brave. How could I leave this world knowing that I had an important role? Maybe I should fight to wake up. Maybe I had a life worth fighting for. Perhaps it was always about beginning: beginning a new life in a new place with a new purpose. Maybe it was always about change. If this was the end, it didn't feel as though I'd served much of a purpose. It felt as though I had not found my purpose at all. And even though it was warm where I was, I felt useless and lonely. Suddenly I wanted to wake up, I wanted to keep going, I wanted there to be a purpose. I wanted to know what it felt like to wake up every day and know that I had a purpose and it was to do something that may help others. And maybe in doing that, I would find myself.

Was I too far gone? The sense of comfort and peace had left me. I didn't feel anything. I was alone, quiet, numb, motionless. I waited and waited. The pain returned. I felt uncomfortable, uneasy, and unsettled. I was floating in nothingness. Is this what death felt like? And then it appeared. That dark, black, and faceless being reaching out to clutch my neck and take every breath out of me until I fell lifeless. I could feel the temperature dropping. There was no light, just a cold haze. I pushed myself away, using what, I don't know. I saw myself for the first time, running. The black figure chased me, inches from reaching out to grab me. I was running, feeling the panic and the relentless fear of evil, and then I suddenly stopped. I watched my body come to a halt and turn to face what I felt was the most threatening and horrifying creature I had ever seen. And when I stopped, it stopped, coming close enough for me to smell the stench of its being, the smell of its own fear and death. It was a smell I would never forget. For the first time, I realized it was the smell of my own fear that had built up and lived inside of me for so long. And at that moment, I couldn't bear to look at it, to be in its presence, and to know that what had been chasing me for so long was looking me directly in the eyes. I was afraid because I was facing my own fear. It was horrible and evil and it shook me at the root of my being. But I held my stance. I wanted to see what I had been running from and fighting against for so many years. It was putrid and ugly. It looked me straight in the eyes and I stared right back at it and held my ground. It roared as loud as anything I had ever heard in my life and I felt myself fall to the ground. I stood back up, clenched my fists, and grounded my feet. I heard a loud roar come out of my mouth from deep inside me. It was as though I was emptying out my lungs, my chest, and my throat. It took every ounce of me to face this gross, despicable creature and I knew if I ran, it would follow me and continue to follow me for the rest of my life. It would be there every time I ran, every time I questioned my ability, every time I faced myself in the mirror, and every time I couldn't make a decision. And I was tired of facing this monster and letting it win. I roared back, I yelled, I screamed, and I raised my fists to its face. I did not back down. I roared again and again. And then I fell silent, saliva streaming from my lips, sweat beading on my forehead, and I looked into its face. It stared into my eyes without a stir. And in that very moment when I felt cold, alone, and full of pain, the dark and putrid being turned and fled. I could smell its stench less and less as it left me, the smell dissipating the farther the creature moved away. I stood watching it become nothing but a speck and eventually nothing at all. The smell was gone, the dark haze floated away like vapors, and I remained motionless, exhausted. I could feel my body giving way, I could see myself falling, slipping away as I fainted to the floor beneath me. I watched my motionless body, my chest heaving slightly as I took in each breath. It seemed like I lay there forever, alone and cold. If there was purpose beyond this very moment, it would not be of my own doing. I had taken on the battle and won. I was free of the fear that had been so deeply buried inside of me, free of running, hiding, and doubting myself. I was finally free of the beast that had walked alongside of me each and every day. I felt a different kind of warm as I lay there waiting. And for the very first time, I felt free.

twenty six

I awoke. The dark had finally left me. My body was tired but I felt reborn and hopeful with a fresh perspective and an eager heart. I had no idea how much time had slipped by. My eyes slowly focused and there above me was the face of a person I had met before, but couldn't quite place. I felt the warm air of the room and smelled the sterile scent of hospital cleanser. Please don't tell me I was in another hospital!

"He's awake, see if you can find Brandon." The person turned back toward me and started to speak. "Sam, you are going to be okay, just a bit of a bullet wound to the shoulder and a knock on the head, but you are fine."

I knew this person, but from where?

"Do I know you?" I slurred my words but he understood.

"My name is Casey Burns. Remember the car accident a few days ago? You witnessed an accident, the guy took off, remember?"

My throat was dry, my voice scratchy. But I was determined to speak.

"Yes, I do remember vaguely. You claimed to know me from a night course we took together. Who the heck are you? What are you doing here? Where are Mr. Tyler and Claire? They know what's going on here and I need to talk to them." I tried to raise myself off the bed but the pain in my shoulder prevented me from doing so.

"Take it easy, take it easy. Lie back down and relax. No one's going to hurt you, no one here is a threat to you. We are here to take care of you."

He looked away from me with a grin on his face. Just then Brandon walked into the room. I looked around and decided we were not in a hospital, but it sure smelled like one. It was a normal bedroom, but exceptionally sterile. Again, I was in a position to ask for answers, and I needed them now more than ever.

"Sam, man, are you doing okay? You finally woke up. That's good, that's good. Look, I know you have lots of questions, but for now, I want to check out that shoulder wound. You were just grazed, nothing serious. Won't take but a minute to do that so sit still while I get that bandage loosened."

"Wait...wait one second before you do anything." I was beginning to feel wide awake and I grabbed his hand to stop him. He was taking the liberty of not answering me at all and just diverting to playing doctor again. This time he was going to give me some answers.

"What happened back there? I don't know if it was today or yesterday, but anyway, where are Claire and Mr. Tyler? I want answers, Brandon, no crap, just give me the truth!"

I saw Brandon give a look to Casey and they both sighed.

"Are you sure you're up to this, Sam? We can wait, there's no hurry."

"No sense in wasting my time or yours, just give me the truth." My stare spoke volumes. I had been patient long enough.

"Alright, here's what happened as far as I know. You have to understand I was not on the same hospital floor when this took place so I am piecing things together as much as I can. They drilled you, you remember that, right? You do remember the test they gave you?"

I nodded my head and asked if they could help me sit up. I was tired of lying down. While sliding me to a sitting position and situating pillows behind me, he continued with his story.

"I was down in the basement running some files on a few guys that Mr. Tyler suspected. He gets information all the time and I run things through the database just to see what I can find out. Well, I was down there when the lights started to flicker. It was about 1:30 a.m. Lights flickering as you have well figured out by now is not a good sign so I stayed put. I have learned enough from the past to know it's best to stay where you are. After all, someone has to be free to poke around without getting hurt. It's just part of the process. It's better to give yourself that chance than to play investigator every time you hear a pin drop, you know what I'm saying? Anyway, I stayed low and the lights went completely out. I heard scuffling, and I knew it had to be Claire and Abraham. They had been going through files for training objectives for you and getting things in order for you to leave the hospital and place you somewhere inconspicuous for a few days. You would not be able to stay at Abraham's house since you were already attacked there. It was no longer considered safe. The Invaders were on to you, even though you had no idea at that time. Don't ask me how they knew; it's unusual that an Invader is that ahead of a Keeper who is to be groomed, like you. With the attack on you, Abraham had some information passed on to him and wanted me to check to verify some who this person was. That's what I was checking when the attack happened at the hospital. Anyway, Claire and Abraham were in the line of attack on the main level. These Invaders had more information than at any other time before. Not sure how it happened and we are going to have to do some research as soon as we get you safe. Claire got roughed up pretty badly, but she's not who they wanted. Abraham, he got worked over pretty well, too, knife wound to the stomach. They had their sights on you, my friend, and there wasn't going to be much to stand in their way. They didn't know I was in the lower level. I guess they didn't do their homework securing the area before making their way upstairs. Abraham always kept something for emergencies on every level to use in case we got caught in the building. Luckily, I was near the storage room and got my hands on a couple of smoke bombs. I threw them in behind them, which caught them off guard and slowed them down while I headed to the barn. The plan has always been that whoever could get to those in danger were to do just that. Claire and Abraham got to you and helped you out of the building. I'm the one who pushed you over in the car and got everyone out of there. And so, you are welcome. We are evaluating Claire and Abraham. Don't worry about them right now. You've been out for about sixteen hours. You got a hit against the head trying to get into the car. We took some X-rays, but they didn't show anything for us to be concerned about. You just needed to rest. You were having bad dreams it seems, lots of twitching and mumbling that didn't make sense. But, at least when that happens, we know you are okay. It's when you lie perfectly still that we have to be concerned. We tried to wake you up several times but you didn't want to cooperate. So, we decided to let you come along on your own. Claire and Abraham are still out so we can't move anybody right now. We are just going to let you rest up and see what happens."

"So, let me get this straight. Mr. Tyler is a Keeper also? How does he fit into all of this?"

"Keepers are moved around, they keep for a while and then hand off. Then they may pick up again. It's all about rotating people in and out so the Invaders never know who they are looking for."

"But wouldn't an Invader try to kill you so they don't have to bother with you again?"

"Well, yes, but getting caught would pretty much end what they do. They are only looking to get the Staff. They are not interested necessarily in killing anybody, at least from what we've seen. They will harm you. But murder, I don't think so. No one has been murdered if that's your next question. But one thing is for sure, they are very willing to keep you from having the guts to follow through. At this point, they are using lots of antics that will scare someone into walking away from being a Keeper. It's not the best life to lead, but we are able to maintain as much safety as possible. The time is nearing, Sam, and the Invaders are well aware of it. So, they have stepped it up. There's no way they want that Staff in the hands of the appropriate people. They are working overtime to make sure of that. We, on the other hand, are keeping our profile low and moving things around even more than before. That's what Abraham works on for the most part. I can't tell you if he has a Staff in his possession. But no doubt, he has knowledge. Before I left the facility, everything on our computers was saved and then removed so no Invader couldn't gain access to anything. I have it with me and will do whatever Abraham wants to do with it."

"So, how many Keepers are out there with a Staff right now? Because if the Invaders are finding people with a Staff and then realize it's not the true one, that number must be decreasing every time they eliminate one. Am I right about that?"

"No Staff has ever been confiscated. It got close a couple of times, but they never succeeded. We have also put Keepers in places just to throw off the Invaders. In other words, some Keepers have a Staff case, but it's just an empty case. The Invaders don't know which one is which until they track someone down. They were and still are very close to tracking you down, Sam. We need to get you hidden, off the grid for a while. So, you have to worry about getting yourself back to 100 percent. Let us do the planning. Get your shoulder back in working order. It won't take but a few days for it to be better. No bones were hit by the bullet, just a lot of flesh, so you should repair quickly. Rest and lots of food should do the trick. They got a little bit too close for your own good. Abraham was in a similar situation once and it is not a healthy place to be. You basically have to convince the Invaders that you have nothing they are looking for. So you have to pass it off to someone you can trust for a while, then gain it back as long as the

Invaders are off your tail. Trust me, they have been eyeing Abraham for a while, and we thought they had turned their attention to someone else since they couldn't turn anything up on him. Somehow they knew to follow you. That's why you don't have your phone any more. Every number in your phone is being checked out. Sorry, but we need to make sure we have cleared every person you have had contact with. Someone passed information on to the Invaders, someone who crossed your path and knew about you. There is no other way the Invaders would take such drastic steps if they weren't given first hand information that you were lined up to be a Keeper. And that Abraham had brought you forward. Someone blew the whistle on you. Even though you technically do not have a Staff in your possession, they assume you do because of Abraham. They started following you right away. The sooner they could scare you off, the closer they are to our mission failing. Do you see how it is playing out? You are under suspicion, that's why they continue to work on you. However, the fact that they were desperate enough to shoot at you to detain you is a new tactic. They usually use brute force, which is what you experienced before. Threats are sometimes enough to scare off the newest Keeper. But using guns and shooting at you, well, they are beginning to get very desperate. Times are getting urgent, they are feeling the pressure."

"Why do they suspect me? I am not the only person that Mr. Tyler has around him. Why would I be under suspicion? What makes me stand out more than anyone else? I mean after all, I just moved here. So, I don't understand how I became such a focus so quickly."

"Here's what I can tell you, the rest will have to come from Abraham. You were chosen, Sam. I don't know how long ago or why you were chosen or how you made it to Boston. But, you were chosen and with that being said, you were probably followed or someone was watching you and saw that you made a move to Boston. You are asking the wrong person. I don't know how Keepers are chosen, when they are chosen, or how they are placed in specific areas to be Keepers. I work from a different angle; I mend those who are broken. I facilitate moving people around and ensure that someone has safety until the next move is made. And I put myself in harms' way for the sake of another and for the mission. That's the part I am trained to do best. Answering questions outside of my scope of ability and responsibility, I simply can't do it. And I understand you have not been able to connect all the dots so far, but you will have to ask Abraham. Things have taken place that have added unusual circumstances, more stress, and less time to work with you than ever before. So, this has been a very rare case."

I felt I had been misled coming to Boston. I thought I had earned a position here and that's what I was coming here to do.

"Do you have a regular job, Brandon? I mean, do you have a normal life outside of what you do for the Keepers?"

"Yeah, I do. I am an online consultant for a medical group looking for expertise in what equipment to use in emergency room situations and where to locate the companies that offer the best. I am the person who does all the legwork and reports back to those who are financing the investments. That's what I do. It allows me to stay out of the office and still do all the work I do for the Keepers. I am at the disposal of Abraham around the clock because I choose to be and I am sure by now you have figured out why. So, that's what I do for a living to earn my keep. My job is to take care of Keepers and get them to a safe place when under suspicion, like you."

His answer was a good one. I had no idea how deeply these people were invested in this mission. I didn't know that having a normal lifestyle would throw the Invaders off enough to keep them an arm's length away at all times. And until now, I had no idea how secure it felt knowing that I was in the care of people who had invested years of their time to protect the mission, never missing a beat, always ready to react to unpredictable situations. It seemed that so far they had been greatly successful, and I was now the next person to come under the protection of this group. They would give their lives and ultimately die for the cause if necessary. Claire and Mr. Tyler took the hit for me, took the beating in order to give me a chance to deliver the Staff, if that was the plan. If I was the one who had the real Staff then I understood they were willing to jeopardize their lives for it. As difficult as that was for me to accept, I understood it. I was beginning to understand that they had already made their decision to move when the situation caused them to move. They are the ones I needed to have close to me, and to always be able to access and trust. Up until now, I had questioned their every move, their secrecy, their motives. I had ended up in places and in situations that had raised question after question. But every time I ask for answers, it seems that it all fits together. I have been the one on the outside and they are the ones who should have a trust issue with me. After all, they know very little about me, I think. Brandon was someone I felt was untrustworthy from the beginning, but I was starting to see it was my lack of understanding and acceptance that made me feel that way. They had been doing this for years and it was difficult to be the new person in the group and not have questions. They wanted me to absorb everything in baby steps, but I had to take on more knowledge because I was under fire quicker than others had been. The Invaders were getting better at what they did; the pressure was building. Was I going to be in the last phase of this mission? Was I going to be the one who handled the true Staff? Was I the one who everyone would work day and night to protect? From what I had gathered, the closer the mission was to completion, the higher the stakes and risk would be for everyone—especially the Keepers. I knew there were others and I wondered if we would ever meet face-to-face. Would I ever meet the founders, the ones who walked this path before I did? I wanted to know them. I wanted to talk to them and hear their stories. I wanted to meet whoever was responsible for finding me and bringing me to where I was now. All the dots needed to connect for me eventually and meeting them would help. Brandon was right, Mr. Tyler was the one I needed to talk to. And I planned on doing just that very soon.

Brandon removed the bandage and looked closely at the bullet entry area. It was clean with no fragments left behind. All it needed now was time to heal itself, reconstruct the ripped flesh to be whole again. He was happy with what he saw and asked Casey to get the salve in the cabinet. Casey left for the other room, and now was my chance to ask my question without any discomfort.

"Brandon, who is Casey? He and I met on the street a few days ago during an accident. He claimed he knew me from college and I was positive I had no recollection of him. And now he shows up here. Tell me who he is."

"I would prefer you ask him that yourself. Like I said, there are areas that I will not dabble, it's just complicated. You will understand what I mean at some point. So, if you need to know, ask him."

Casey came back in a matter of minutes. By the look on his face, I was sure he knew we had brought his name up.

"From the look on your face Sam, I can tell you have a question for me."

"So, Casey Burns, we have met before. Tell me how you are connected to all of this."

Brandon continued to put the salve on my wound.

"Yeah, well, let me start from the beginning. My job with the Keepers is to make sure I distract an Invader when someone is being followed or set up for, let's say, an abduction. There are those who have been following you according to Abraham's direction, and I am one of them, but for other reasons. I had some information on you, where you were living, where you went to school, college, the year you graduated, what you did with your time, that type of stuff. That accident was no accident, it happened on purpose. You were to be abducted that day and probably scared off. Everyone around would be looking at the accident and it was a perfect setup for you to be taken by an Invader. The guy in the car and the girl were paid, and we are speculating that, of course. So, an Invader created an accident to get everyone's attention on the accident and away from you. Once the accident happened, the crowd milled around just as they planned, and many of the people milling around were Invaders, put in place on purpose. The driver of the car was able to get out unnoticed after setting off a smoke bomb and he blended into the crowd without anyone knowing the difference. Everyone thought the smoke was coming from the engines. The girl would draw all the attention to herself. There was a van that pulled up right behind the accident a few seconds after it happened that was meant for you. What they didn't plan on was you taking the dog back to the house first, that was the first thing that went wrong. They quickly lost track of you and when they couldn't find you, they had to stick around and people were beginning to see their faces. Then you came back and they felt they still had a chance without being noticed. When the police showed up quicker than expected, that was the second thing they didn't anticipate. They were watching and trying to get closer to you when the police came over to talk to you. It was when you stepped back away from the accident that they saw their opportunity to snag you. That's when I stopped you and insisted I knew you, taking up the time they would need to grab you. They couldn't do that with me there. I would have involved the police and they would have been tracked. They had to decide to let you go at that point. Once the van split, I split and remained out of your eyesight. You didn't need to see my face any longer. I watched you and drove several cars behind you until you made it back to the hospital. You never even noticed me following you, did you? The plan died out for them and you were spared, at least that time."

"So, you are not someone who was in a night class I took? Do you know how crazy I went trying to remember you?"

"Yeah, but it was for your own good. My real name is not Casey Burns. I never use the same name twice in order to protect myself. Sorry I had to do that, but the reality of it is that you needed to be protected from getting snagged or roughed up enough to make you leave Boston. Trust me when I tell you that I know how close you were to leaving. I realize that there has not been anything enjoyable for you since you got here, and I would want to head out of town and go back to what was working for me just as much as you did. We had to do whatever it took for you to stay here and get you into the mission. You were being tailed much sooner and quicker than we had anticipated so lots of planning has gone into getting our grip on you. I won't apologize for any of that."

"Unbelievable. Has anything since I got here been real?"

"No, not really. But, with all due respect, you were brought here to be a Keeper, not to lead a normal life. Keep your focus, my good man, and everything will make sense to you eventually. We just haven't had the time or opportunity to explain everything that we normally would. We have been putting out fires and keeping you safe and alive. Listen, what we need from you, Sam, is to be tough. We need you to do now and ask later because we are running out of time here. We are going to patch you up and get things going, that's what we do. Time is working against us and it's just best if you start responding to the responsibilities. I would love to ease your mind, but I don't have time. You are going to be asked to do some things that may not make sense to you but it is imperative that you just do them. We need to move forward. Make sense?"

He was so matter-of-fact it was startling. This was all just normal procedure for these guys and I was having a really hard time digesting it all. But, I had made the decision to do what I could and that's what I would do.

The bandage was replaced, the salve felt cool against my skin, and I knew it was working already. Brandon was dedicated to patching people who needed mending, and he was excellent at what he did. He stayed out of things that didn't concern him, remained cool, and gave direct answers. I was going to be ready as soon as they said jump. And I would take whatever knowledge with me that I could.

Brandon came back in and his face had changed. He looked stressed. I could tell that something had gone wrong. I held my tongue and didn't ask.

"This house you are in belongs to another servant to the mission. His house is a safe haven we use from time to time. It's best we move you, but it's just not a good idea right now. So, we are going to wait for another twelve hours and then go. I am taking a risk waiting that long, but feel you need that time to gain your strength. Please don't ask questions. And, before you ask, I don't have any news on Claire or Abraham. Keep focused, Sam, as it is the only thing that will keep the mission successful. At this time, you are to put Claire and Abraham out of your mind and concentrate. You are a brave man, Sam. You have come into this project with little knowledge and what has happened to you would scare most people away. But you have stayed and pursued the truth through counsel from Abraham. He has given you strength and drive, and I admire that. Please keep your focus. You will need it to remain safe and do what is necessary. Remember your mission."

"Where are you moving me? What am I doing, for crying out loud? I don't have a plan. I have nothing to go on, nothing! And you think I'm brave? And you tell me to stay focused? On what?"

Brandon had left the room by the time I had finished my rant. I was sure my outrage of frustration was what he expected and he wasted no time in leaving. I wasn't expecting him to respond, but I did want to know what the plan was. After all, these people were in control and I was completely at their mercy. How could I stay true to something that hadn't been shared with me? My shoulder was starting to ache. I wondered if I would get any pain-killers to help me sleep. Maybe they weren't expecting me to sleep. I looked around and didn't notice a button to push for assistance. Then I remembered this was not a hospital, it was someone's home. This must be the basement because there were no windows. I wasn't quite sure what to make of the lack of direction from Brandon. At best, I could sleep for a while and hope there were no dreams. I was truly left with no choice but to sleep again and wait.

twenty seven

It felt like the middle of the night when I awoke from the noise outside my room. This very same scenario had played out just a night or two before. I was no longer sure of the duration of time between events; I just knew time according to injuries and healings. My room was dark. The voices became louder and people were approaching my room. I tried to remain calm and reassured that I was safe and no longer on the run. I needed to stay focused and positive.

The first to come into my room was Casey, or whatever his real name was. He turned on the light and it was a blinding change from the pitch black I had been lying in. I squinted, finding it hard to see at first.

"Sam, oh good, you are awake. Brandon wants to get you ready to move. How's your shoulder feeling? Is it bearable for you to get out of bed and ride in a car? Things have settled down a bit and we need to use this time wisely. What do you say, are you up for a short ride?"

I didn't understand why he seemed so cheerful and upbeat. He used the tone as though asking me if I wanted to grab a beer and watch the football game.

"Well, Casey, or whatever your name is today, what time is it? What day of the week are we on? And good God man, do you really care how much pain I'm in since you didn't bother to check on me last night before I went to sleep? No pain meds?"

"Yeah, sorry. We got busy and figured you would yell if you needed something. We don't read minds here, Sam, we just try to keep them healthy and focused. Must not have been too bad, I didn't hear you yelling or anything. Now, let's get you up, check that bandage, and get some more salve on it for healing. I won't tell you the ingredients because you wouldn't believe me if I did."

I sat up and let Casey check the bandage. Although I had some scrapes on my face and arms and a good size bump on my head, my shoulder was the only source of pain. And even that had dissipated to just an ache. Whatever they did put in that salve was just shy of a miracle drug. They could be millionaires overnight if they put it on the market. But I didn't ask. Right now, I had other things I wanted to know.

"So, Casey, where to now? And how long did I sleep? What time is it, and for that matter, what day is it?"

"Today is Friday, it's two o'clock in the morning and I don't know where you are being moved. I just know they need to keep you mobile and out of the limelight until the Invaders have exhausted all ways to track you for now. Your shoulder is looking great, better than I thought. You didn't seem to have any nightmares this time while you slept. Must be you have made some peace with your demons, yes?"

"I don't know what you are talking about. Bad dreams happen to everyone, I'm no exception."

Casey had a look on his face that told me he knew better. He had come across others with intense nightmares—those who stayed to fight and those who let the demons take over. I had no doubt he had experienced it himself.

"Sam, do you think you're fooling me? Each of us who has taken on a role in this project has had to face our own demons. You are no exception. Some of us have dreams, some have visions, sometimes so real that we can't tell reality from dream. We have had a few people end their lives feeling that it was too much misery to take on and too much of a nightmare to carry around. We have suffered through those times and are sorrowful for not being able to help them gain the insight, courage, and faith we knew they needed. But you, my friend, you are different. You have gained in just a few days what others have had to gain in months of training. When you were chosen, someone knew exactly who you were and what you were capable of. It is an honor to be chosen and you have done well. Abraham is very proud of you and knows that you will honor the mission. He has a very deep faith in you; do not let him down. Now, I realize all the pieces of the puzzle have not been presented to you yet, but they will be. Remain patient, for all good things come to those who wait, as you know.

He chuckled as he continued with the bandage, trying to give me words of encouragement. At two o'clock in the morning, it was definitely what I needed. Amazingly, I did not feel tired. The sleep I had was restful. In fact, it was probably my most restful sleep since I set foot in Boston.

With my bandage back in place and my shoulder on the mend, I assumed I was ready to leave. Casey left and came

back in with a huge plate of fried eggs, home fried pota-
toes, steak, wheat toast with jelly, fresh fruit, and a huge
glass of orange juice. I didn't realize how hungry I was
until I smelled it. I ate like it was my last meal.

Brandon came in with a smile on his face and seemed
to be in a much better mood than before.

"I see Casey brought you something to eat. Was it
delicious?"

"Well, delicious doesn't even come close, Brandon.
This has to be the best food I have ever had. Seriously,
whoever did the cooking should open their own restau-
rant, they would be millionaires in no time at all."

"Thanks, I appreciate that. I did the cooking this time
since Casey was busy with other things. Not bad for a medical supply consultant, huh?"

"You cooked that? Where did you learn to cook like
that?"

"I have had some time in my life when I have been
on my own without much to lean on. During that time, I
decided to learn how to cook what I liked or starve. So, I
tried different things and here I am today to share it with
you. Not bad, huh?"

"Not bad at all. Thank you for making such a feast for
me. Makes me wonder what is coming my way once I leave
here. By the way, where are we?"

"Sam, it's best if I don't divulge locations to you. People
remain safe because information is not shared. You have
to understand, you would be putting another in danger if
you talk about certain things. Remember when Abraham
gave you the rundown—things to do and not to do in order
to survive. You have been with us for less than five days,
that's not very long. There's very little that you know. But I

will tell you this much. We are no longer near your apartment. Don't panic, but we needed to get you away from there. We have someone watching Mr. Tyler's home, of course, because your apartment would be the first place someone would look for you. The other folks who live in the building are okay; you have nothing to worry about. Your belongings are intact and your dog is taken care of. Take those things off your mind because we have it all taken care of for you. I know you have friends who must be worried and concerned about you. But you have to understand how urgent it was to take you off the grid. No one can talk to you right now because it could be traced, and you could be followed. That's how they found you in the first place. Their ability to catch up to our Keepers has become more sophisticated than it was in the past, thanks to technology. Most of our Keepers were safe and untraceable. But, there was a leak of information somewhere, and you were found out relatively quickly. So everything had to be put into motion quickly and quietly to get you hidden."

"What about people who work in the office building where I was hired? They are innocent. And the other people in Mr. Tyler's house? Are those people in danger because of me?"

"Let me tell you this much. Some of those people were put in place to keep you safe. They work for the Keepers. Once Mr. Tyler brought you to Boston, people were put in place to protect you, and they were meant to cross your path. What we didn't anticipate was the Invaders knowing as much as they know."

"Are you serious? You mean, me getting this job was no accomplishment for me, it was arranged so that I would

move to Boston and meet Mr. Tyler? His available apartment was intended for me? Everything was predesigned?
Holy crap, are you kidding me? How far back does this go?
Does Jake know anything about this? What about my parents? Are they all safe, because I have to tell you, if they are
harmed in any way, I am out of here. It's not worth it for
my family and friends to be involved. They are good people
and don't deserve to go through this stuff. My gosh, Jake's
mom is in the hospital, he doesn't need to deal with anything right now regarding me. Oh my gosh, I can't believe
this. This is unreal."

"And this is why we share as little as possible. Do you
hear yourself? Do you think we haven't thought of those
things already? Sam, you need to listen to me. We don't have
much time before we leave here. Everyone you knew from
Cleveland is safe, they are all being watched and cared for.
People are in place to be around them and to guard them
if necessary. Nothing is going to happen to your family or
your friends. You are no good to this mission if you don't
believe me and let go of them for right now. It is critical
that you leave them behind to handle your responsibility,
do you understand me? We need your undivided attention to this for however long it takes. We are taking care
of everything else. Trust me when I tell you that. Do you
think I don't have family and friends that I worry about?
But I have to trust what I have been told and the people
who are guarding my loved ones. You are not the only one
who has gone through this. Remember the reason you are
doing this, for the mission, for a greater cause. To finally
bring truth to the forefront, to take that stand in order to
prove that your faith has reason and that what you believe
will change lives. That's bigger than life itself. And you are

a part of that, Sam. You are a piece of something greater than your own life. You are a part of something that will change people in the long run and will give them faith. The words were written so long ago and people have lost their way, lost what purpose they had. This is something that can change lives, Sam. It really is something extraordinary and worth every bit of pain, every bit of energy, loneliness, and suffering we may go through in order to bring even one person to the light and the saving grace that is extended to each and every one of us. We are not in this to make friends or to be put on a pedestal. We are here because we have been chosen to perform a mission, and we will do whatever it takes to see it through. You have what it takes, Sam, I see it in you already, in just a few short days. You have turned a corner and you will not back out or back down. You will persevere; I see it in you. I see that you do have a passion for doing what's right, and you have a strong love for your family and your friends. You are brave, you have strength, and you will do whatever it takes to see this mission to the end. You need to let go of what is behind you and step up to take on what is ahead of you. Otherwise, you will only be as good as you are right now and nothing more than that. You were designed to be more, but you have to have the faith that someone greater than you has a plan for you. And you need to have faith that you will be protected to see it through. And if you don't have faith in that, then you are free to go. You can walk out this door right now and we will leave you alone. It's a choice you get to make, not me. I am not here to force you against your will. But I will tell you this: I believe there is a will on all of our lives and we will battle our will against God's will every day if we can. But sooner or later, we will pay the price for ignoring his will. You have to ask yourself—am I strong enough to believe in his will for my life, and am I willing to let go and trust in his love for me. Or am I going to continue to live my life as I see fit and be what I choose to be and nothing more. We all face that choice sooner or later. And if someone tells you otherwise, they are lying to you. Some of the most difficult things to admit are the things we have desired to control, knowing how wrong we were in doing so. But the bravest are those who will admit they can give it all to him and let him guide them through the path he has chosen. And I stand here today, I am living proof to you that I had to be that person, I had to make a choice. Not easy, not easy at all. So, when you are alone here in a few minutes, you can think about this. I'm not in control of you, I am just doing what I can to keep you safe. You may think I am holding back information from you. I understand that you don't understand it all, but you will. And then you may have to teach someone in your lifetime. I don't know. But, I'm glad I have learned what I have and I sleep well at night knowing that I did well today, that God looks at me and says, 'Good job, Brandon, good job.' That matters to me. Now, I'll be back in later. Let that salve work into your shoulder and it won't be long until it will be healed enough to be considered brand new."

I felt the emotion rising in my throat, my eyes filled with tears, not because of self-pity, but because I really did believe what he said to me. I really wanted those things to matter more than anything to me. I wanted to look in the mirror and see someone better, someone stronger. I wanted to be someone who was grown up, responsible and who my family and friends could be proud of. I needed to realize that I was a small speck in a big world, one of trillions of beings that are alive and doing something every day. I just wanted to do something that mattered and somehow made a difference. I sat back down on the bed, letting the salve do its work. My shoulder felt a hundred times better than it did an hour ago. I am convinced it is because of that miracle salve.

I wanted to invest my time in learning the program, the process, and how to handle myself once I had a Staff in my possession. I imagined I would become a different person and it would be a good thing. Having a purpose that was not all about me seemed like the right thing. I almost looked forward to it.

Brandon and Casey came back after about an hour.

"Alright, now that we are all in the same room at the same time, we need to share some information with you, Sam. We are going back to your apartment tonight. The Staff that you will be responsible for is there. I was not aware of this, but apparently Mr. Tyler incorporated it very wisely and cleverly into the structure of the home so no one would ever suspect it to be there. He was once a Keeper, but he stepped away from it to keep Invaders off his tail after losing Elle. He is now ready to pass it on to his chosen Keeper. That's you, Sam. So, while Casey and I get the Staff, you need to grab a few things that belong to you, change of clothes, toothbrush, small stuff that can be put in a backpack because you will have that with you at all times. I suggest you have a writing tablet, a couple of pencils, a place to record names, places, times of day, that kind of thing. Casey and I can show you what we carry. It's always ready and always available. Just a part of life, right, Casey?"

"Yeah, that's all we know for now. We have instructions as to where the Staff has been kept over the years and it has not been discovered. We have people who have been watching the building and they feel right now would be a safe time to go there and grab the Staff and make as little or no spectacle of ourselves as possible."

"What do you mean, grab the Staff? Mr. Tyler has the Staff at his house? And we are going alone? Just the three of us without any help? How do we know we will not be ambushed or that there aren't Invaders hiding somewhere just waiting for us to show up? What kind of guarantee do we have? Because, personally, I don't think I can go through another beating of any kind right now."

"Good questions, but we have to go when the least amount of possibility exists that an Invader would be around. And now is the time. So, let's get going. And Sam, stop asking questions. You will get your answers later. Right now isn't the time."

And that was that. I was walked out a doorway that was level to the outside, no stairs, just around a lot of corners and through some doors, one that was replaced with a solid wall. This place was hidden quite well, almost like a survivor bunker with an underground tunnel. It was quite a distance to get to the door that led us outside, and I welcomed the fresh night air. A truck was parked just outside the door and we climbed into our respective places. Brandon was driving, Casey in the passenger seat, and I was alone in the back seat. Brandon and Casey threw their gear in the front next to them so they had access to it in case of an emergency. They were not kidding when they said it was with them at all times. They had small electronic devices, phones, but no computers, some kind of handheld device that must hold a lot of information. Brandon said he had downloaded all the documents they needed when he left the hospital and he had them with him. I trusted that he was high on the list of people the Invaders would like to capture and harm. It seemed as though he possessed a lot of vital information that others did not have. I wanted to question them about Claire and Mr. Tyler but I remembered what he said about looking forward and focusing. I was sure they were safe. But it was difficult for me to not think about them.

The ride took several hours and it was disturbingly quiet the entire way. Apparently they had moved me quite a distance away from Mr. Tyler's house. It would be early morning before we got to Mr. Tyler's house. There would be little going on and movement would be easy to spot. I hoped we had enough support and backup to pull this off. I felt we were taking a big chance. I had no idea that Mr. Tyler had the Staff, much less where he kept it. I noticed it wasn't raining or storming and that made me feel a little better.

We drove up to the house and Brandon turned the truck off. I asked him about the other tenants and if they would hear us. His answer was simply, "It's all been taken care of." I didn't know how these guys communicated, but I was thoroughly impressed. I wanted to learn from them. We discussed what each of us was to do according to the plan. I would go to my apartment and quickly grab whatever I needed. They threw me a backpack. It reminded me of one I used when I was younger and went camping with my family. I was told what to put in it and what to leave behind. The rest of my belongings would be handled later. I was not to pay any attention to Bailey's things as he was already taken care of and I should ask no questions. They were starting to understand how difficult this was for me, to let go. But I was beginning to understand how badly I needed to let go for the sake of my own personal safety. Casey and Brandon put on black sweatshirts and threw me one to wear. They had stowed a few tools in their pockets. They did not tell me where the Staff was. They would be five minutes at most and then back in the truck. I was to do my task quickly and make my way back to the truck, all in a matter of five minutes. I was breathing deeply and questioning my ability when Brandon turned around and said to me, "Hey, Sam, just do it. Don't think about it, don't worry about it, just do it. Alright? The plan is all worked out and we need you."

"Yeah, I'm good, I'm good. Just breathing deep and staying calm. I got this."

I was to go first, leave the truck on my own with no protection around me. I was told to just keep going. My door was already unlocked and I was to go up the steps and not look back. With that being said, I opened the door reluctantly, put both feet on the ground, and headed up the back staircase Keeping focused, I reached the top of the staircase, tripping again on the top step. I had always meant to mention that to Mr. Tyler. I reached for the doorknob and walked inside. It was dark and smelled musty from being closed up. Everything was left exactly as I remembered it. No one had ransacked my belongings. I guess that was a good thing. I tried to focus and grab just the things I needed. I raced around trying to remember what I was there for. I was starting to feel the anxiety rise in me. I grabbed a pad of paper in the kitchen and headed for the bathroom, where I took my comb, toothpaste, toothbrush, bar of soap, rag, and a small towel. I ran to the bedroom and stuffed jeans, sweatpants, sweatshirts, underwear, socks, and t-shirts into the backpack. I quickly put on a clean set of clothes. I needed to get out, my five minutes was about up. As I made my way to the front door, I saw Bailey's things on the coat rack—his extra collar, his toys on the floor. I took notice that his food and water dishes were missing, as was his regular collar. Without giving it any thought, I grabbed his spare collar and threw it in my backpack. I ran out the door, not wanting to be late getting back to the truck. I felt for a fleeting moment how horrible this must be for Bailey, not knowing where I was and having a stranger taking care of him. No one knew him like I did. Jake was the only other person Bailey knew, and he was back in Cleveland with his mother.

I flew out the door, closing it quietly, but firmly. I heard it latch and turned to make my way down the staircase. This time I was careful of the top step, knowing I had tripped on it every time since I moved here. I didn't see Brandon or Casey so I decided they must already be back in the truck. I made my way down, scrambling quickly. As I was taking my last step around the corner of the house, I heard a car approach. It was moving fast and the tires were squealing. Within seconds Brandon and Casey were out of the truck. The car stopped behind the truck and I panicked. I wasn't prepared to take on another fight and sustain more injuries. My mind was racing. I couldn't leave Brandon and Casey to take on this battle. Mr. Tyler's words echoed in my mind, the words I struggled with so badly, to take care of myself instead of others, to always think of my mission and keep myself away from harm. I struggled with the idea of others getting in harm's way in order for me to be safe. I understood it, but refused to believe it was the best option. However, at this very moment, I struggled with involving myself in another round of battle. It was no surprise to me that I could not make a critical decision. I was not the man for this mission, clearly.

There was shouting and words being exchanged I could hardly understand. But this I heard very clearly. The words "where is he" rang through my mind in a way I will never forget. I knew I was in danger but prayed Brandon and Casey would not reveal my whereabouts. I slowly inched my way around the corner to see who this person was. If I could get a clear view of his face, I was sure I could avoid him in the future. If I had a future.

The fighting had begun. The stranger made his first attempt at taking Brandon down, swinging his arms to give a harmful blow. Brandon, much taller than the Invader, took advantage of his body size and gave his best swing back. A second man appeared out of nowhere and made his way toward Casey. I stayed hidden behind the corner of the house while two much braver men battled for me. I could hear the grunts and groans as each hit took its toll. The fight lasted for what seemed like eternity. I felt frozen to the ground from fear. I listened from a cowardly distance, knowing it could very well be my body taking the painful beating. There was yelling. I heard Casey say he would never divulge anyone's whereabouts. They responded by saying they wanted the Staff and wouldn't stop until they had it. I peered around the corner of the house and saw Casey drop to the ground, a body standing over him ready to hit him again. Brandon was on the ground, wounded, and barely moving. The two Invaders had accomplished what they set out to do. One of them walked over to the truck door and grabbed the wooden box that held the Staff. It was in their hands now, and

Brandon and Casey were left wounded badly. I watched the Invaders get into their car and drive away. It was the longest few minutes of my life. I felt helpless and I knew I would have to live with the fact that I had hidden in the face of danger. I heard a groan coming from the sidewalk near Brandon's truck. With what little bravery I had, I ran over to help whoever I could. Casey lay on the sidewalk, his face swollen, blood seeping through his shirt. He was knocked out, but still breathing. Brandon was groaning in a great deal of pain and blood covered his entire face.

"Brandon, tell me what to do!"

I felt nothing but panic. It was taking over my ability to think clearly. I needed to get control of myself. What would Mr. Tyler tell me to do?

"Alright, Brandon, hold on. Just hold on. I'm going to somehow get you in the truck. You and Casey both. Oh, man, I'm sorry, I'm sorry I took the coward's way out."

I needed to get myself in control and get these guys out of here.

"Brandon, can you stand up at all? I need to get you guys in the truck and get out of here. We need to get you somewhere safe and take care of your wounds. Can you move at all, Brandon?"

All I heard was a groan. His eyes were swollen shut, his mouth bleeding. He was hurt badly, bleeding from his left side. It was obvious to me now the two Invaders had knives. There was no way this guy was going to answer me. I needed to take action.

I opened the back door of the truck and threw everything to the floor to make room for Casey and Brandon. I ran back to Brandon and locked my arms under his arms from behind, hoping to get him into a standing position.

Brandon was a big guy and outweighed me by sixty or seventy pounds. Getting him into the truck would be a miracle. It had started to rain, adding insult to injury. I could barely move Brandon, much less stand him upright. He moaned as I continued to yank his body around, trying to lift him any way I could. There was no movement from Casey and I feared he was fatally wounded.

A car turned the corner a few blocks away and was heading down the street toward us. I couldn't tell if it was the same car the Invaders drove or not. The rain was coming down heavily, blinding me. I continued to try to lift Brandon, him moaning even more than before. I was sure if he had any broken bones, what I was doing would only multiply his pain. But it was better than dying.

My breathing became labored and heavy, panic was taking over. The car was closer as each second passed. If the Invaders were returning, I would fight them the best I could..

The car pulled up and stopped suddenly, a man stepped out and began to walk toward me. I kept my head down. The rain drenched my body. My clothes were now clinging to me like another layer of skin. The man came closer and I looked up briefly to see his face. I knew him from somewhere. He said nothing to me, but pushed me out of the way and lifted Brandon into the truck. Brandon was barely awake, his pain evident with each agonizing groan he gave. He swung Brandon's legs into the back seat and slammed the door shut. I stood with my mouth open, not knowing what to make of this. I knew this person, but from where I couldn't remember. He approached me.

"Sam, get in the truck and get out of here. I'll take care of Casey. Just get in the truck and haul butt out of here. You have no time to argue or try to figure me out, just go."

"Wait, where do I know you from? At least give me that."

"Get out of here before they find us. We are going to split these two up, hopefully well enough to confuse them. Did they see you at all? Do they know you are here?"

"I don't think so, I was just coming down the back stairs when they came around the corner. I stayed out of sight until they left."

"Okay, that's all I needed to know. Now get out of here."

I swallowed hard. "They took the box with the Staff."

The words were like knives cutting open my throat. The one thing I was supposed to do was to protect the Staff above all things and I couldn't even do that. The man before me did not change his expression. He didn't even sigh.

"Get out of here, drive somewhere you know is safe."

I knew this man. How did he know we were here?

He got Casey into his car, I could see his arms hanging as this man picked him up, placed him in the vehicle, and shut the door. And he was gone. It would come to me how I knew him. It would come to me.

I took a t-shirt out of my backpack and pressed it against Brandon's side to ease the bleeding. He rolled his head in pain, barely conscious but alive. I realized he was counting on me to do the right thing. I was heading out of Boston.

I needed to calm down and collect my thoughts of where to go. "God give me strength" was all I could ask for. I started the truck and began the long drive.

twenty eight

"Hold on, Brandon, I am getting you to a safe place and to someone who can help you. Hang in there, buddy, I am not going to let you die. Not you and not me and not today.

I drove in silence for miles, driving back roads, trying to whittle my way out of the city through the countryside as best I could. Although I was blessed with a great sense of direction, I stopped at one point to search the backpack for a map. And believe it or not, there was one. I needed to make sure I stayed on back roads. There was no movement from Brandon, but I could hear him breathing.

I needed to be brave, insightful, and stay aware of my surroundings. There were people who were looking for me, searching out my path, waiting for me. I was not going to let them win. I wondered how Claire and Mr. Tyler were. I needed them right now and at best all I could do was wonder if they were even alive. I wondered about Jake, about his mother. I wondered if they were okay. I wondered about Bailey and how he was doing with all of this change.

I drove on along unfamiliar roads that would take me to the next safe port.

twenty nine

"Perseverance is a positive, active characteristic. It is not idly, passively waiting and hoping for some good thing to happen. It gives us hope by helping us realize that the righteous suffer no failure except in giving up and no longer trying. We must never give up, regardless of temptations, frustrations, disappointments, or discouragements."

~Joseph P. Wirthlin~

We drove for hours it seemed, the quiet balanced by Brandon slipping in and out of consciousness, mumbling and murmuring things I couldn't understand. At one point I thought he was crying. His mind was still alive and working, but his body was struggling.

It had started to rain even harder. I hoped there was enough gas to get me to where I was headed. Staying on back roads was making the journey longer. I kept driving, stopping briefly to look at the map. We had about another half hour to go. The last stretch of road was mountainous, but drivable. Every mile I made was one step closer to safety. I was growing tired.

Despite being hungry, tired, and uncertain, I persevered. I thought back to the incredible food fed to me right before leaving our last safe house. I promised myself that when this had all come to a close and I was safe again, I was going to find that house. I was going to thank those people who took me in, saved my life, and put themselves in danger for me. Being frightened for your life is bad enough, but not knowing where to go when you feel that way compounds your fear.

The rain came down harder, thunder rolled above our heads, and lightning streaks flashed before my eyes. I hated storms. Nothing good came of them for me. Even as daylight broke, the storm clouds kept it darker than usual.

The last road before our turn was no more than a mile ahead. I had not seen much traffic during this journey. It was either a blessing or a nightmare in disguise; I wasn't sure which. I was tired and scared. I needed a safe place to be.

Brandon was still out, mumbling from time to time. The road was becoming treacherous from the rain. Large puddles filled with mud were forming. Most people would have taken the road on the other side of the mountain. It was a two-lane road and safer by all means. I chose to take the less traveled route, which meant putting myself into a more dangerous situation. It seemed danger was with me no matter what choice I made. Brandon always said to keep out of the public eye. On this road, I didn't have to worry about being seen.

My head was throbbing from the stress. Finally I saw our destination. I pulled off the road on to a long driveway lined with large boulders, exactly how I remembered it. This was the back entrance and no one ever used it. The mud had thickened and the truck started to slide. I kept pushing it because we were almost to the back door. We slid again, this time the truck went sideways and hit one of the boulders. It broke the front headlight. I put the truck in reverse to straighten out the wheels and then had to rock it back and forth a few times to get some traction. After a couple of tries I eased on the gas and this time we didn't slide. Brandon was moaning. At least he was still alive.

The house was just a few feet away. I lay on the horn to get some attention. I put the truck in park and jumped out to get Brandon. As I was reaching for the doorknob, someone came running out of the house. A familiar face at last.

"Oh my God, Sam, what happened to you? What on earth are you doing here?"

Before me stood my sister, Hannah. She was just as beautiful as I remembered. Her hair was soft and blond, her eyes deep brown and shaped like those of a doe. Everything about her was sweet, kind, and gentle. And here I was hoping to take refuge and get the best care I could find.

"I'll explain later. You have to help me."

I grabbed her close to me and hugged her. I felt hopeless and weak. I needed her help. I didn't have any answers or strength. I just needed shelter and hope.

"What do you mean you need help? What's happened to you? My God, what on earth has happened? Sam, what's going on here?"

"Please, Hannah, you have to help me. I have someone in the truck who is critically injured. I need your help. I need to stay here and be out of sight for a while. And I need to hide this truck. Hannah, please help me without questions. I couldn't think of anyone who could help me right now better than you."

"Of course, Sam. Calm down a bit. It's going to be fine whatever it is. Now, show me this person? What do you need me to do?"

"He's hurt bad, Hannah. I don't know if he's going to live or not but I needed to try. I needed to try. Just help me get him out of the truck. Hannah, I will try to answer your questions later, but right now, I just need you to help me."

"Alright, calm down, just calm down. I'm going to help you. I will do what I can. Where is he?"

"He's in the truck, I strapped him in with the seatbelt. Hannah, prepare yourself, he is hurt really bad. I'm just trying to prepare you."

"Alright, alright, let's just get this guy inside and help him in any way we can. Why did you come here, Sam? Why didn't you take him to a hospital?"

"It's a long story, Hannah. I'll tell you later. Help me get him out of the truck, that's what we need to do first. He's a big guy, Hannah, so prepare yourself."

"Okay, come on, let's do this. Are you able to do this, Sam? Are you okay? Are you hurt? Because you don't look too good. We'll help this guy out and then I'm making you something good and warm to eat and you can get some rest. Then we can talk."

She was trying to ease my mind, bring me down from the ledge, and make me calm. She was good with people, with situations that were unsettling. She was gifted in that way, and I loved her for it. She was an amazing person. The shameful thing is that I am nothing like her. Everything is over the top for me; everything is a crisis and unbearable if not in the realm of my ability to cope. She was the one and only person I thought of to bring Brandon to. She would know exactly what to do and she would never lose her cool. I needed her right now.

"I'm fine. I'm tired, and I'm falling apart at the seams. I just need your help."

I opened the back door and turned to Hannah. She stepped in next to me and her face turned white, her eyes grew large, and she raised her hands to her mouth as she held in her reaction. I didn't know what to do. I reached for her, grabbing her by the arm. I needed to make sure she was all right, that the sight of this man and the condition he was in would not upset her. I had warned her about him. I tried to prepare her.

"Hannah, talk to me, for God's sake, talk to me. I told you it was bad, I told you."

I was shouting, the rain was coming down so hard. Hannah just looked at Brandon as tears streamed down her face. The one person I was sure I could count on had no words at all. Please God, help me here.

She went to Brandon, moving quickly to unbuckle the seatbelt. I heard her whispering to herself, loud enough to be heard even over the pounding of the rain on the top of the truck.

"Oh my God, no, please no God."

"Hannah, talk to me, you have to talk to me!"

"Sam, I need you to focus, I need you to get a grip and help me."

She snapped her words at me, hoping to bring me back to the reality that she needed from me. She needed my help.

She had composed herself and was working quickly, a strength I so many times wished I possessed. I knew I could depend on her; she had the strength of a hundred people put together. I came to the right place, the right person. I knew Brandon would be in good hands. I knew Hannah would know what to do. And although she was working diligently to free Brandon from the seatbelt, I saw tears running down her face, mingling with the rain. I was confused, but didn't underestimate the compassion my sister truly had for others in times of trouble. It should not surprise me at all that she felt pain for this man who was so badly injured.

She stopped for a brief moment, only to give me an order.

"Sam, go to the back door and yell for Owen. Yell for him to come help. Do it now!"

I ran to the door, trying desperately not to slip in the mud. I opened the door wide and yelled for Owen to hear me. He hollered back and said he was on his way.

I ran back to the truck, Owen right behind me. I watched Hannah as she drew in a deep breath, her hair hanging in her face, tears streaming down and blending with the rain. She wiped her face with the back of her hand and looked at me.

"Sam, this man..."

She stopped and took another deep breath.

"This man is my husband. Brandon is my husband. We married three years ago. Do you understand me, Sam? This is my husband that none of you know about. And now you know why it was a secret. Everything, you know everything. If you know Brandon, you already know who he is. Do you understand me? You already know! Don't ask me any questions right now. I need you to get yourself together and help me carry him inside. I need to get this bleeding stopped. I need to know how serious his wounds are."

She turned back and continued to work diligently on removing Brandon from the truck. I stood there in shock. I couldn't move my feet. I didn't know how much more

I could take. My life had been turned completely upside down. I felt dizzy and sick to my stomach. I felt myself fall to the ground and everything went black.

My eyes opened, again from what was seemingly a long sleep. I felt the warmth of a fire on my face and the comfort of a soft bed. It felt like home. I laid still, taking in the silence of that moment. There was a knock at the door and it opened a slight crack. It was Owen.

"Sam, are you awake?"

I tried to push myself into a sitting position, only making it halfway.

"Hey Owen, yes, I'm awake. Come in, please come in."

He had a tray with a small bowl of soup and a few crackers. "I thought you might want a little bit to eat. You've had a pretty rough day."

"Owen, where's Hannah? Is Brandon going to be okay?"

"Brandon is going to be just fine. Don't you worry about that right now. Miss Hannah is handling everything. She's got a good head on her shoulders and she's going to take care of everything."

Owen was about the wisest and kindest old gentleman I had ever met. Everyone loved his gentle soul and mild way of speaking. He was the caretaker at the Old Door Inn and he'd been there with Hannah since she opened the doors to the public. He's family to her.

"Owen, did you know that Hannah and Brandon were married?"

"Sam, I think it's best if you save your questions for Miss Hannah. She would respect having the opportunity to tell you the things you need to know. Why don't you try some soup and we'll go from there. One step at a time."

He turned and left the room just as passively as he had come in. I followed his suggestion and ate the entire bowl of soup including the crackers. So many things were running through my mind. I sat for just a few more minutes before I decided to find Hannah and try to get some answers. I felt it was the least I deserved.

I made my way from the bedroom to the main room of the inn. It was a large open room with a fireplace big enough to stand in. As always, on a cold rainy night, Hannah had a roaring fire burning. There were sitting areas tucked into nooks and corners, places to sit, visit, read a good book, or just relax. Hannah had done an amazing job creating an ambiance suiting to the New England flavor. I loved coming here.

I sat down on the sofa in front of the roaring fire. I could feel the stress melting off my shoulders and relaxation taking over. As I slowly tipped my head back and closed my eyes, I heard small footsteps coming up behind me. It was Hannah.

"Sam, how are feeling?"

"I'm better Hannah. How is Brandon?"

"He's going to be just fine. He has a knife wound to his side but nothing life threatening. It will heal. Stand and give me a hug. I never even said hello to you. Sam, I'm so sorry for this to have happened and for you to find things out this way."

I stood and hugged my sister, the longest hug I have ever given her.

"Thank you for being here. I don't know what I would have done if I didn't have you to come to. A now, finding out that you and Brandon are married, I made the right decision I guess."

"Come on, let's sit down and talk. I know you are loaded with questions and I don't blame you."

"Not without me you won't." We both turned and saw Brandon standing in the doorway behind us. Hannah quickly made her way to his side, letting him lean on her to walk.

"Brandon, you shouldn't be up. This wound could get worse if you don't stay off your feet and let it heal."

"Hannah, help me over to the sofa. I will sit with my feet up and take the pressure off my side. Don't worry, I'll be okay." He leaned his face towards her and gave her a tender kiss. I turned my head, giving them the private moment they deserved.

I made my way over to Brandon to help him walk over to the sofa. Once done, we looked around to each other not sure who would start the conversation.

It was Brandon who broke the silence and began the story of how he came to know and marry my kid sister.

"About four years ago, I and a Keeper were being tracked. We were told of a place in the mountains of New Hampshire that was off the beaten path and we could take refuge there for a few days. We made the trip here and stayed for about a week. And that was when I met your sister and just fell in love with her. Even though I am a few years older than her, we hit it off instantly and decided to try and see each other whenever we could. I told her I was a medical advisor in Boston and I could travel here to see her whenever possible. Unfortunately I had to keep my real job from her because I did not want to jeopardize her safety. It became complicated though and I finally divulged to her the mission and my involvement in it. We kept our relationship quiet and made sure even family did not know. And we got married privately three years ago because we were in love and wanted to spend our lives together. I remained in Boston and came to see her occasionally, whenever it is safe for us to be together. And she comes to Boston when she can."

I looked from Hannah's face to Brandon's. Their story sounded uncomplicated and sweet. But, for some reason, I felt there was more. I decided to approach them for more information and see what happened.

"Hannah, are you telling me everything? For some reason, I feel you are not sharing the complete truth with me. Who knew Brandon could come here and be safe? I mean, there's tons of places he could go and be in seclusion for a while. So, why here? Who knew you?"

"I did."

I recognized the voice. I felt flushed from surprise and as I turned to look, my mouth dropped open.

Mr. Tyler was standing in the entry way of the room. He held his side as he walked to where the three of us were sitting. I rose from the sofa and hugged this little humble man who I was sure I would never see again. I fought back the tears welling in my eyes and tried to speak without choking.

"Oh my God, I didn't think I would ever see you again. I can't believe it's actually you." I was talking and crying at the same time.

Sam, I'm fine, I'm doing just fine. Come on, let's sit down. I know this is a shock to you, so let me explain some things that I haven't had the chance to.

Hannah, the exceptional hostess that she was, made her way to the kitchen. "Let me put some coffee on, this could be a long night."

Mr. Tyler read me like a book and was quick to ease my mind . "Before you ask, Claire has been taken to a safe house in another location. We have had no contact with each other. That's all I can share with you about her. I just wanted you to know. Now, let me start filling you in on where and how you came into the picture."

After a few minutes, Hannah came into the room with coffee for everyone. She knew we were going to be a while.

Mr. Tyler continued.

"Twenty some years ago, Elle was asked to attend a conference regarding Child Abuse and how to recognize it in hospital cases. She went and met a woman there who she became good friends with. In that friendship somewhere, this woman shared with Elle about this group of people who were called Keepers and what their mission was. This friend told her she knew of it through her father and his brother whom she overheard talking one night. Elle was intrigued at the thought of a secret mission and wanted to find out as much as she could. Elle and her friend eventually talked to her father and he told them to let it go, it was nothing they should be concerned about. Elle decided to do just that and she went about her normal life. Several years later, Elle came home from work and told me that her friends' father approached her at the hospital about this mission of the Keepers and she was excited. He explained everything to her, how he chose her, how she could never tell his daughter, and as she spoke to me, I could see the excitement and conviction in her eyes. I asked her to walk away from this, it sounded risky and our lives would be changed drastically if we didn't walk away. But she continued to speak about it, and if you had known Elle, you would have understood that once she became convicted, that's it. I eventually told her I would be supportive to this mission but I needed to know everything. So, it was through this gentleman that Elle became a Keeper, not I. We lived a very normal life, enjoyed every moment and kept the Staff in a safe place, hidden from sight and from our minds. There were those who watched us and protected us without us even knowing. It was a few years later that Elle was asked to join a team of doctors and nurses who were conferencing in Cleveland for a week and she accepted. She was at the hospital doing emergency room duty when she first met Hannah. She was the one who took care of her until the doctors came in. Hannah was just a young girl but Elle was captivated by her. I remember when she came home she couldn't stop talking about the look in Hannah's eyes. Hannah became a person of interest for us and Elle recorded her name in her book of future Keepers."

"Wait, wait, Mr. Tyler, back up here. You mean while I sat in the emergency room with Hannah, your Elle was there and I was there in the same room with her and we actually met?" I got up from the sofa and started to pace back and forth. I felt overwhelmed and was trying hard to take in this whole story. All these years it was Hannah that was watched and called upon. And then me.

"Hannah, do Mom and Dad know this? Does anyone else in the family know this?"

Hannah looked at Mr. Tyler, unsure of how she should answer me.

Sam, Mom and Dad have no idea. No one else knows. I was approached by Mr. Tyler when I was eighteen, you were off to college at the time. He said he knew me through his wife who took care of me at the hospital. So, we agreed to meet and the more he talked, the more intrigued I became. To be a part of something so big and to be a place where people who need to be safe, I was on board immediately. He asked me to open a safe house in the mountains in New Hampshire. He had a location already picked out and I could make it my business and he would finance most of it if I needed him to. I told Mom and Dad that I was interested in opening a Bed and Breakfast and that I had found one on-line. It needed repair but I could do things myself. Mr. Tyler arranged all the fake paperwork to make it look as though I had taken out a loan to buy and repair the Bed and Breakfast. It was an excellent cover. He mastered the whole plan. So, I am not a Keeper, I am a safe house. It was during that initial conversation that Mr. Tyler told me I had met Elle years ago when I was younger, in the emergency room. Elle had mentioned to Mr. Tyler about you and how as my older brother you were so concerned and how much you cared. The more we talked, the more Mr. Tyler wanted to watch you and see if he thought you could take on the roll as Keeper. He saw potential in you Sam and your name was recorded as a future Keeper. I asked him to please not involve me in the decision any further and he honored that for me. And that's how you came on board. Mr. Tyler has many people behind the scenes that make things happen and appear to be the real thing. You going to Boston was no accident, the apartment you have is no accident, the job you have is no accident. It was all designed so you would leave the influences of Mom and Dad and Jake. Sam, I feel very honored and privileged to be a part of something so immense, something that has so much meaning to so many people. I truly do feel that way."

"How did you know you could trust him?"

She replied to me, "The same way you do. You just do."

My head was swimming. So much of what I thought to be real was unraveling as predesigned and predestined. I looked into Hannah's face and I saw her sincerity and sweetness. She was one person I had always trusted and admired. I reached out to her and hugged her, knowing that she was being honest. I hugged her for a long while, and tears rolled down both our faces. I trusted her and realized that she would always have my back. She was always a safe haven for me. I stepped back and turned to Mr. Tyler and Brandon.

"Mr. Tyler, you have been telling me that I just needed to be patient and I would hear the truth. I had no idea when I brought Brandon here to hide him that I was actually bringing him to his wife's safe house. It was pure coincidence that I chose to come here. My gut told me this is where I should go. And Brandon, you knew things and you said nothing to me, nothing. You knew my sister was involved and you said nothing!"

Brandon defended himself. "I told you, it's not my place to do so."

Mr. Tyler, in his calming way, spoke up. "Sam, have faith and be assured that you were guided to come here. And now that you have heard how you were chosen, it's time for us to begin our talks of what will come along from this point forward. There is still much to tell you and as time goes on, I will share everything with you. But right now, the Invaders are becoming anxious and aggressive. They too must be feeling the time is nearing and they cannot afford to lose their opportunity to close in on the Staff. Our level of danger has increased. We need to begin to plan our next move."

"But, there' still so much I question. If Elle was the Keeper, why was the Staff still at your home even after she's gone? And another thing is that there's faces of people that keep popping up at every corner I turn and they are people I have seen before. I'm curious, the big guy who carried Brandon into the truck, where have I seen him?"

"It was Keith from your office. He was purposely placed in your office for you to meet him and his part was to keep an eye on you when I needed him to. Many of those people in the office were placed there for a reason. As I have told you Sam, there is still much for you to know and learn, but now is not the time to spend explaining everything."

"How do you do all of this? How do you make so much happen?"

It was Brandon, who after sitting quietly throughout this entire time, carefully and slowly stood and said what made the most sense to me.

"Sam, there's things in life that are just hard to accept and difficult to explain. I have learned to accept that Mr. Tyler has mastered the ability to guide people through times when there is little to no reason for us to believe in any of it. Other than the fact that he walks by faith and not by sight. He believes in what he does and he believes in the people he surrounds himself with. I believe in this mission and I believe that the people I am surrounded by believe in it too."

His words were sincere, just as Hannah's were. I nodded, and in that moment, I settled it in my soul and in my mind that my ending was my new beginning. That each day now would be a day dedicated to my mission. I didn't know where I was headed and I certainly didn't know the ending. But, I knew this much. I belonged to something that was greater than myself. I simply had to walk by faith.

The ringing of the phone in the dark of night was never a good thing.

"For crying out loud, what time is it?"

He rubbed his eyes to clear them of the deep sleep he had fallen into. His vision still blurry, he glanced at the clock . The numbers were too small to read without his glasses. He cursed the middle of the night.

The voice on the other end was harsh and non-compassionate. "Never mind the time, we need you here. Get your things and get on the road....now!"

The time on the clock read just after midnight. He dressed quickly and packed what he would need. Things had changed, he needed to prepare to be in place. The rain was heavy as he drove for endless hours, avoiding the main highways. It was important he remained unnoticed as much as possible, leaving nothing to chance of being recognized by anyone crossing his path. The scope of the operation had changed, a Staff has been confiscated.

He felt drowsy, talking out loud to stay awake. The rain continued its' relentless spatter on the windshield as he drove on for miles. He drove through cities and towns, the cars diminishing in number as he continued. He was alone on the road, like many times before and his mission was all he focused on.

<u>Coming Soon</u>

The Keepers
Part II
"The Storm"

www.ingramcontent.com/pod-product-compliance
Lightning Source LLC
Chambersburg PA
CBHW020242180626
46810CB00006B/2324